FIRST COMES PASSION

"Kiss me, Avis. We'll only go as far as you wish," he whispered.

She had no control of her head as it slowly lowered toward him. Using only the slightest of touches, she caressed his lips with hers. But it wasn't enough. She wanted the fire. She wanted to be seared by his passion if only to prove to herself that plain, old, spinster Avis could indeed flame Banning's desires.

As she parted his lips with her tongue, he groaned. He tasted like scones and chocolate . . . or was that her? Either way, it was delightful.

Banning deepened their kiss as he rolled her over onto her back. She stiffened and then forced herself to relax. No easy task when he trailed hot kisses down her neck. A moan escaped her. Never in her twenty-six years had she imagined a sensation as exciting as Banning's lips on her body.

As he undid the pearl buttons of her nightrail, cool air swept over her right breast. His kisses stopped. Avis peeked at him through her lashes. He stared down at her breast with a sensual smile on his face.

He skimmed a finger down her chest until it reached the tip of her breast. Tremors coursed through her body at his light touch. She wanted him to do more than just tease her like this. But what? What more did she want?

Everything.

BOOK YOUR PLACE ON OUR WEBSITE AND MAKE THE READING CONNECTION!

We've created a customized website just for our very special readers, where you can get the inside scoop on everything that's going on with Zebra, Pinnacle and Kensington books.

When you come online, you'll have the exciting opportunity to:

- View covers of upcoming books

- Read sample chapters

- Learn about our future publishing schedule (listed by publication month *and author*)

- Find out when your favorite authors will be visiting a city near you

- Search for and order backlist books from our online catalog

- Check out author bios and background information

- Send e-mail to your favorite authors

- Meet the Kensington staff online

- Join us in weekly chats with authors, readers and other guests

- Get writing guidelines

- AND MUCH MORE!

**Visit our website at
http://www.kensingtonbooks.com**

EVERY NIGHT I'M YOURS

CHRISTIE KELLEY

ZEBRA BOOKS
Kensington Publishing Corp.
www.kensingtonbooks.com

ZEBRA BOOKS are published by

Kensington Publishing Corp.
850 Third Avenue
New York, NY 10022

All Kensington titles, imprints, and distributed lines are available at special quantity discounts for bulk purchases for sales promotion, premiums, fund-raising, educational, or institutional use.

Special book excerpts or customized printings can also be created to fit specific needs. For details, write or phone the office of the Kensington Special Sales Manager: Attn. Special Sales Department. Kensington Publishing Corp., 850 Third Avenue, New York, NY 10022. Phone: 1-800-221-2647.

ISBN-13: 978-1-4201-0351-9
ISBN-10: 1-4201-0351-2

First Printing: February 2008
10 9 8 7 6 5 4 3 2

Printed in the United States of America

To my husband, Mike:
Thank you for believing in me and
pushing me to do the thing I love most.

I love you!

I would never have come this far without my fantastic critique group, The Tarts. Kathy Love, Janet Mullany, Kate Dolan, Kate Poole, and Lisa, you ladies rock!

A special thanks to Kathy Love and Sheryl Fischer for reading this book more times than any person should have to. And another thanks to Kathy for giving me the hardest villain's name to type.

Mom, thanks for all the support the last seven years!

Thank you, Laura Bradford, for getting this book where it needed to be for publication. You're amazing!

Mike and the boys, I love you all.

EVERY NIGHT
I'M YOURS

Chapter One

London, 1816

"Let me love you."

The shadowy figure moved over her, not quite touching her. Yet she felt him with every fiber of her body. His heat, his strength, his desire. Or maybe it was her desire. She burned for him, ached for his touch.

Helplessly, she writhed, begging with her body for his touch. Her body understanding more of what she wanted than her mind did. The shadow shifted. He was closer. Right there, his body nearly grazing hers. Each barely there touch, making her throb with this uncontrollable need. His warm breath caressed her skin, his rich, almost spicy scent making her dizzy. His lips, strong yet velvety soft, brushed the side of her throat. She whimpered, reaching for him, wanting to feel the pressure of his body. She needed something more substantial than this shadowy lover. But when her fingers would have brushed his chest, his shoulders, his dark, spectral hair, his voice stopped her.

"Let me love you."
This was what she wanted, what she needed.
"Yes. Yes. Please."

No! Avis Copley sat upright, blinking against the watery light that still managed to make her bedroom seem unbearably bright. Not that dratted dream again. She yanked out the secret volume she'd stashed under her pillow last night and threw the book against wall. This was entirely the book's fault.

Ever since she found the volume among her late father's belongs two weeks ago, she'd been plagued by dreams. Not just any dreams. Sensual, erotic nightmares that tormented her with feelings of longing, until she awoke drenched in perspiration and aching for the one thing she could never have—a man.

She groaned and pulled the coverlet over her head, cocooning herself in darkness. In her seclusion, the images of her dream revealed themselves in vivid detail and her traitorous body responded again. Her breasts ached to be touched, and she gave into the need, hesitantly skimming her hands over the cotton of her nightrail. Beneath the fabric, her nipples puckered and became even more sensitive. What would it really feel like to have a man touch her this way? Touch her bare skin? Suckle her breasts and draw her nipple into the hot recesses of his mouth as her dream lover had?

The thought alone made her body tingle, the flesh between her legs pulse. Would it feel as good if she touched herself there? She squeezed her legs together to stem the growing ache but realized her efforts only added to her torment. Wrenching up her nightrail, she lowered her hand and slipped her fingers between the moist folds—

"Good morning, miss."

Oh Lord, this morning couldn't get any worse. "Good morning, Bridget," she mumbled from under the coverlet. Heat scorched her cheeks with the mortification of being caught with her hand between her legs. She quickly adjusted her nightrail but refused to leave her sanctuary under the covers.

"Happy birthday, Miss Copley!"

Her birthday. Clearly, her morning *could* get worse. It wasn't horrid enough that she was regularly dreaming of a man in her bed, or that she had nearly been caught in a very private position, now she was reminded that she was twenty-six years old. Twenty-six and she'd barely experienced anything in life.

"Just leave my breakfast on the table, please."

"Yes, miss."

Avis listened as her maid placed the tray down and walked out the door. Slowly, she emerged from her hiding place. Staring up at the coffered ceiling, she knew she couldn't go on like this, playing at really living. It was time.

The time had come to make a decision that could affect her life forever.

Chapter Two

"I've decided to take a lover."

Avis couldn't believe she had just blurted out her news in such an indelicate manner. It was not quite the way she'd imagined telling her friends.

Jennette held her floral teacup halfway to her lips. Sophie's mouth gaped open. Hardly the reaction Avis had expected from either of them. Silence filled the small room, deafening her with the empty sound.

"You cannot be serious," Jennette finally said.

"Think of your reputation," Sophie added. "You have always managed to keep your reputation intact even when you scorned your cousin's generosity and decided to live on your own. Taking a man to your bed will ruin everything you have strived to keep sacred."

"Why would you do such a thing?" Jennette implored.

Avis stood and paced the carpet by the fireplace. "I have given this much thought." She had thought of little else for the past week. She knew she couldn't tell them the truth. They just would not understand. Instead, she recounted to them the lie she'd practiced all week. "I never feel I capture the true . . . true . . . essence of the relationship between my characters. I don't understand physical love."

"Surely you have been kissed before?" Sophie asked.

"No," Avis denied far too quickly and then turned to avoid Jennette's prying stare. Only Jennette knew about her one and only kiss. A kiss on a wager, and not *her* wager.

"Really?" Sophie shook her head as if unable to believe a person could reach the age of six and twenty and never have kissed a man.

"Avis, why now?" Jennette asked.

"What do you mean?"

"You haven't been yourself since your birthday last week. Is there something you're not telling us?"

Avis sighed. "I am twenty-six. There are nineteen-year-olds who know more about what happens between a man and a woman than I do."

Sophie tilted her head and asked, "Can't you just read a book about it?"

She had tried that already and look where she landed—feeling even emptier than before. "A book will not give me the answers I need," she finally replied.

"You must rethink this plan," Jennette started again. "Your reputation would be at risk. Everything you love—your chances of publication, the parties and balls you enjoy, even our friendship. My mother would never let me associate with you again if word of this reached her ears."

"And if you get with child?" Sophie asked softly.

Avis had to admit this one complication had not

crossed her mind. A child. She could never have a baby—a child meant a husband and she would never have one of those. "It will only be one time. I certainly won't get pregnant the first time."

Jennette chuckled. "Remember Susanna Lindsay?"

"How do we know she really did that only one time?" Avis asked.

"She swore it was one time in the garden at Lady Wentworth's ball." Jennette twirled a strand of black hair around a finger. "One time, Avis."

"There are ways to prevent conception," Avis countered. Although she had no idea what that might entail.

"There are ways to prevent an unwanted pregnancy but they aren't foolproof," Sophie said. "I'm a perfect example of that. I wouldn't be here today if these methods were perfected."

Avis supposed a bastard daughter of an earl and an actress might just know a little about prevention. She sighed and sat back against the sofa, deflated.

"What if you change your mind regarding marriage?" Sophie asked. "Many men would not be pleased to learn you're damaged goods."

"I will never marry," Avis replied with conviction. "I understand my reputation might be at risk, and I understand the other risks. If I get with child I can sell my house and move to the country as a 'widow.'"

She sipped her tea and continued before her resolve weakened any further. "But I have decided on the perfect man. One who would never let a soul know what we have done."

"Who is your victim?" Sophie asked.

Of course they wanted a name. "I really shouldn't say."

"I daresay she doesn't wish to kiss and tell," Sophie said with a laugh. Her comment brought giggles from Jennette.

Her censorious glare did nothing to stop their irreverent laughter. "Very well. Emory Billingsworth."

All laughter stopped and a strident silence filled the salon. Sophie frowned. Jennette looked concerned and neither of her friends spoke for a full minute.

"Mr. Billingsworth?" Sophie echoed.

Jennette shifted in her seat. "I'd heard a rumor of him with Lady Hythe recently. They have become quite close. Some even speculate she would be willing to accept an offer from him."

"I am quite certain he would have told me about that," Avis said with a wave of her hand in dismissal. "He tells me everything."

"Why would he tell you about another woman when you are—"

"He tells me everything," Avis said before Jennette could speak of the money Avis loaned Emory when he needed it. Only Jennette knew about the money, and only because she had overheard them one day.

"I know my brother thinks rather poorly of him," Jennette remarked.

"Why?" Avis asked, not that it mattered one way or the other what Lord Selby thought of Emory. She had known Emory for three years and he was a perfect gentleman and friend to her.

"I don't know for certain. I just know he doesn't have a good thing to say about him."

"Have you spoken with him yet?" Sophie asked.

"No. The last time he called was on my birthday. He's been occupied writing his book."

"Oh," she said in obvious relief. "Are you certain he is the right man for you, Avis?"

"Of course. He is a writer like me. He's a wonderful and caring friend."

"Yes, but do you truly desire him?" Sophie asked softly.

Sophie's question stopped her short. Emory was quite handsome with his blonde hair and brown eyes. Just because her dream lover appeared to have much darker hair didn't mean anything. Besides, Emory would do anything she needed and not because he was in wild, passionate love with her, but because they were close friends. She had no need for wild, passionate love. She only wanted to discover what happened between a man and a woman and how it felt. Perhaps then her dreams would stop frustrating her.

"I do think Emory is perfect for me."

Sophie's gray eyes bore into hers. "If you say so."

"I will talk to him at my cousin's ball tomorrow night. It will be far easier for us to slip away from the crowd unnoticed." Avis smiled up at her friends. "You will be there, won't you?"

"I have plans with my Aunt Harris," Sophie said quickly. Which Avis knew meant her cousin had scratched Sophie's name off the guest list.

"Yes, my brother said Lord Watton has some business to discuss with him so we must attend," Jennette replied.

Avis wasn't surprised. The new Lord Watton had not been pleased when he discovered the title came with the ancestral pile in Wiltshire and not much else. The majority of wealth her father had generated during his lifetime went to Avis upon his death two years ago. More than likely her inheritance provided him some relief from his guilt, not that the money offered a salve to her wounds.

A knock on the door sounded and Lord Selby's low voice resonated from the hallway.

Jennette glanced toward the doorway then leaned in closer. "Think carefully on what you are about to do, Avis. You might be making the biggest mistake of your life."

Avis grimaced. "I am quite certain I am not."

"Only time will tell," Sophie said in a haunting voice. "Only time will tell."

Avis looked over to see Jennette's highly annoying older brother Banning standing at the threshold. She pressed a hand to her stomach at the sight of the Earl of Selby. His black hair gleamed from the drops of rain he hadn't yet wiped away.

He was wet, dripping water all over her marble floor. Now was her chance. She had waited weeks to get back at his last spiteful comments to her.

"You look like a drowned rat, Selby."

His lips twitched slightly. "Hardly a rat, Miss Copley. Much more like the legendary selkies of Scotland."

A selkie! The arrogance of the man astounded her. "Oh but I think the human form of the selkies is supposed to be irresistible."

"And most women would say that was true of me," he said with a wink and a smug smile.

"Not all women," Avis replied tartly.

"I understand you recently had a birthday. So just how old are you now?"

"Still younger than you," she bit out.

"Also true. But an aging man is seldom looked upon in the same light as an aging, unmarried woman."

"Banning," Jennette exclaimed. "That is enough."

Avis turned her back on him for a moment. She hated how his comments always struck so deep with her and once more, he'd responded only to her waspish tongue. She should have bit her tongue rather than behave like such a shrew. Why after eight years couldn't she put their animosity behind her?

"So where is the rest of the Spinster Club?" he drawled, leaning a broad shoulder against the door-frame.

The Spinster Club. The name he coined for the five of them years ago, before they were even considered on the shelf. Now most of the *ton* thought of Avis and her four friends as spinsters.

"Victoria and Elizabeth could not join us today," Avis replied.

"Banning, I think we should take our leave now," Jennette said.

"But I would be remiss in not wishing Miss Copley a belated happy birthday," Selby retorted. "Happy birthday, Miss Copley." He took her bare hand and gently kissed the top of it.

Sparks leapt up her arm from the brief contact. She tugged her hand back and looked away from him.

He moved back toward the doorway near Sophie but didn't leave the room.

"I forgot to show you what Mr. Billingsworth gave me for my birthday," Avis said to her friends. She held out the small pearl chain.

Selby muttered something, which made Sophie's

eyes widen but Avis couldn't make out his comment. Most likely another derogatory remark about her age.

"It's lovely, Avis," Jennette said.

"Yes, lovely," Sophie concurred, and then sent another strange glance toward Selby.

"Happy birthday, Miss Copley," he said. "We really must take our leave now."

"Good day, Lord Selby," Avis said. She breathed a sigh of relief as his footsteps echoed down the hall.

Banning climbed into the carriage after Sophie and Jennette. The two women seemed unusually quiet after their visit with Avis. But after calling on Lady Ledbury's daughter, Anne, and listening to her endless prattle about the musicale she attended last night, the silence of the carriage was more than welcome. There wasn't one young woman currently out that made him want to consider marriage. His father had always spoken of the importance of finding the right woman for a wife. She must come from a good family, no scandals attached to her name, and wealth would only be a plus.

Lady Anne had all those qualifications, but the idea of spending the rest of his life with her set his stomach roiling. He had promised his mother he would seriously pursue marriage this Season. At one and thirty, he knew it was long past time to settle down and have children. The idea of children made him smile. The idea of a wife set his lips in a downward position.

Sophie's light cough drew him out of his musing. Banning glanced at both women and knew something was going on between them today. Instead of talking, they kept giving odd looks to each other, which they appeared to understand, but he certainly did not. He wondered if he should ask them about their lack of conversation and then decided it was best to let the normally chatty ladies stay quiet.

Until Sophie could no longer hold her tongue and blurted out, "We can't let her do this."

"This is not the time," Jennette warned, with a quick nod toward Banning.

"This may be the perfect time. Your brother might just be able to help us."

Help them? With what? Instead of asking, he decided to wait to see what they would do. He leaned back against the velvet squabs of the carriage and crossed his arms over his chest.

"Sophie, she needs *our* help. Banning could never help her."

Sophie raised an eyebrow. "Tell me, Lord Selby. What do you know of Emory Billingsworth?"

Warning signals flared throughout his brain. Was there more to Billingsworth and Avis's relationship than friendship? "He is not a man I would want a friend of mine associating with."

Sophie gave Jennette a smug smile.

"Why not?" Jennette asked.

"He's not a man to be trusted," Banning said.

"Could you give us a little more information?" Jennette complained. "Why can he not be trusted? What has he ever done to you that leads you to believe he is not a good man?"

Banning grimaced. Dreadful memories flashed through his mind. He couldn't tell them everything he knew about Billingsworth, but he could give the women a reason to warn Avis if she was indeed the reason they were worried.

"Emory Billingsworth has a sordid past. His last three books have not sold. He is living on handouts and not just from Miss Copley."

Sophie played with the folds of her gown. "So Mr. Billingsworth is using Avis for his own gains," she concluded.

"I believe you understand me."

The carriage pulled to a stop in front of Selby House in Grosvenor Square. Banning climbed down and held out his hand to assist both women from the carriage while a footman attempted to cover them all with an umbrella. Assuming their conversation finished, he walked inside his home, handed his wet greatcoat to Battenford and headed straight for his study. He didn't need to know any more about what Avis Copley had in her head. In fact the less he knew, the better . . . at least for him.

Banning flexed his fists in frustration as he paced in his study. The woman made him insane.

What was she about? And how was Billingsworth involved?

Bloody hell. Avis Copley meant nothing to him.

Instead of thinking about her any further, he walked to the decanter on the corner cabinet and poured a brandy to chase away the chill from the cool June rain. The smooth liquid eased his irritation and warmed him. He dropped into the leather chair behind his mahogany desk, determined to put the infinitely frustrating woman out of his mind.

He stared at the papers in front of him. Only a few more weeks of Parliament then he could leave London and Avis behind for a few months. He shuffled through the missives and invitations until he heard a delicate cough. Glancing up, he saw Sophie standing there but looking behind her as if she wanted to make sure no one saw her.

"Miss Reynard?" He stood up, waiting for her to say something.

She turned her head back toward him. "Lord Selby, I must speak with you in private."

"Where is Jennette?"

Sophie walked into the room and closed the door behind her. "Your mother needed her upstairs. I don't have much time before she returns looking for me."

"What is the matter?" He waited for her to take a seat across from him before returning to his chair.

"It's Avis."

"I assumed that from our conversation in the carriage. What about Miss Copley?"

"She plans to take Emory Billingsworth as her . . . her . . ."

"Her what?"

"Lover," she whispered. Her cheeks reddened in embarrassment.

Banning's blood went cold. "I had no idea she was in love with Billingsworth," he said, staring at the desk.

"I don't believe she is. They act far more like friends than lovers or even people in love with each other. If they love each other at all I fear it may be only in a sibling manner."

"Then why?"

"She told us she believes this will help her write more realistic characters."

Bloody hell it would. Yet something in Sophie's

voice gave him pause. People said she had visions and read futures. He wondered idly if perhaps she sensed the truth about Billingsworth.

"But you don't believe her, do you?"

"No." She raised her head slowly and looked him square in the eye. "But I don't know her true reason. It might come to me in time, as in a dream. But for now . . ." Sophie shrugged.

"So why are you bringing this matter to me?" Avis Copley could do whatever she wished with whomever she wanted.

"Because I believe you have information that could stop her."

He might, but Avis would never believe him. She thought far too highly of Billingsworth.

"And *you* must stop her," Sophie whispered.

"Miss Copley and her love affair is none of my concern," Banning replied harshly.

Miss Reynard glared at him. "Indeed? She is your sister's dearest friend. Do you want Jennette's reputation sullied by her association with Avis if she takes that libertine as her lover?"

Banning clenched his fists on the desk. As much as Jennette might not care if her reputation were tainted, he cared.

Miss Reynard continued to glare at him. "You will stop her."

"Why me? You should stop her. After all you are her friend, not I."

"I have no information about Mr. Billingsworth that would influence her. I'm quite certain you do. Tell her what you know about the man."

"It is highly unlikely that Miss Copley would even believe me."

"You must try," she implored in a quieter tone. "If not for Avis, then do this for your sister."

"Very well." He stood to his full height and crossed his arms over his chest. "Miss Copley despises me. How exactly do you propose I prevent her from involving herself with him?"

"I am certain you shall devise something," she answered sweetly. "If all else fails, lie to her."

She rose and quickly headed for the door. Before she reached for the knob, she looked back at him.

"She intends to slip away at her cousin's ball tomorrow night with Mr. Billingsworth. He normally leaves for his crumbling estate in Devon as soon as the Season ends. Prevent her from asking him before he leaves. Hopefully by the time he returns, she will have forgotten her mad idea." She inclined her head toward him. "Good day, my lord."

He mumbled something as she shut the door behind her but it certainly wasn't "goodbye."

One day.

He had one day to determine the best course of action. How had he allowed himself to be pulled into this? He did not even like Avis Copley. Well, that wasn't exactly the truth. But like and lust were two very different emotions. It was the lust that always caused his frustration with her. Every time they were near each other they bickered. It kept the desire at bay and seemed a much better course of action than carrying her to his bed and keeping her there until their attraction waned.

Keeping her away from Billingsworth would not be easy. She would be wary if he suddenly followed her around at a ball. And Billingsworth would be suspicious if Banning attempted to befriend him after all that was between them.

Banning would have to make certain she never had the opportunity to speak with Billingsworth alone. It sounded like a simple plan, but everyone in the *ton* knew he despised Billingsworth, and everyone in the *ton* knew Avis Copley despised Banning.

The *Ice Maiden* had a long memory.

"Excuse me, my lord," Battenford said from the doorway. "Lord Kesgrave is here."

"Show him in." Perhaps Trey could help him.

"Banning, I have news you might not want to hear," Trey said upon entering the room. He sank into the nearest chair, pulled out a handkerchief, and wiped the droplets of rain from his face.

Banning poured a brandy and handed it to Trey before picking up his own snifter and slipping into the leather chair across from him. "All right, go ahead."

"I stopped by Tattersall's this afternoon and discovered Arthur's Pride has been purchased in a private sale. It's a damn shame. He would have made a great addition to our stables."

"Yes, he *will* make a wonderful addition to our stables. Mate him with Delilah when she is ready."

Trey shook his head. "Damnation, Ban. Do you get your way in all matters?"

"I certainly try," he said with a smile. "Besides, I couldn't let you get outbid. We needed another stud."

Banning sipped his drink, wondering how to bring up the subject of Avis Copley and how best to solve her problem.

"Are you attending the Watton affair tomorrow?"

Trey asked. "I understand he is very interested in investing some money. He might wish to throw some money toward the horses."

One dilemma solved. "Yes, I am attending. And I could use your help, but not with Watton."

"Oh?"

"I need to stick close to Emory Billingsworth."

Trey raised a brow in question. "I see."

"I need to keep someone from speaking with him."

"Anyone I might know?"

Banning glanced down at the amber liquid in his glass. "I don't believe you do."

Trey leaned his head back and laughed. "Right. In other words, you are trying to prevent someone, and by someone I can only assume a woman, from contacting him."

"Perhaps."

"I know how you loathe the man. Of course I can help you."

"And no questions about whom I'm trying to protect, or why?"

"Absolutely not," Trey replied with a slight grin. "So how am I to help you?"

Trey sipped his brandy, then swirled the remaining liquid around in his glass as if bored with their conversation. Banning knew him well enough to be certain Trey was anything but bored.

"I need to stay close to Billingsworth, and you know it would be too irregular for me to suddenly interject myself with his crowd."

Trey's always-present smile faded as he stared into the empty firebox. "So we must find a mutual friend in Billingsworth's group that we can talk to."

"Anyone come to mind?" Banning had only one thought, but he wasn't certain Trey would agree.

"Unfortunately, it has to be Somerton."

Banning blew out a long breath. "Are you certain?"

"Yes."

There was no one who could discover information on people like Somerton. He had contacts everywhere. And Banning wanted to know exactly what Billingsworth was about now.

"I shall talk to him." Trey blew out a long breath. "Somerton and I go back to Harrow. While we may move in different circles now, I believe he may still owe me one favor."

"So, if he agrees, then all we have to do is pretend I wish to speak with him."

"*We* wish to speak with him. You don't know Somerton as I do. Which is more than likely a good thing."

"Very well, then," Banning replied, holding his glass up in salute. Now he had to determine how to deal with Avis Copley's anger if she discovered his plan. The woman was more stubborn than a mule. Like his sister, once Avis had an idea in her head there was no dissuading her. But he would stop her, for her own sake.

Chapter Three

As Avis dressed for her cousin's ball, she continued to tell herself that everything she had designed was for the best. Emory Billingsworth was a gentleman and would not speak a word of their affair. As a writer and a friend, he would be a good choice to initiate her into the passions of the flesh.

As her maid placed the final pins in her hair, Avis reviewed her list of the benefits and disadvantages of her planned affair. Discovering the truth of what happens between a man and a woman—to satisfy her curiosity—was most definitely a benefit. Putting a stop to these persistent dreams, another plus.

Yet, being ostracized by Society wasn't something she desired. And the thought of pregnancy terrified her. Since her friends had reminded her of the consequences, Avis had thought of little else.

She enjoyed meeting with her friends and attending the balls and the theater. But she was twenty-six-years old. She wanted, no needed, to discover what she was missing by remaining a spinster. The way her married friends giggled and whispered about their husbands when they thought no one could hear them had only increased her curiosity. Assuming she could find her courage to go through with the idea, she would spend only a night or two with the man anyway.

Once she had contained her inquisitiveness, they would end their time together and resume their platonic friendship. She had worked out every detail of their relationship from how she would ask him to how they would end as friends. Everything would work out perfectly.

Closing her eyes, she tried to imagine Emory Billingsworth kissing her. Unfortunately, the only image that came to mind looked nothing like Emory and far too much like Lord Selby.

She clenched her fists in her lap. Selby was a cur. She hated him. She most certainly did not want to kiss him . . . again.

"All done, ma'am," her maid said with a satisfied smile.

Avis stood up and walked to the mirror. While not an "Incomparable," tonight the woman reflected back at her appeared different, almost alluring. Highly unusual for her normally rather bookish self.

The lower than normal neckline on her new emerald gown might have something to do with her bold feelings. The dress gave her a sensual look, not something for which she normally strived. Her brown hair was piled into curls upon her head with long, spiral tendrils framing her face. There was a hint of confidence in her smile; hopefully, that same self-assurance would reach her mind, too.

With a nod of determined satisfaction, she departed for the ball. She would make the arrangements with Emory tonight. Everything was organized. She could sneak him into the house after dismissing her servants for the night. Then all she had to do was make sure he left via the back entrance before the servants awoke for their morning preparations.

The carriage rolled to a stop in front of her former home. As the maroon and gold liveried footman opened the door, a familiar ache touched her soul. She did not miss the house, only her mother. She had been dead for ten years, yet the pain remained. Her heart wept for all the wrongs that had played out in that house, misdeeds a child couldn't fix and a wife should never have to endure.

With a deep breath for courage, she walked up the steps. Bateman opened the door and smiled broadly at her.

"Miss Avis, welcome home," he said as if this was still her home.

"Good evening, Bateman. Is everything ready?"

"Yes, miss."

Avis walked up to the first floor and gave an approving nod. The ballroom was exactly as she and Celia had ordered. Long pink and white roses stood in crystal vases at every corner and near every entrance to the room, just as she'd requested. Glancing up at the ceiling, she was taken aback to notice the yellow silk draped across it like the blazing sun on a summer afternoon.

That girl knew nothing about decorating a room for a ball.

"Avis!"

She turned to see the new Lady Watton all but running to her. She remembered what her mother said about controlling her temper—breathe, count to ten. *One, two, three, four, five*—

"Why is the ceiling draped in yellow?" At least she'd made it to five.

"The room is perfect, isn't it?" Celia twirled around as her jonquil dress flared out and her golden tresses spun with her. She looked like a golden canary in her elaborate birdcage.

"I thought we had agreed on the pale pink silk for the ceiling?"

Celia twisted her bow shaped mouth into a frown. "But pink wouldn't go with my new gown."

"That is true," Avis said, resigned.

The sound of voices from the hall announced their first guests, saving her from a whimsical conversation about the importance of fashion matching the ball decorations.

"I must go and greet my guests," Celia said with a slight giggle. She and Lord Watton took their positions at the entrance to the ballroom.

Avis watched the people arrive and greeted many of her acquaintances, but she searched for only one person. Finally she glanced back to the entrance relieved to see Emory assessing the room. His perfectly combed back, graying blonde hair drew attention to his broad forehead and brown eyes. He wore black form-fitting breeches and a well-padded emerald jacket that spread across his narrow shoulders like moss on a tree. The cravat he wore was tied in some new fashion. They would look splendid dancing together.

He scanned the room once more but did not seem to notice her.

She was determined to rectify that.

While she still had her courage, she strolled across the deserted dance floor, her gaze locked on her victim. Halfway to him, a large body bumped into her. The man caught her close to keep her from tumbling to the floor. She looked up into sparkling blue eyes and wanted to scream.

"Selby, you oaf! Don't you ever look where you are going?"

"I must apologize, Miss Copley. I barely recognized you," he said with a pointed look at the valley of her breasts exposed by her dress.

She yanked herself away from him. "You are a beast."

"Hmm, probably so," he said with a rakish grin.

Avis strode away from him, still looking for Emory, who had managed to disappear into the crowd. The musicians finished tuning and the dancing was set to begin. Avis moved off the dance floor, glaring over at Selby. He irritated her in so many ways she couldn't begin to count them.

She finally located Emory in a crowd of men, which meant she wouldn't get the chance to talk to him until later. Everything was fine. It was only a small change to her plan. She could talk to him later. Strolling out of the room, she headed down the hall to her father's—no, Watton's—study.

As she sat in the overlarge chair, memories of watching her father working here overwhelmed her. She glanced down at her arm and the faint jagged scar still visible after almost twenty years. Looking over at the raised hearth, she wondered if the servants had ever cleaned all the blood off the bricks. All she'd wanted was a hug from her father. Instead, she had this constant reminder that business had been more important to him than her love.

She shoved those dreadful thoughts away, picked up a piece of paper, and dipped the quill into the ink. After penning the note that would seal her future, she sanded it and waved the paper to dry.

It was done. She would give herself up to the passion she had inside of her and allay her curiosity. The only thing left to do was get the message to him before midnight.

After returning to the ballroom, she scanned the room for him. She found Emory only two feet from the man she wanted to ignore. While Emory didn't appear to notice her stare, Selby naturally did. It seemed the wretch was spying on her tonight, though she had no idea why. Instead of dwelling on Selby any further, she waved a footman over.

"Yes, miss?"

"Bring this to the man by the terrace door," she whispered, pointing toward Emory.

The man hesitated.

"Over there," Avis said, again pointing to Emory.

"Ah, yes, miss."

She couldn't watch. Instead, she turned and walked toward Jennette knowing her plan was in motion.

Banning continued to make inane conversation with Billingsworth's friends, wondering when Avis would try to contact the man again. He hoped he had forestalled her first attempt when he jostled her on the dance floor. Letting Billingsworth make a fool out of her . . . or worse was not an option.

Banning would do everything in his power to make certain Avis didn't give herself to that letch.

"I have great news to announce tonight at midnight," Billingsworth said to his small crowd of admirers.

"About what?" one of the men asked.

"My latest novel. *Walking with Emily* is going to be a huge success."

Banning smiled along with the rest of the group but wondered exactly how Billingsworth's unpublished novel would be a success when he couldn't find a publisher. Banning watched as a footman headed toward the group with a note on a silver salver. He'd seen Avis talking to the same footman and could only assume she meant the missive for Billingsworth. Banning moved slightly closer to him, ready to grab the note if necessary.

"Sir, I believe this is for you," the footman said to Billingsworth.

"Actually, if the note is from Miss Copley, it would be for me," Banning said with all the arrogance an earl could possess.

The footman turned toward Banning with a bow. "My mistake, my lord."

"Are you certain, Selby? Perhaps the lady had an assignation with me in mind," Billingsworth said with a coarse laugh.

The men in the group chortled, except Trey and Somerton who both gave Banning curious looks.

He slipped the paper into his jacket pocket. "It is a note regarding some business I am supposed to have with her cousin, Lord Watton."

"Of course. The *Ice Maiden* wouldn't have anything to do with assignations when she can keep herself warm with her words," Billingsworth said, raising chuckles from his toadies.

The urge to strangle the man forced Banning's hands into fists. How could the bastard talk so poorly about her when he greedily took her money and pretended to be her friend? And Banning hated how people called her the *Ice Maiden,* especially since he'd coined the term for her. But that had happened a very long time ago.

He moved away from Billingsworth's group, found a secluded corner and opened the note.

Meet me in the study at midnight . . . A

He would certainly do just that. He crumpled the paper back into his pocket and checked the time— quarter past eleven.

"Lord Selby, have you forgotten our dance?" the tinny voice of Miss Olivia Roebuck sounded from behind him.

The woman would not leave him alone. She had been after him the entire Season. Banning turned and faced the young woman. Her blonde hair styled into a halo of curls, and her big blue eyes looked angelic, but he knew better. Several times in the past few months, she had tried to get him into a compromising position. He only agreed to dance with her tonight because the girl's mother pressed him into it.

"Of course, Miss Roebuck. I believe this is our quadrille."

"There is a waltz coming up next if you would prefer to wait?"

"No," he said a bit too roughly. "I would love to dance with you now." *And be done with it.*

He only prayed the quadrille wouldn't last too long. He had to keep his unexpected appointment with Avis.

Miss Roebuck droned on about some new *on-dit* as they walked to the dance floor, but Banning kept his eyes on his prey. Avis stood in the corner with his sister, talking about something, and he doubted it was the latest gossip.

As soon as the dance ended, Banning returned the pouting girl to her mother and searched for a corner to pass the next few moments. His gaze landed on Avis as she stood across the room. She leveled him a glare before averting her eyes to the dance floor. He loved the way her cheeks turned rosy when he stared at her. As the minutes passed, he wondered what he would say to her. Some measure of the truth, but just how much? He'd never told anyone what he'd seen Billingsworth do to those girls all those years ago.

Miss Reynard had suggested lying to Avis, and it might just come to that. He skirted the crush on the dance floor and reached the hallway just in time to see the door to the study close behind her. Standing outside the room, he stared at the door.

A rush of apprehension overwhelmed him. He suddenly felt as though he could be making the biggest mistake of his life. But he had to stop her. He'd failed the others. He would not fail Avis.

Forcing the unease away, he slipped inside.

Avis turned at the sound. Her mouth dropped open, and her amber eyes widened in surprise or shock, he wasn't sure which.

"Wh—What are you doing here?" she sputtered.

Banning smiled. "Were you expecting someone else?"

He hadn't thought her eyes could get any bigger, but they did. She backed herself against the large, cherry desk.

"You must leave—now!" she exclaimed, pointing to the door.

"I cannot do that, Avis."

"Selby, get out of here!"

Slowly he advanced on her until he stood only inches away. Her chest rose and fell in quick succession emphasizing her full breasts, which she seldom exposed to this degree.

"I'm expecting someone," she cried. "You must leave before he arrives."

A loud cheer from the ballroom turned both their heads toward the door.

"He won't be coming."

"Who?" she whispered, looking up at him.

"Emory Billingsworth."

Chapter Four

She slapped her hands down on the desk behind her as if to brace herself. "What are you talking about, Selby?"

Why couldn't Billingsworth meet her? There had to be a good reason. Thank God, he had actually listened to Jennette's gossipy prattle at breakfast about Lady Hythe.

"That cheer was the *ton's* congratulations on Mr. Billingsworth and Lady Hythe's engagement. He won't be coming in here."

"His engagement?" she whispered. She blinked as if attempting to keep tears at bay. "Did he send you in his place, to inform me?"

"No."

"Then how did you . . . ?" Her face blanched with comprehension.

He held up the note she'd written until she grabbed it out of his grip. "How did you get this?"

"I took it from the footman."

She pushed him away and walked around the desk. Leaning over the desk, she stared at him before saying, "You took my private message and read it?"

"Hardly private, Avis. There wasn't even a name on it."

"Regardless, you shouldn't have read my note," she retorted. "Besides, his name wasn't on the note. How did you know it was for Mr. Billingsworth?"

Damn good question. How did he know? "I made the assumption and thought to save you the embarrassment of asking a newly betrothed man to meet you alone. Highly scandalous, Avis, and so unlike you."

He sat down in the chair by the desk. Her emerald gown shimmered in the candlelight. But it wasn't the lovely dress that caught his attention. Her light brown hair shined with burnished gold strands, highlighting her amber eyes and heart-shaped face. His gaze moved lower, admiring the amount of snowy skin exposed to him. For a small woman she had ample curves everywhere a woman should.

"Now what did you wish to speak with Billingsworth about? A problem with your current story? Did you need him to assist you?"

"It is none of your concern." She stood upright and crossed her arms over her chest.

Slowly, Banning stood and then leaned in closer to her until only a desk kept them apart. Avis stood her ground, but her breathing increased.

"I'm quite certain *I* can help you," he whispered with a ghost of a smile.

Her mouth dropped open. "Oh my God! Did Jennette tell you?" Her voice raised an octave. "Did she?"

Heat crept across his cheeks. He felt like a damned schoolboy accused of cheating on his exams. His sister had told him nothing of any consequence, but he could not tell Avis about his conversation with Miss Reynard. "No. I overheard my sister and Miss Reynard talking."

She paused as if taking in his words. "What exactly did you hear?"

"I believe you decided to have a love affair with Mr. Billingsworth. I'm here to stop you from making the biggest mistake of your life."

Her face grew pallid. "This is none of your concern, Selby."

"I'm making it my concern."

"Why?"

Banning sighed. "Emory Billingsworth is the worst kind of man—"

"Unlike you," she interrupted. "You're simply an angel, are you not?" Her eyes, normally a soft amber, hardened as she glared at him.

"I never claimed to be an angel, Avis. But nothing I have ever done can compare to Billingsworth. He will rip your reputation to shreds. Why? Because he shall think it a great joke."

"I don't believe you. I have known Mr. Billingsworth for the past three years, and he has been nothing but a gentleman to me. Unlike you."

Banning clenched his fists. "Avis, he is not the man you think he is."

"Why should I believe *you*?"

"I was at Eton when he was there. I know things about him that he has been able to keep quiet—things that could ruin him if they became public."

"That was years ago when he was barely a man. I would be surprised to find a man who didn't have some slight scandal to his name, even you," she whispered the last two words.

"Avis," Banning said, trying to contain his frustration. "You cannot do this. At least not with him, think of Lady Hythe. She would be devastated if she discovered her betrothed with another woman."

She closed her eyes and stood still. After what seemed like minutes, though in truth was only a few seconds, she opened them again. "Very well then. I shall have to find another man."

"No!" The words tumbled out before he could stop them. "If you want someone else, choose me."

Damn! Where had that come from?

He walked slowly around the desk with his fingers sliding across the smooth wood. He took two more strides and then drew her against his chest.

"Let me go, you—"

"Dear God, please stop calling me an oaf."

Her lips twitched. "I will not do this with you, Selby. And you know why."

His head dipped toward her ear. "That was eight years ago, Avis. And I was a fool."

"No. Not you," she said with a slight catch to her voice. She pulled out of his arms, walking only a step backward before she stopped.

"I wasn't?" He'd felt like one back then. Kissing the *Ice Maiden* had been a prank, but the joke had been on him when he realized he might have lost control if she hadn't backed away.

She poked her finger at his chest. "Yes, you were a fool. And I was an even greater one for thinking I was anything but a wager to you. Melt the *Ice Maiden* and win the bet. I won't be that foolish again."

"I never meant to hurt you."

"Well you did and on more than one occasion."
She walked toward the door. "I believe we should
leave."

"One kiss."

She whirled around with a swish of green silk.
"What?"

"One kiss to convince you that I am the man you
want. If after one kiss you decide not to accept me,
I shall leave you in peace. And I won't speak of
your plans."

Her face screwed into a multitude of emotions as
she contemplated his request. "That's all it would
take to be rid of you—one kiss?" she asked hesitantly.

"That is it." *Say yes . . . say yes,* he silently urged as
he walked closer to her. He wanted her kiss like a
drowning man wanted saving.

"Very well then. Let's get this over with."

Every seduction skill he had ever learned would be
needed for this one moment. With exacting preci-
sion, he drew her against his chest. Slowly, he lowered his head until his lips touched hers with the
briefest of contact. It took every ounce of self-control
not to drag her even closer to him. Instead, he
sucked her lower lip into his mouth and slid his
tongue across it. She whimpered—one battle won.

He pressed her closer to him and deepened the
kiss. The light scent of her jasmine perfume infused him. He wanted her. Damn. He wanted her
more now than he had eight years ago. Touching
her warm skin and tasting the hint of wine on her
tongue sent his pulse thrumming.

Her whimper turned into a soft moan as she responded to him. One more battle down but the war

was far from over. He skimmed his hands down her back and squeezed her derrière tightly against his rising erection. She started to draw away but he refused her. He bent his head over her mouth again and played with her tongue until she wrapped her arms around his neck and pressed her warm body closer to him. This time, he moaned.

His lips trailed a path to her ear. "Say yes, Avis," he whispered. "Say yes."

"One night, Selby."

Banning pulled his head back—one night? "A month wouldn't be enough time to teach you everything you want to know."

"One week—"

He cut off her protests with another passionate kiss. Lifting his head, he said, "Three weeks."

"One—"

Again, he kissed her until he hoped her protests would cease.

"Two," she said breathlessly. "That's my final offer." She thrust out of his arms and walked unsteadily toward the door. "Call on me to finalize the details tomorrow," she said with a quiver to her voice. The door shut quietly behind her.

What the bloody hell had he done?

He was only supposed to prevent her from having an affair with Billingsworth, not exchange places with the man. Banning pressed his palms against the desk. He had made the situation even worse. The quiet, reserved woman he had known for years was suddenly doing everything in her power to ruin herself, and *he* was helping her.

It wasn't as if he needed a lover. Any number of married or widowed women in that very ballroom would jump at the chance to be his mistress. But with Avis, he was playing with fire. There was every possibility that someone would discover their liaison and as an innocent, she would be ruined. If he didn't marry her to spare her name, he'd be an utter bastard. Not that he would ever let that happen. If this insanity was ever discovered, he would live with the consequences.

He thought about the word consequences for a moment, weighed it in his mind, and released a heavy sigh. It wasn't too late to stop this madness. But no matter how hard he tried to think about consequences and logic and morals, he knew one thing for certain. He wanted this. Consequences be damned. He wanted Avis. If someone discovered them, he would marry her.

Marriage to Avis . . . he waited for the usual aversion to strike him. And yet, it didn't. After years of avoiding marriage, he'd expected to feel repugnance, not the quiet, warming calm that spread over him.

Marry Avis Copley?

He slid into the chair behind the desk and examined the idea from all sides, searching for flaws. Other than the possible exception of her hating him, he couldn't find any fault. And after that passionate kiss, he was inclined to think she didn't hate him as much as she professed.

He did need to wed. That had been the plan for this Season, after all—find a bride. Because of their past history and the fact that she was Jennette's best friend, he had never considered her a candidate for his wife. He tapped his fingers on the desk. She wasn't a silly girl like Miss Roebuck or Lady Anne.

Avis had a maturity and intelligence he admired. She had her writing to keep her busy when he became embroiled with the estates or Parliament. She had a body any man would love to keep in bed for days.

This was truly a mad idea.

Still, she was the daughter of a viscount, wealthy in her own right, and from an excellent family with no scandals. She would have met all of his father's requirements for a wife. Except she had no interest in marrying . . . anyone. The thought made him smile.

He so loved a challenge. Women had thrown themselves at him since he was an adolescent. Most just wanted the title and money he brought to a marriage, while Avis had no desire for either. The other women were easy conquests. But in all the years he'd been with women only Avis rejected him. Only Avis would respond to him with cutting remarks. Only Avis argued with him in front of any number of people. Only Avis could respond to his kisses and make him forget everything, including his own control.

Only Avis.

Why had it taken him this long to realize she was exactly what he wanted in a wife? Guilt. He still regretted being involved in that bloody wager. If not for that kiss, he would never have realized how much he desired her. Still, they couldn't be in the same room without making sneering comments toward each other.

He had to admit that most of the time he only made derogatory comments to keep her at arms length. And surely his behavior had only supported her dislike of him. They would spend their days bickering and their nights making passionate love with each other.

He smiled.

She had made a bargain with the devil. How had it happened? How had she let him take control of the situation like that? Avis leaned against the ballroom wall and clutched her stomach. The one man she knew she would never be able to manage had turned her plan upside down.

And all because of one simple kiss.

Although, in truth, Selby's kisses were never simple. They were heated, mind-altering medicine that made her say and do the most foolish things, such as agreeing to have an affair with him. How could she have been so stupid?

There had to be a way out of this mess. She couldn't go away with Jennette's brother.

"Are you all right, Avis?"

She looked up to see *his* sister staring at her with concern. "Just a little dizzy, Jennette. It's a bit stifling in here."

"I meant with Mr. Billingsworth's announcement. Are you going to concede your idea is foolish and not continue with it?"

Well, she certainly couldn't tell Jennette who her new target was. "I shall have to decide on another man."

"Think carefully on it, Avis. You need a man you can trust, one who would never tell a soul about your affair. There are not very many men who fit into that category."

Could she trust Selby? She wasn't sure she could. After all, he had wagered he could kiss the *Ice Maiden* before any other man. And he had. Yet, as she thought about it, he had never gloated about their kiss. Perhaps Selby was just the man she needed, and she certainly desired him.

Avis glanced away from Jennette only to notice Selby and Lord Kesgrave strolling toward them. She couldn't face him again so soon.

"Jennette, would you excuse me? I need to give my felicitations to Mr. Billingsworth."

Avis slipped into the crowd on the dance floor and strolled to the other side of the room. She glanced around until she sighted Emory dancing with Lady Hythe. Avis let out a small sigh, feeling no pain at the sight of them together. With Emory, it wasn't as much a physical attraction as a mental appeal. They shared much in common with their writing. She had nothing in common with Selby.

The dance ended and Emory left Lady Hythe with a group of her friends. He walked toward Avis with a smile. "Miss Copley, how wonderful to see you tonight."

"Thank you, Mr. Billingsworth."

"I assume you heard my announcement?" he asked, straightening his already perfect coat.

"You must be very pleased."

"Of course. It's not every day Prinny invites a writer to join him in Brighton for a month in the summer. I do hope that his support will help my book to be published sooner."

Avis shook her head. Prinny? Brighton in the summer? "I thought your announcement might be an engagement to Lady Hythe."

Emory released a high-pitched, almost whiny sounding laugh. "Lady Susan Hythe? *And me?*"

"No?"

"She is a sweet, young widow but hardly a suitable wife for a man like me. Her husband left her but a paltry sum."

Avis scanned the room until she found Selby. A smug smile touched his lips as he stared back at her. Anger washed over her when he raised a sardonic eyebrow at her in question. She had no doubt he knew exactly what just transpired during her conversation with Emory.

"Congratulations on your accomplishment, Mr. Billingsworth. Excuse me, I must speak with Sel— someone."

"I shall call on you after I return, Miss Copley. I'm quite certain you will wish to hear all about my month with the prince."

She waved a hand at him in dismissal and walked toward Selby. Before she made it to the middle of the ballroom, he clasped her elbow and propelled her out to the terrace. A few people mingled in the shadows but Selby found a secluded spot for them before he released his grip.

"Is there a problem?"

Avis turned to face him. "Of course there is a problem. You deliberately lied to me about Mr. Billingsworth so I would be forced to accept your offer," her voice lowered to barely a whisper.

"Oh? There is no betrothal?" He twisted his lips as if attempting to contain a smile. "No matter. I'm still the better choice for you."

The arrogance of the man astounded her. "You are wrong on that point. Now that I know Mr.

Billingsworth is unattached, I have decided to return to my original plan. I shall just delay my proposal for a few weeks. I no longer need you, Lord Selby."

His mouth turned upwards into a wry smile. Why couldn't she take her gaze off his full lips? Lips that had warmed her mouth, and entire body, only moments before in the study.

"I'm afraid you cannot do that, my dear."

In the dim torchlight, she could just make out the darkness in his pale blue eyes. They reminded her of the sky just before a strong, summer storm.

"Why not?" she finally asked. She really needed to keep her concentration on his words not his eyes and mouth.

"Because I shall walk into the ballroom and tell everyone of your plan."

Avis stood there, unable to say a word. The Selby name was held in far more esteem than the unmarried daughter of a viscount. If he did as he threatened everyone would believe him, and she would be completely ruined. Her perfect plan had come tumbling down because of him. She should tell him she didn't care about a disgrace, but she really did care, and she was certain he knew it.

"Why? Why would you want to ruin me?"

"You made a bargain with me, and you will abide by it," he said roughly.

"You can't possibly want me—"

"I think I proved I do in the study."

"You can have your choice of women. You don't need me."

"You're right. I don't *need* you." He leaned in

closer to her ear until she could feel his warm breath tickle her. "I *want* you."

Banning Talbot, the sixth earl of Selby and quite possibly the most handsome man among the *ton*, wanted her. And he wanted her in a wholly improper fashion. A searing heat flowed through her body and centered between her legs. The only time she felt such desire was when he was around or in her dreams.

"There are just a few things you need to understand," Selby said. "You are to stay away from Emory Billingsworth."

"What?"

"Stay away from the man—"

"I will not!"

"There you two are," Jennette said. "Arguing again. Just once I would like to see you both together and not fighting."

If they didn't fight, they kissed, and she doubted Jennette would like to see that either. Avis wondered what other conditions Selby wanted to put on her, but that could wait until tomorrow when he called on her.

She had a dreadful feeling their two weeks would be nothing but arguing and making love. Perhaps even arguing while they made love. It would be the most difficult fortnight of her life.

Chapter Five

Banning sipped his tea and looked down at his congealed breakfast. Nothing appealed to him this morning. He dreaded his upcoming confrontation with Avis because he knew she would do anything to get out of their affair. The more he thought about it, the more certain he became that she would make a perfect wife for him. The last thing he wanted was her trying to get out of their arrangement.

"Are you unwell this morning, Banning?" Jennette's lilting voice brought him out of his musing.

"I'm quite well, thank you."

She sat down in the chair next to him and patted his hand with her own paint-splattered one. "Bloody hell you are. You look dreadful."

"Jennette, how many times do I have to tell you it is completely unladylike to swear?"

"Probably a few hundred more," she said with a laugh.

His sister might just be the death of him. At least that would spare him this valiant need to keep Avis from Emory Billingsworth. Banning had seen what

Billingsworth could do when angry with a woman, but he knew Avis would not believe him . . . at least not yet.

He should have put a stop to her association with that bastard years ago. Not that he'd had any way of doing so. Until now.

He knew the real Billingsworth. The man who wore a mask of gentility while in truth was nothing more than a violent, cruel beast. The same man who had beaten a prostitute because she tried to take the money due her from him. Banning closed his eyes against the images that rose to the surface. Not even years could eradicate those haunting memories. That girl writhing and moaning in pain as he carried her to the carriage. The gasp from the physician when he saw Banning holding the battered woman out to him. His own blood-splattered clothing ruined over the few shillings the poor girl needed to survive.

And she wasn't the only girl Billingsworth had beaten. But he would never lay a hand on Avis.

"I need to go out for a short while," Banning said.

"At this hour?"

"This isn't a social call, Jennette. It's business."

"Oh, well then have a marvelous time," she drawled. "I believe Mother and I have some shopping that must be completed."

"You might wish to use a bit more turpentine on your hands before leaving." He stood and smiled down at his little sister. "The shopkeepers might get distressed if you touch their fabric with those hands even with gloves on," he teased.

Jennette laughed as she stood to leave. "Followed by a course of rose scented lotion to hide the foul odor. Never fear, no one shall learn of my scandalous secret, brother dear."

Banning shook his head. Her scandalous secret was far from scandalous and far from secret. Most people knew of her painting, though few knew she painted the most beautiful oil landscapes he had ever seen. And even fewer people knew she planned to move to Italy after she gained Grandmama's inheritance. He sighed. Jennette's future was an issue for another day.

He decided to skip Parliament today and rode straight to Bruton Street and the house where Avis lived. His coachman stopped a few houses away from her home. As Banning stepped down, he looked up at her white, brick home and noticed it looked no different from any other on the block.

Except an unmarried woman occupied this house.

After skirting a couple out for an early stroll, he walked up the steps to her door. Reaching for the knocker, he let it slip from his hand to bang against the brass plate.

An older man with a stern expression opened the door for him. "Lord Selby?"

"I am here to see Miss Copley." Banning gave the butler one of his cards.

"Please wait inside, my lord. I will see if Miss Copley is at home."

Banning entered the small receiving room and smiled. This room suited Avis perfectly—functional furniture with no frills. He strolled around the small room idly as he waited for the servant to return.

"My lord, Miss Copley will see you in the study."

He followed the butler down the hall and into

the study only to find Avis sitting behind a large, masculine mahogany desk. With her stern gray dress and dour expression, she looked as if she were prepared to transact a business arrangement, not determine the location and details of an illicit affair.

"My lord, thank you for coming by on such short notice," she said as the butler closed the door. Once the door was firmly shut, the Avis he knew so well went on the attack. "You are such a beast. I cannot believe you think to blackmail me into an affair with you."

"Do we really need to discuss this again?" Banning sat in a soft leather chair on the other side of the desk. He glanced around the room, impressed by the décor. "Lovely rooms, by the way."

"Thank you, your sister helped me with the colors." She folded her arms over her chest. "I have decided not to go through with this."

"Oh?"

She tilted her head slightly. "I don't believe you mean to go through with your little blackmail scheme."

Banning gave her a half-smile and leaned in closer to the desk. "I wouldn't wager on that if I were you."

"Why?" Her face paled in the sunlight streaming in the windows.

"Because I have every intention of making love to you."

Her eyes darkened but he doubted it was anger causing the change. Whether or not she wanted to admit it to herself, he knew she was attracted to him.

"What?" she sputtered.

Banning stood and leaned over the desk. "I am going to make love to you, Avis. I'm going to touch every inch of your body. Taste your skin with my lips. Fill you completely and then I will watch your face as you cry out in release. And then," he paused, leaned closer and whispered, "then . . ."

"What?" She whispered with wide eyes.

"I'm going to do it again."

Avis whimpered.

Banning sat back down into his seat and watched the play of emotions cross her face.

She gaped at him and finally blinked. As if realizing any more arguing would be futile, she cleared her throat and said, "Shall we get down to business, then?"

"That may be your first problem, Avis. An affair such as ours has nothing to do with business."

She cocked her head and raised a tawny brow at him. "When blackmail is involved, I believe it becomes a business arrangement."

Banning casually leaned back in his chair and laughed. "I hardly think what I did was blackmail."

"And what would you call it?"

"Getting my way."

"And what about my way?"

He glanced at her and almost laughed again. Her amber eyes glared at him. But even from his seat, he could smell the sweet fragrance of her jasmine perfume. The scent gave her a totally feminine air that was in direct contrast to her masculine study and stern clothing.

"I believe my solution lets us both get our way," he finally replied.

"I chose Emory Billingsworth for a reason."

"Are you in love with him?"

"No," she mumbled.

"Then what reason?"

She looked away from him. "He's a writer like myself. I believe he would be able to help me with more than passion."

"Being a writer doesn't qualify him as a lover," Banning retorted.

"He can also help me with my characters . . . to make certain they have enough depth and—"

Banning's chuckle cut her off. "Sounds like you want a reader, not a lover."

"Well I don't want you," she retorted.

She had issued a challenge. He rose from his seat and rounded the desk. Avis scrambled out of her chair but couldn't move fast enough to avoid him. Pulling her up against his chest, he smiled down at her.

"You do want me, Avis."

She struggled against his grip. "I do not!"

He brought his lips to the outer shell of her ear and whispered, "Yes, you do."

He moved his lips down her jaw until he reached her full mouth. She trembled slightly as he lowered his head to kiss her. Dear God, he wanted her. He deepened his kiss, letting his passion run free for a moment, imaging her naked against him. With only a slight hesitation, she kissed him back.

He kissed her until he moaned from the simple pleasure of his tongue caressing hers. Knowing she would be his was a heady aphrodisiac. He pressed her back until she was stuck between the desk and his chest. Slowly, he trailed hot kisses down her slender neck until the idea of making love on a desk in her study overwhelmed him. He could lift her up onto the desk, strip her of all those damned layers of clothes, and find her sweet warmth.

He wanted to forget her innocence, but could not. If he didn't stop soon, he might not be able to stop until she surrendered to him.

He drew away from her, trying to catch his breath. "Seems we have a penchant for kissing in studies," he said lightly.

She turned away from him, but not before he noticed her high color. "So we do," she whispered.

"Still believe you don't want me?"

She only shook her head.

"All right. Shall we finish our arrangements?"

This time she nodded.

He smiled, satisfied anew with this decision.

"Parliament should be done in a week, so I will be free to leave London then. I have a place near Southwold we can travel to and have some privacy. My family won't think of going there because they don't care for the place. Since I tend to take a holiday there every summer, it won't seem odd to them."

"You don't wish to meet here, after the servants retire? Surely you could find a way to sneak in?"

"Too risky. Southwold is more secluded."

Her eyes widened and color tracked across her cheeks. "Shall I meet you there?"

"Meet me at the Wayside Inn in Chelmsford next Tuesday. You can tell your servants you are meeting Lady Elizabeth and going away with her for a few weeks."

"What if someone discovers the truth?"

"No one will. And who would suspect the two of us going away together?"

"Very well." She glanced down at her desk before continuing, "Selby, just how many servants do you have at this estate?"

He smiled down at her. "Only two and they can be trusted to keep quiet about who I bring with me."

"Only two?" she whispered with a frown.

"Would you prefer more?"

"No—no, I just assumed a large house would have many more servants," she said in a quick odd tone.

"For the most part it will just be the two of us. Mr. and Mrs. Hathaway stay in a cottage on the estate." Banning circled back around the desk and picked up his hat. "I must be off. I'll see you in a week then."

Avis slid into the leather chair as Selby closed the door behind him. One week to prepare herself for a fortnight with only him. She could not stop the shiver from enveloping her. What if he was like her father?

She knew she wasn't like her mother and would never allow a man to strike her, but with no one there to protect her. . . .

When she had planned this affair, she knew she would have to spend some time alone with a man. Only she had assumed it would be a night or two in her home and the man would leave during the day. She could always call up on her servants if she needed them. Selby's arrangement meant two weeks with him, and him alone. All day and all night.

Perhaps she should bring a pistol with her. Not that she imagined she could shoot him, but at least she might threaten him with it. She laughed aloud at the image of her holding a gun to Selby's head. He was several inches taller than she and outweighed her by several stone.

She was being ridiculous. He was Jennette's brother. Selby wouldn't do anything that might make Jennette angry with him.

Avis pushed aside all her negative thoughts and concentrated on positive things. Which brought her back to Selby's kiss, definitely an optimistic thought. She had never imagined kissing could be so—so intense. Today, he could have taken her right here on her desk, and she might not have stopped him.

A light knock sounded on the door to her study.

"Yes?"

Grantham opened the door. "You have callers, ma'am. Your friends."

"Show them into the salon, Grantham. And set out some tea and biscuits."

She hadn't expected a visit, but knowing Sophie, she wanted to discover what happened at the ball last night. With a deep breath to steady her frayed nerves, Avis walked to the salon.

All four of her friends were seated in the room, waiting expectantly for her.

"Well?" Sophie said before Avis even sat down.

Avis leveled Sophie a glare.

Sophie waved her hand at Avis. "Oh, of course I told them. They are our dearest friends and would never tell any soul. We all care about you, Avis."

"Mr. Billingsworth is otherwise occupied this summer," Avis replied as she dropped onto the settee.

"Good. Now you can forget all this nonsense and get back to your writing," Victoria commented.

Avis looked away but not before she noticed Sophie's prying stare. "Perhaps I shall do just that, Victoria."

"Of course, this is God's way of telling you it is wrong," Victoria added. Leave it to the daughter of a vicar to bring God into this mess.

Avis knew she had to get this discussion on to an ordinary topic. "What is everyone doing during summer?"

"Father has decided we should leave for the summer," Elizabeth said, thankfully changing the subject. "Apparently, even though it has been a cool summer he's packing us off to the Lake District."

Thankfully, it worked. "I have decided to start a new book to put this whole plan out of my mind. So I will need some time alone."

"Oh?" Jennette murmured. "What will you write about this time? I would love to hear more."

"It's too soon to talk about it. I am not certain where it is heading yet and besides, I'd rather get a bit of it on paper before talking it out. Emory is always telling me I shouldn't diffuse the muse. When I see you in a few weeks, I shall let you know more."

"At the Kesgrave summer party," Jennette said. "You promised me you would pay no heed to your sickness and come. I'm certain Mother will want to go to Talbot Abbey for a few weeks this summer so I will be there with her."

Avis had forgotten about the country party, and her dreadful motion sickness. She seemed to forget everything with Selby near. How would she manage in a carriage with Selby for hours? She would have to do what she always did, sleep. Assuming she could sleep with him so near.

"Avis?"

She glanced up to see Jennette giving her a peculiar look. "Yes?"

"You are attending the Kesgrave party, are you not?"

Selby was friends with Lord Kesgrave so he would certainly be there. She wondered how awkward it would be to see him so soon after they parted ways. Of course, they were bound to run into each other at balls and parties so she'd better get used to the idea. Had she chosen Emory, they could have remained friends. Since she and Selby were not friends to begin with, she had no idea how thing would end between them.

"Yes, I will be there," Avis answered.

"Well," Victoria said, looking into her teacup, "I have to admit, I'm happy to hear everyone will be busy this summer. I had an offer to assist a dear friend of mine who is starting an orphanage. I've been hesitating to accept, but now I shall."

"Good, so we will not have any regular meetings until we all arrive back in town?" Elizabeth asked.

Sophie bit her lower lip. "I suppose not."

Avis wished there was something she could do for Sophie. She wasn't completely accepted in Society, so she had very few friends. Most summers while the *ton* departed for their summer homes, Avis and Sophie and Victoria stayed in the city. But for at least two weeks, Sophie would be alone.

And Avis would be alone . . . with Selby.

* * *

Avis tried to ignore the strange sensations that overwhelmed her every time she saw Selby, but she couldn't. Each night she attended a different function and there he stood, against the wall, staring at her. Only with each passing night, the looks he gave her bordered increasingly on scandalous.

Tonight was no different.

Even from across the room she could feel the hot looks he sent her. Everyone else melted away until there was only the two of them, hungering for each other from across the room. She endeavored to look away but found it impossible not to stare at his handsome face. Her reprieve finally arrived when Mrs. Roebuck brought her daughter, Olivia, to Selby. Avis couldn't help but smile as he took Olivia to the dance floor with a deep scowl on his face. He looked completely irritated with the interruption.

Lady Bolton's ball was the culmination of the Season. The young women in their pale pastels searched desperately for a mate before they left for their summer estates, while the single men tried their best to avoid them. And then there were the married couples who, after one quick dance with their spouse, spent the rest of the night flirting with others. Was it any wonder she had no desire to marry?

"Oh dear, why is Olivia Roebuck dancing with my brother again?" Jennette asked then sipped her lemonade. "The poor girl is quite pretty, but have you ever tried to talk to her?"

"Unfortunately, I did. She proceeded to tell me all she knew about the greatest authors from history." Avis looked up at Jennette and shook her head. "She could only come up with Shakespeare and she called him Hamlet."

Jennette stifled a grin then frowned. "What if she ends up as my sister-in-law?"

"If your brother falls for her trap then he deserves what he gets."

"True. She would bore him to tears." Jennette sipped her lemonade again. "But I know he is serious about getting married."

Avis choked on her drink. "He is?"

"He's spent most of the Season searching for a wife."

"Well, there certainly are enough eligible ladies. Why hasn't he chosen one?"

Jennette shrugged. "I believe he finds them all as dull as Miss Roebuck. He needs a strong woman. One who will stand up to him, a woman with some brains in her head. You have to admit there are not very many of those here tonight."

"I take exception to that," Avis said with a grin.

"Indeed you should. I meant, there are not many intelligent women who wish to *marry* here tonight," Jennette said with a laugh.

Elizabeth came up to them. "What are you two giggling about?"

"Giggling?" they asked together.

"Well, perhaps cackling is the better word," Elizabeth said with a smile.

"We were discussing the lack of intelligent women my brother has to choose from," Jennette replied.

All three women shook their heads. Avis went still as she realized Selby was walking right toward them and staring directly at her.

"Ban, please tell me you shan't marry that girl," Jennette pleaded when he finally reached them.

He smiled, causing his dimples to deepen. "You have nothing to worry about there." His gaze slid to Avis. "What are you all discussing tonight?"

"Watching the young women panic as they realize the Season is complete and they haven't won their husbands," Elizabeth replied.

"Must be dreadful," Selby said, rolling his eyes. "I came over because there is one dance left, and I have no partner." He held out his arm. "Anyone care to save me from another dance with a woman like Miss Roebuck?"

Elizabeth shook her head. "I have danced enough for one night."

Avis looked away as Selby tried to coax her with a smile.

Jennette spoke up, "I shall save you from all the vapid young women hoping for a final dance with you." She linked arms with her brother and they headed for the dance floor.

A stab of envy struck Avis's heart as she watched Jennette go off with Selby. She should have taken his offer but could not. It would appear far too odd if she suddenly decided to dance with him after all these years.

"Now there is a good man," Elizabeth mused, watching them dance.

"Selby?"

Eizabeth nodded. "Yes."

"Then why don't you marry him?" Immediately she wished she hadn't said that in such a spiteful tone.

"Oh come now, Avis. Even you would have to

admit he is a Corinthian, even if he isn't into the sporting life."

"Not into the sporting life? Selby has always been an avid hunter."

Elizabeth blinked as if in surprise. "Really? Last year he refused my father's invitation to join him at the hunting lodge. He said he had too many other invitations. Then I found out from Jennette that he'd been at the Abbey the entire time."

"Oh," Avis replied. While she didn't mention any more about situation, she did find it odd because she knew Selby loved the hunt. At least he had years ago.

Elizabeth stared at the dance floor and sighed. "Still, with those dark looks and bright blue eyes, it's a wonder no woman has caught him yet. A man such as Selby might even make me think twice about marriage."

"Well, I wouldn't say that," Avis replied. Not even his potent kisses would change her mind on marriage.

Chapter Six

The rest of the week flew by in a rush of activities for Avis. However, there was still one item she had not completed before she left with Selby. She had yet to speak with Sophie about prevention. Avis dreaded this conversation but understood she couldn't bring a child into this world, especially without a father. Or more importantly, with her as the child's mother. With her resolve strengthened, she knocked on the door to Sophie's home.

"Yes, Miss Copley?"

"Is Miss Reynard at home, Taylor?"

The grandfatherly butler smiled at her. "I am certain she is. Come inside and wait in the drawing room."

While Avis liked stronger, vivid colors in her own home, Sophie loved pastels. The drawing room was a pale green with lovely jonquil curtains. She sat in a moss colored chair while she waited for Sophie.

"Avis? What are you doing here today?"

Sophie entered the room smelling of a floral

breeze. Her dress swirled around her legs as she turned to sit on the settee.

"I need to speak with you privately," Avis said, staring at the open door.

"Taylor, please bring us some tea and close this door."

"Yes, ma'am." The door instantly shut, bringing them into a cocoon of privacy.

"Now, what do you need?"

Avis shifted uncomfortably in her seat. It was best to get this over with. "I need you to tell me what you know about prevention."

Sophie's black brows rose in question. "I thought Mr. Billingsworth was unavailable?"

"He is."

"Oh. And I suppose you have no plans to give me any more information than that?"

"Exactly," Avis said with a little grin.

"All right, I believe I understand," Sophie replied in a knowing tone.

Avis only hoped Sophie didn't know what Avis had planned or with whom. Sophie waited while the footman brought in the tea. Once he left and the door was firmly shut behind him again, she began. "My mother told me about two methods of prevention. The first is a small sponge with a string attached to it. The sponge must be soaked in vinegar then inserted into . . ." Sophie's face brightened with color. "You do know where?"

"Yes, I believe I do," Avis replied, feeling her own face flare with heat.

"However, this method will not work until after the first time."

"Why is that?"

"Oh dear, you do understand what happens between a man and a woman?"

Avis looked away. She knew the rudiments of the act, but nothing further.

"Avis?"

"Yes, I do."

"Your virginity will be in the way until this man rids you of it."

"Of course," Avis replied. She wondered how much that would hurt.

Her face must have given her away as Sophie said, "Don't worry, you shall be fine. It's only the first time, or so my mother said. After that, if you have a good man, he will make certain you feel pleasure too." Sophie spoke with all the confidence of a virgin daughter of an actress.

Would Selby be a good man? Avis certainly hoped so. "What is the second method, Sophie?"

Sophie's cheeks blotched with color. "The man must withdraw his p—penis before he—he, ahh . . . explodes."

Explodes? A man explodes while making love? She really needed to learn more about all this.

"Are you all right, Avis? You look a bit peaked."

"Do you think it hurts when he . . . he explodes?" Thinking back to the book she'd read, the men always seemed to find great pleasure in the act.

Sophie frowned. "I doubt it. Why would men always want to do something that hurt?"

"But what about for the woman?"

"Well, based on the noises my mother made, she enjoyed it . . . or was a better actress than I thought."

That was certainly something to think about. "Thank you for your time, Sophie. I have a few more errands to run. Do you know where I might find these sponges you talked about?"

"My mother made sure I had plenty. I believe she expected me to follow in her footsteps. I must be a great disappointment to her," she said with a chuckle. "Wait here and I'll bring you a few."

Sophie left to retrieve them from her special cache of prevention secrets. Avis sipped her tea in thought. She had never been one to act out of impulse. Yet it seemed as if she'd lost control of everything since agreeing to Selby's kiss in her cousin's study. She should have walked away while she had the chance. Although, she wondered if Selby would have blackmailed her even without his intoxicating kiss, just to get his way.

"Here you are." Sophie handed her a small, wrapped bundle.

Unable to contain her curiosity, Avis opened the package to find five small sponges with red thread attached. "Five?"

"Wash them out after each use, but make sure they stay inside you for at least eight hours after he . . ."

"Explodes?" Avis supplied for her, then giggled.

"Yes," Sophie shook her head and laughed. "I cannot believe I had this conversation with you. I always expected it would be Jennette first."

Knowing Jennette's impulsive personality, she nodded. "Me too."

"Have a care, Avis. Lord Selby is a gentleman and the perfect choice for you, but he might want more out of this affair than you wish to give."

Avis's mouth gaped open. "How did you know it was Selby?"

Sophie smiled as her eyes glazed over, as Avis had

seen many times when Sophie experienced one of her visions. Avis wished she could see what her friend saw.

Sophie blinked. "The man I have seen for you has dark hair and is very strong, in other words, the exact opposite of Mr. Billingsworth. Plus, I arrived at your home first last week. I noticed Selby's carriage driving away and made the assumption that you had changed your mind. For the better, I might add."

"You mustn't—"

Sophie hugged her tight. "I would never tell Jennette or anyone else about this. Just have a care."

"I shall at that." Avis pulled away from Sophie. "Can you tell me what else you see for my future?"

Sophie closed her gray eyes and smiled fully. "You shall be very happy."

"Any more specific information?"

"No. If I tell you more you shall do everything in your power to thwart your future."

Avis frowned. "Why would I do that?"

"Because it may not be what you think will bring you happiness."

With those mysterious words, Avis left, pondering her future and what would bring her such happiness.

Where was she?

Banning glanced around the grounds of the Wayside Inn once more. He had arrived nearly two hours ago and night would be falling soon. She should have joined him by now. His thoughts ran to the obvious—she had changed her mind.

He kicked a small pebble toward the road. He

should have called on her before leaving town. It might have been best if he'd skipped the rest of Parliament, allowing them to leave earlier in the week before she had the chance to change her mind. But he could not neglect his responsibilities. He blew out a breath and kicked another stone.

What if she had decided to go away with Billingsworth? The man was a complete cad and scoundrel. The man would take whatever Avis offered and leave her alone and pregnant or worse, alone and battered. He looked up at the sound of gravel crunching under the wheels of a plain black carriage.

"Lord Selby, what a surprise to see you here," Avis said, stepping down from her carriage. "Is your sister with you?"

He turned at the soft sound of her lilting voice. "No, Jennette is still in town, Miss Copley."

Her coachman frowned. "Ma'am, I know it is not my place, but I would never forgive myself if some harm came to you—"

"We have been over this many times, Smith. Lady Elizabeth may even be here already."

"Still, we should wait to make certain."

Avis glanced over at Banning. "Lord Selby is here. Lady Jennette's brother would never let any harm come to me."

Banning took his cue. "Of course not, Miss Copley. Actually, I do believe Lady Elizabeth arrived a short while ago and now rests in her room."

"Thank you, my lord," she replied with a slight nod. "There, it is settled. You may take my valise up to my room and then depart. I shall be home in a fortnight."

"As you wish, ma'am." The coachman gave Banning a look that said he knew exactly what had just transpired. He took the large valise down and carried it inside.

Banning released a long held breath. He looked around but noticed no one familiar to him. "You're late," he whispered harshly.

"Your darling sister paid me a visit this morning. Perhaps if you had prevented the call, I would have been on time."

"Where are the rest of your things?" he said, now irritated with both himself for getting angry, and Jennette for delaying her.

"Smith took my bag inside already."

"That's all you need for two weeks?" He'd expected a trunk, or two. His sister rarely traveled without two trunks, sometimes even three.

"I didn't believe I would need that much. Unless you have a ball or soiree planned that I wasn't aware of?"

He smiled at her cheeky tone. "No. Ever practical, Avis, bringing only what you need. We shall stay the night and continue on in the morning."

"Very well." She started to walk to the inn. "Goodnight, then."

So much for starting their liaison tonight. Then again, Chelmsford was a much larger town than where they would stop tomorrow night. There was far more chance of being seen here. He would have to wait until they reached Stowmarket.

"We could have supper together?" he asked, surprising himself.

She stopped and turned toward him with a frown. "I hardly think that would be wise, my lord."

Perhaps not. "Still, you do need to eat."

"I will have a tray sent up."

Damn. "Tomorrow we shall dine together."

"We shall see about that," she replied with a smile and then opened the door to the inn.

Banning blew out a frustrated breath as she slipped inside the inn. He had hoped to have some time alone with her even if it was just a quiet conversation over dinner. Anything to get to know his future wife better.

Banning awoke before dawn and ordered a large basket of breakfast items to be packed. By leaving early and eating on the road, they could get to Stowmarket before nightfall. And he had great plans for tonight. He glanced around the hallway before knocking on her door.

Nothing.

"Avis," he whispered. He heard a groan from in the room. "Wake up. We need to leave. I shall wait for you downstairs."

He waited for an answer but only received another groan in reply. His coachman had readied the carriage by the time he walked back downstairs. After another fifteen minutes, Avis strolled out of the doorway, yawning, and then clamored into his carriage. Leaving before the sun rose afforded them the most privacy.

"I had them pack us a breakfast."

She nodded but did not look terribly happy with the prospect of eating in the carriage. Or perhaps it was the idea of eating with him.

"Are you ready?"

Her brown eyes looked away from him and clouded with apprehension. "I believe I am."

They departed in silence. Avis looked out the window as they headed east toward Southwold. He could only see the profile of her heart-shaped face, but he didn't need to look at her. He knew her face like his own.

She'd dressed in her usual conservative fashion. The neckline of her high-waisted, sage gown was cut so high that barely the hollow of her slender neck showed. He closed his eyes and imagined her in the emerald dress she'd worn the night of her cousin's party. He would never forget how beautiful she looked that evening.

"Selby?" she whispered.

He blinked and smiled at the confusion on her face. "Yes?"

"I didn't mean to wake you—"

"You didn't. In truth, I was remembering you the night of your cousin's party."

"Why?"

"Because you looked more beautiful than I had ever seen you, Avis."

She swallowed visibly.

He loved watching her face as she realized just how much he wanted her. Her brown eyes widened and a pale rosy color tinted her cheeks.

"Selby—"

"I think you should call me Banning."

"Right. Banning, we need to come to some agreements about this . . . this affair."

What was she up to now? "Agreements?"

"Yes. I cannot get—get pregnant. I brought some

personal items that should prevent that from happening, but I was told I can't use them the first time."

"What exactly do you want me to do, Avis?"

Her cheeks flushed bright red with embarrassment. "I—I need you to . . ."

"Yes?" he prompted, hiding the smile that threatened to give him away.

"To withdraw your p—pe—"

"Ahh, I think I understand," he interrupted to stop her stammering.

"Good. Then you will do the appropriate thing the first time?"

"I shall do whatever you wish me to." He stared at her until she understood his sensual meaning. Crooking his finger, he said, "Come here."

She shook her head. "I don't believe that is a good idea."

"You want to learn about passion, don't you?"

"Yes," she squeaked. "But not in a carriage where the coachman might hear and people passing might see and—"

"I have no plans to make love with you in a moving carriage," he murmured. "I just want to kiss you."

She bit her lower lip as she appeared to think this over.

"Avis, what exactly are you afraid of?" Certain she would never admit her fear he expected no answer.

She raised her gaze to meet his. "You," she finally whispered.

"Me? Why?"

"I am not quite certain. I can't seem to figure out who you really are. Jennette always told me you were such a gentleman and *overly* nice to women.

But you've never been that way with me. You kissed me to win a wager. You blackmailed me when I tried to get out of an arrangement you coerced me into." She threw her hands up in exasperation. "And every time we're in the same room we end up making rude comments to each other."

All right, he definitely had to make some changes in his manner with her. "You don't make it easy."

"What do you mean? I am a very easy person to know and like! You are the only one I cannot seem to get along with."

"Perhaps that is because we both have always known what might happen if we did get along."

"Oh? And that would be what?" she answered in a sarcastic tone.

"This," he said, sliding to the seat next to her. Slowly, he brought his mouth down to hers.

Avis knew she should push away from him and deny his accusation. But his mouth caressed hers in such a sweet manner she had to respond. Slowly, he parted her lips and they tasted each other. The action drew a moan from deep in her throat. She let her hands move up to his hair and touch the silky, dark strands.

She wanted him to be wrong about their attraction to each other, but at least from her perspective, he was right.

She had been attracted to him since that first kiss over eight years ago. She had thrust away from him that night, terrified by the sensations he invoked. This time, she wouldn't have to push him away.

He pulled back, smiling down at her. Her cheeks blistered with heat and disappointment.

"I think we had better stop before I go back on

my word and make love to you in this carriage," he said in a husky voice.

Expecting him to move back to his seat, she didn't know what to say when Banning dragged her up on his lap, holding her against his chest. She thought about scrambling off, but the clean, spicy scent of him and the motion of the carriage were lulling her to sleep. And sleep would keep her from the motion sickness that always plagued her when she rode in carriages. She'd deliberately stayed awake most of the night just so she might be able to sleep during their trip. As she drifted off, she realized just how nice a man Banning could be, for a blackmailer.

Chapter Seven

The carriage came to a halt in front of the coaching inn Banning used whenever he took this route. Normally, he would enjoy the good food and even better women the inn had in service, but tonight he would have Avis. His cock twitched in anticipation.

She turned toward him with a frown. "Why are we stopping?"

"It will take us another day to get to the cottage. We have to rest the horses so we shall stay here tonight."

"We will do no such thing!"

He cocked his head at her. "Oh?"

"If someone sees me getting out of your carriage, I will be ruined."

"You weren't overly concerned about getting into the carriage with me this morning."

"It was barely light when we left this morning. And no one was around then."

"We have no choice. I will take care of everything." The coachman opened the door. "Wait here."

Banning walked toward the inn, dodging a

mother duck taking her ducklings for a stroll. The familiar scents of meat pies and ale engulfed him as he entered the coaching stop.

"Lord Selby." The owner greeted him with an overly large, semi-toothless grin.

"Mr. Owens, I hope you have a room for me tonight."

"Only the best for ye, milord."

Mr. Owens shuffled through his papers and then found his register. Banning took the time to glance around for any familiar faces. His luck held. There seemed to be no one of his acquaintance in the tavern or the dining room.

He walked back to the small table where Mr. Owens waited for him. With little thought, he signed the register Mr. and Mrs. Talbot. He tossed Mr. Owens more than the appropriate fee for the room and board.

"We would like dinner in our room."

"I understand, milord," Mr. Owens replied with a nod. "I shall bring yer supper up personally."

"Thank you."

Banning headed back out to retrieve his *wife* for the night.

"Selby," a man's voice called at a distance.

He recognized that voice. Banning looked up as a shriek erupted from his carriage. Dammit! Somerton must have opened his carriage door thinking he was inside and seen Avis. Of all the rotten times to meet up with a man like him. Running toward the coach, he heard Somerton's reaction to finding her.

"My, my, this is a surprise, Miss Copley."

"Somerton," Avis replied in a cool tone.

Banning clamped his hand down on Somerton's

shoulder and pulled him away from the carriage. The grin on Somerton's face said it all.

"Interesting company you're keeping these days, Selby."

He continued to drag the viscount away from the sputtering Avis. "Not a word of this to anyone, Somerton."

Somerton threw his head back and laughed soundly. "Now what fun is that?"

"And what fun would it be if the entire *ton* learned of your background?"

"As if I cared," Somerton answered with a nonchalant shrug. "Most of them realize I'm not good enough anyway."

"But would they be pleased to learn that the somewhat respectable Viscount Somerton makes his money from renting buildings to brothels?"

"It's only one. And besides," he said with a chuckle, "I get a discount that way."

Banning struggled to keep his control. Somerton was a cunning scoundrel, and Banning doubted he could trust the man. Perhaps a better threat would do the trick.

"Keep my secret for now and you can continue to live," Banning stated calmly.

Somerton only laughed. "You'd never kill me."

"Don't tempt me."

"And with what would you kill me? That small dagger you keep in your boot?" Somerton eased away from him. "We both know you'd never use a pistol."

Banning's fists clenched tight. He could not think about what had happened in France or in

London. He had to focus on the present. "Just keep this quiet."

"Very well."

He hated to ask this question, but Somerton was the best person for this type of work. Leading him away from the carriage he said, "I need some help that you have the expertise for."

"Oh?"

"I want to know everything about Emory Billingsworth. I know some things from his past but I want to know about his financial conditions and what is happening with his writing."

Somerton smirked. "I can do that, but I expect a favor in return."

"What favor?"

"I may need some business advice in the near future. You will give it to me."

Business advice? Good Lord, this most likely had something to do with that brothel he owned. "Very well."

Somerton walked toward his own carriage. "I shall keep your secret as my own."

Banning could only hope he would. Now to settle Avis down. With the door to the carriage still cracked open, he peered inside to see Avis with her arms crossed over her chest. She mumbled something about a cur. He could only hope the cur was Somerton and not himself.

He opened the door, and noting her hard gaze, realized he was, in fact, the cur in question. If her eyes were daggers, he'd be dead by now. And perhaps he should be. After all, this was hardly the best way to catch a bride.

"Shall we?" he said, holding out his hand for her to take as if nothing had happened a few moments ago.

"No, I don't believe we shall."

"Avis, I talked to Somerton. He will keep this quiet."

Her eyes widened to the size of saucers. "And you believed him? Everyone knows what a scoundrel he is."

"True. But he wants something from me, so we made a pact."

"Take me home, Selby."

He scrambled back into the carriage and shut the door. "No."

"This was a mistake," she cried. "I should never have tried to do something so impulsive. I'm not an impulsive person. I'm just boring, plain, old, spinster Avis. The one everyone turns to when they need someone to listen to their problems."

He grabbed her hands in his own. "Avis, you are not old, not plain, and certainly not boring. You are one of the most exciting and interesting women I have ever met."

"You're only saying that to get me into your bed," she replied with a sniff.

"Maybe," he said with a smile. "But I want you there because you are none of the things you just said you were."

He brought her hands up to his lips and gently kissed them. "You may not be impulsive. But for once in your life, do something rash and see if you like the results."

"I don't like to take risks," she whispered.

"I know, but try it anyway."

She looked up at him with her soft amber eyes,

and he was lost in their depths. He drew her closer to him. Slowly, he lowered his lips to hers. A low simmering heat suffused him as she responded to his kiss. Every time he kissed her his control went out the door, his brain concentrated on only one thing—getting her into bed.

She ended their heated contact far too soon. "I think we should go inside now."

"Put the veil down on your bonnet so no one will recognize you."

For once, she did as he requested without an argument. As she tied the blue ribbons under her chin, he jumped down from the carriage to assist her. Even with the veil covering her face, she kept her head down while they walked into the inn.

"Do you think anyone saw us?" she whispered to him as they reached the stairs.

"I don't think anyone took notice. We appeared to be just another couple seeking refuge for the night."

"Thank God," she mumbled under her breath.

He led her into their bedroom. The room was light and airy, although the bed appeared lumpy. Since he did not intend to sleep tonight, it would not matter.

"How far away is your room?" she asked after viewing the room.

"You're standing in my room."

Her eyebrows lowered into a deep frown. "Then where is my room located?"

"You are here, with me."

"Oh," she whispered. She walked to the window and with a trembling hand moved back the curtain to stare outside.

Noticing her nervousness, he didn't know what to say. He'd had great plans for tonight and that lumpy bed. Damn.

"I shall sleep on the floor," he said.

She turned and gave him a curious look, then a small smile. "No. I slept for quite a while today in the carriage. You take the bed. If I get tired, I'll sleep in the chair by the fireplace."

He could never let a woman sleep in a chair while he slept in the bed. Before he could tell her that, a knock scraped the door.

"Mr. Talbot, it's Mr. Owens with yer supper."

"Come in," Banning called.

Avis turned herself back toward the window so the proprietor could not see her. Mr. Owens entered the room and quickly glanced about for a table to set down the food. Unfortunately, the only table large enough was right next to Avis.

"Excuse me, ma'am," he said.

She tried to turn her head away from the man to no avail. Mr. Owens caught a glimpse of her.

"Fresh fish tonight, milord. I hope you like haddock."

"That will be all, Mr. Owens."

Mr. Owens passed Banning toward the door. "Goodnight, milord."

"I'm sorry," Banning said after the proprietor departed.

"This is a dreadful mistake," she said. "First Somerton and now this. I truly believe it would be best if we forget our plan and return home."

"Avis, we cannot do that."

As she whirled away from the window, her anger

blew around with her. "Of course," she said sarcastically. "You will tell everyone that I'm a h—h—harlot."

"You are not a harlot," Banning replied in a soft
even tone. Slowly, he approached her. "But you are
not going back on our agreement."

He cupped her cheeks. He would have to go slow
with her. Leaning in closer still, he bent his head.
His lips coming nearer to hers, his breath mingling
with hers, but before he could kiss her as he'd intended, she pushed away from him.

"Shall we dine?" she asked.

With a frustrated sigh, he sat down across from
her. As they ate, he watched her every move and
learned more about her than he'd ever known. She
ate her fish with enthusiasm, barely touched the
wine, and played with her peas but never ate one.
Either she wasn't used to making dinner conversation, or she was still miffed at him. Knowing she
had been raised properly, he could only assume she
had no desire to talk with him.

He supposed he could not blame her. Although,
he yearned to know more about the sultry vixen
who had no idea just how special she was.

"Tell me about your childhood," he started.

She choked on her wine. For a second he
thought he might have to pound on her back to
help her.

"My childhood?"

"Yes. Did you spend it at the country estate? Did
you ride horses and climb trees?"

Avis stared at the wine still lapping at the sides
of her glass. She had heard stories of such idyllic
pleasures. Perhaps she should lie to him and tell

him how she had the perfect childhood but the words wouldn't come out that way.

"We stayed in London while my father visited the estate during the summer. So, to answer your question, I never climbed a tree."

"Why didn't you and your mother accompany him?"

Because it was the only peaceful time they had. "My mother preferred London," she replied softly.

He nodded. "I understand. My own mother has much the same inclinations. Although, she does enjoy a sojourn from the summer heat in town, now and again."

She had to get the subject of their conversation off her childhood. "Tell me about yourself."

"Dreadfully boring stuff, I assure you," he said with a grin.

"I doubt that." She smiled imagining him as a young boy. "I daresay you caused your mother nothing but heartache as a child."

He laughed, nodding in agreement. "She was thrilled to have a little girl after me. Although I believe Jennette has most likely given her far more heartache than I ever did."

He stood and offered her his hand. Without a thought, she accepted his assistance and they brought their wine to the more comfortable chairs by the empty fireplace. She really did want to know more about the intriguing man across from her.

"How did it feel to grow up knowing you would someday inherit the earldom?" she asked.

"Actually, I was born the second son."

"You were? I had no idea you had an older brother. Jennette never mentioned having another brother." She sipped her wine hoping he would continue.

Banning shrugged. "Jennette doesn't really remember him. Geoffrey died when she was only four. Besides, unless Geoffrey impacted her shopping life it is unlikely that she would have even noticed him."

"Banning!"

"You must admit it's true," he said with a lop-sided grin.

And it was. Jennette shopped more than any woman Avis had ever met. Luckily, her brother spoiled her rotten and never minded her expenditures.

"Very well, it is true. So you were how old when your brother died?"

"Eleven." He glanced over at her and smiled. "And you still want to hear all about this, don't you?"

Avis nodded eagerly.

"My father had a first wife who bore him a son, Geoffrey. Unfortunately, it became apparent as he grew older that he was afflicted with the same weak heart his mother had succumbed to years before. Geoffrey married at twenty-one and did his best to give Father an heir."

Banning sipped his wine before he resumed his story. "After a few years, his health deteriorated and he still had no son to inherit. My father decided he'd best marry again."

"My goodness, he must have been getting on in age by then," she said.

"He was well into his fifties when he met and married my mother."

"Your mother must have been quite young."

Banning shrugged. "Yes, but it was the typical marriage of the day. The union strengthened both families."

"No love, just money and position," she added.

"Yes," he said stiffly.

Avis wondered how he really felt about his parents' marriage and about love in general. Jennette had told her that her parents loved each other madly. She almost asked him but stopped. Personal topics such as love and marriage were not subjects they should discuss. It mattered not to her. Most men she knew believed love had nothing to do with marriage. Position, money, and land strengthened a marriage. Perhaps they did. Her mother had married for love and it certainly hadn't made her happy.

Sometimes in the dark of night, she wondered if all marriages were as dreadful as her parents'. Or if two people could truly fall in love and stay in love for a lifetime.

She highly doubted it.

Chapter Eight

"Wake up," a deep voice whispered in her ear, drawing Avis from her peaceful nap.

She kept her eyes closed for minute, savoring the feel of her head resting against Banning's strong chest and the sway of the carriage. His hand gently caressed her hair. After talking most of the night away, she'd fallen asleep soon after they left in the morning. Quite a nice way to spend a day, tucked firmly in his arms.

"I know you're awake."

She could almost hear the smile that must be on his face. Keeping her eyes closed, she thought about his smile. He had two deep dimples and white teeth that would be perfect except for the way the bottom front teeth overlapped ever so slightly. She liked that imperfection in him. No one should be too perfect.

"Avis," he whispered.

"Go away," she muttered against his lapel.

He chuckled softly. She could stay here all day, in

his arms with his heart beating in her ear and his hand caressing her hair.

The carriage rolled to a stop.

A stop!

They had arrived at his home, and she was still sitting on his lap. Avis scrambled to the seat across from him, quickly smoothed her hair and replaced her bonnet.

"You look perfect," he said with a grin.

"I must look as though we've . . ."

"Not yet, but you will."

She blasted him an angry scowl. "You are a beast."

"I know," he answered with a boyish grin. He tucked an errant strand of hair behind her ear and winked at her.

Banning jumped down, then reached back inside to assist her. The scent of salty air wafted by her as she stepped down and the breeze fluttered her bonnet ties. She looked at the house in front of her, surprised. It was the most beautiful cottage she had ever seen. A large green vine crept up the brick to the gray slate roof. Colorful flowers of every sort escorted guests along the stone pathway to the door.

"I expected something more in the manner of your estate in Surrey." She had been to his family's formal estate once for a ball and the house was enormous.

"This is a bit smaller, I believe," he replied with a laugh.

This house could fit into the drawing room of his Surrey home. In the distance, Avis heard the crashing of waves onto the shore. "It is beautiful."

Banning smiled broadly. "I'm glad you like it. But

you might wish to see inside before you make your final judgment."

He walked along beside her until they reached the door. He swept the door open but before she could take a step, he bent down, picked her up and carried her over the threshold. The meaning was not lost on her.

"My lord, welcome home!" an older woman said from the far end of the hallway.

"Do you escort all your women friends through the door in such a manner?" she whispered as he placed her down in the entranceway.

"You're the first woman I have ever brought here."

She swallowed the rest of her condemnation.

"Mrs. Hathaway, you look prettier than ever," Banning said to the portly, gray-haired woman.

"My, my, you have finally brought us your bride." The woman clapped her hands together, releasing a cloud of flour dust. "I always knew you would find a woman to love."

Oh my indeed, Avis thought. "I'm not—"

"Of course you're ready to be introduced, darling," Banning said, pulling her close to his side. "Mrs. Hathaway understands that you have been in a carriage most of the day."

"Of course, my lady," Mrs. Hathaway said. "You must be exhausted after such a ride."

"Just play along," he whispered in her ear.

"Lady Selby," Mrs. Hathaway curtsied, "it is a pleasure to serve you."

Anger at Banning threatened to overflow, but Avis had been drilled in proper etiquette since she was able to talk. "Thank you, Mrs. Hathaway."

"My lord, you stated in your note that you and

your bride wanted privacy. So I will bake your favorite items for breakfast tomorrow. I will leave them in the dining room so you may eat at anytime you wish," she said, her cheeks turning pink. "Of course I will knock discreetly before I enter the house. Now that you are here, I shall set out your supper and have Harry bring up a bath. You two must be dreadfully hungry."

"Perfect," Banning replied. "Please set the table in the dining room while I show *my bride* around."

He gripped Avis's elbow and turned her toward a room awash with soft greens. "This is the drawing room, darling. Let me show you to our room so you can change before dinner."

He led her up the stairs to one of two bedrooms. "Not a word until she leaves us in peace. Once she's gone you can rail at me until you're blue in the face, but I won't have you embarrass yourself in front of her."

Avis ripped her arm out of his steely grip. "Very well. But once she leaves, I have a few words for you."

"I'm certain you have." Banning grimaced. He studied her from head to toe. "Change into something less severe for dinner."

Less severe? Oh, she'd show him less severe. She had brought only a few dresses with her, including the emerald silk he seemed to like so much. But this called for something drastic. She waited for him to leave before pulling out her long-sleeved brown muslin and grinned—perfect.

She glanced out the open window while she waited for Mr. Hathaway to bring the bath water upstairs. The air here was so clean, unlike London.

Once the heat hit town, the vile smells became most unbearable.

"My lady, I have your bath for you."

Avis opened the door to find an older man who appeared to be well into his sixties, but still fit and trim. "Mr. Hathaway?"

"That'd be me," he said as he hoisted the copper tub from his shoulder to the floor. "The water will be up in a moment."

"Thank you."

As Mr. Hathaway brought buckets of water up to her room, Avis looked over at the dress lying on the bed. It truly was a dreadful thing. She normally wore the dress for writing since it had more ink stains than she could count. She twisted her lips. No, she would prove to him that she wasn't the type of woman who would bow to his every demand.

"All ready, my lady," Mr. Hathaway said, then quietly closed the door behind him.

The tub looked positively delightful. She added her jasmine-scented oil then removed her traveling clothes and hung them back up to air. Easing her body into the warm water, a long sigh escaped her. Even though she wasn't the least bit tired after sleeping most of the way here, she closed her eyes and leaned her head back against the tub.

She couldn't believe she was here, at Banning's cottage, naked in a tub of water where he could burst into the room at any moment. She didn't take risks. And she wasn't an impulsive person. She normally thought everything through with an eye for details. Yet, something about him brought out an imprudent streak in her that she never knew she had, and if she had to be honest with herself, she was starting to enjoy it.

She savored the way her body heated when he looked at her with desire in his eyes and how moisture pooled between her legs when he kissed her. She loved the way his blue eyes sparkled when he laughed. This peculiar attraction to him had intrigued her for years.

"Any warm water left?" he called to her from the hallway.

"Yes." *If you want to smell like flowers,* she thought with a smile. "Just give me a moment to finish in here."

After getting out of the tub, she added a bit more of the scented oil to the bath. She released her hair from all its pins, brushed the curly mess and pulled it into a tight chignon. She dressed in her ugly brown dress and placed a lace fichu around her neck.

A quick glance in the mirror told her the image was exactly what Banning Talbot deserved.

Avis strolled downstairs and peeked into the drawing room where Banning sat, reading a book. She rushed past the room. "I am finished with the water. Enjoy your bath. I must help Mrs. Hathaway in the kitchen."

She stopped around the corner of the kitchen and waited. The book landed on the table with a thud and heavy footsteps slowly made their way up the stairs. Her shoulders lifted with a suppressed giggle. When he returned he would smell as sweet as a June day.

Mrs. Hathaway placed steaming platters and bowls on the table. Avis had offered to help, but the caretaker told her to rest in the drawing room.

"I'm all finished here, my lady. Everything you need is on the table. Just leave the dishes, and I'll see to them in the morning."

"Goodnight, then," Avis said, walking back into the dining room to stare at the feast. Her stomach rumbled in complaint of the delay. She turned at the sound of footsteps coming down the stairs.

"What the devil are you wearing?" he asked with a laugh as he entered the room.

She could not believe the gall of this man. "Would you please stop laughing at me?"

"Hmm, I seem to remember telling you to wear something less severe and yet here you stand looking as if you were going to meet your maker, not your lover." He crossed his arms over his broad chest. "Now what should I do about a disobedient *wife?*"

She narrowed her eyes. "I—I . . ." her voice trailed off as he stepped closer to her.

A disobedient wife.

She'd heard those words so many times growing up, right before her mother would receive a slap to her face. Why hadn't she thought about his possible reaction? She was no fool. She knew the nature of men.

Menacingly, Banning backed her against the table.

"W—What are you doing?" she stammered.

He only gave her a slow smile that made her heart skip a beat. Oh dear Lord, what was he doing? White-hot panic sliced through her, paralyzing her movements. Was this how her mother felt before Father struck a blow?

She'd promised herself all her life that no man

would ever harm her. Fighting her alarm, she stared back at him. She could have sworn that she saw a glint of humor in his eyes.

"Since you cannot comply with my one simple request, I shall have to alter your outfit for you."

He placed his hands on the chairs beside her, effectively blocking her exit. Panic threatened to turn to anger. She couldn't let her fury get the best of her. She wouldn't do something mad.

He yanked the fichu off her neck. The lace landed with a swish across the room. He reached for the pins holding her hair in place. One by one, they hit the table and floor with a tinkling sound. He caressed her head as her hair fell from its tight confines.

Avis refused to move. Not a muscle. "How dare you!" she finally found her voice. "You are a libertine, a rake, a scoundrel, a defiler of innocent wom—"

He cut her off with a heated kiss. Her mind spun with passion and anger, but rage won. She would show him that Avis Copley was not like her mother.

She pressed her body closer to him, feeling the hard length of his arousal. Forcing herself not to fall victim to his kisses, she concentrated on his every movement. Blast! He was supposed to smell sweet with the heavy aroma of jasmine. Instead, the scent of his spicy soap had mixed with the floral, giving off an intoxicating fragrance.

His lips trailed a hot path down her throat until he found her erratic pulse. She reached behind her and grabbed the first thing she found. Her fingers wrapped around the cold metal handle of a sharp knife.

All she had to do was bring it up to his neck. She wouldn't actually hurt him.

Avis swallowed. *No*, she told herself.

Put the knife down.

Banning would never hurt her.

But he'd blackmailed her. He'd kissed her on a wager. Who could say what he might do if he felt justified? She wouldn't let him hurt her.

Her grip on the knife tightened.

But nothing happened. She couldn't bring her hand up to his neck. And his kisses were intoxicating her with their wicked sweetness, lowering her resistance to him. Deep in her heart, she knew the truth.

He wouldn't hurt her.

And more importantly, she wouldn't hurt him.

Banning slid his lips farther down her slender neck. Need shot through him until he knew he had to have her now. He'd expected her to struggle against him, show some sign of resistance, but she hadn't. Instead, she melted into him, clung to him, returning his kisses with passion and desire.

A clunk of metal hitting wood made him pull away. He glanced down to see a dinner knife that must have fallen from the table. He looked up to Avis staring at the knife as if she'd dropped it on purpose.

He shrugged.

"I'm sorry," she whispered. Her hands trembled as she tucked her hair behind her ear.

"Sorry? For what?"

She shook her head and then glanced up at him. Her face appeared ashen, and her eyes still held a bewildered look. "I accidentally dropped the knife off the table."

"And you need to apologize for that?"

Avis blinked and smiled in a half-hearted manner. "Well, now one of us will have to get another one."

"I'll get one from the kitchen," he said then walked toward the hallway.

While there were plenty of knives in the dining room sideboard, he felt certain she needed a moment to recover. But recover from what? Their kiss? It was a rather heated kiss. But no more the ones they had shared in her study a week ago.

He grabbed a knife and returned to the dining room. Avis had taken her seat. The silver knife glittered on the floor as the waning sunlight hit it. He bent down to retrieve the knife.

"Shall we dine now?"

She frowned and opened her mouth but nothing came out. Instead, she nodded.

He took his seat at the table. "Soup?"

She nodded.

Banning ladled the soup into her bowl then did the same for himself. A sliver of guilt slid down his back when he glanced at her pale face.

"I must apologize for my behavior," he started. "I am not in the habit of removing women's clothing without their permission." Though the idea of completely removing that dreadful dress and any undergarments had merit.

Her face turned that beautiful rosy tone. "I owe you an apology too."

"So you keep saying. Yet, I believe I was the one at fault, certainly not you."

She looked away from him. "If you say so."

"I do."

The atmosphere in the room slowly relaxed as they ate their dinner.

"Tell me about your story," he said, then took a sip of his wine.

She waved her hand in dismissal. "You would not be interested in my story."

"Yes, I would."

"Truly?"

"I wouldn't have asked otherwise."

"It is a romantic tale of two people who fall in love. Lord Shipley had lost his first wife only two years before the story begins, and he believes he shall never find true love again."

"And your heroine?"

Avis held up her finger as she took a sip of wine. "Sarah. She is an impulsive young girl who comes to London for the Season, hoping to find a man to love. But her mother only wants a high title for her."

"And Shipley has one."

She nodded. "An earl, of course."

He smiled at her. "Of course."

The wonderful food and wine relaxed Banning and appeared to do the same for Avis. A contented look replaced the early tension-filled glances she'd given him. He slid his chair back, stood and held out his hand. Her eyes flickered with panic.

"Come have a brandy with me."

"I don't normally drink spirits."

"Just a sip then." He led her to the room at the back of the house. His pianoforte took up a corner of the comfortable room and windows lined the back wall displaying the sea's wild beauty. This was his favorite room in the house.

Avis sat on the red velvet sofa that faced the windows. After pouring them both a brandy, he sat down next to her. He noticed her stiffen when he moved closer to her.

"Thank you," she murmured, gripping the brandy snifter under her white knuckles. "You have a beautiful home, Banning."

He sipped the smooth liquid, enjoying the deep flavors. "I'm surprised you like it so much. Most women I know would prefer Talbot's Abbey."

"Your estate in Surrey is lovely, but rather large. This is comfortable for an . . ."

"Intimate gathering?"

"Well, yes." Avis took a long sip of brandy then choked from the strong liquid.

"Take a small sip."

"I'm not used to brandy," she replied in a hoarse voice. But she did as he suggested and drank a smaller amount. "It's actually quite nice. Rather warming, isn't it?"

Avis relaxed back into the soft cushions of the sofa and drank some more. "Are you trying to get me drunk?"

He smiled. "It might help both of us, at least the first time."

"Are you as nervous as me?"

"No." He poured another splash of the dark liquid into both their glasses. "But I've never done this before."

She cocked her head and grinned. "Never?"

Banning threw his head back and laughed. "Never with a virgin."

"Do you think it will hurt overly much?" she whispered, staring out to the sea.

"Oh, Avis." He caressed her soft cheek with his hand. He longed to pull her into his arms but feared she might not be ready for his comfort just yet. "I don't know. I will do everything in my power to ensure you will enjoy it too. But I have no idea if a woman even can find pleasure the first time."

"Thank you for telling me the truth."

He moved his hand to touch her tawny hair. "We can take this slowly. We have a fortnight, and if you would prefer to wait a few days, I can accept that."

"That might be a good idea," she whispered. "If we get to know each other better before . . ."

"I think that might be best too."

"Thank you, Banning."

He kissed the top of her head. "You're welcome." The throbbing in his breeches was near to killing him, but if she needed time then he'd give it to her. Although, she had better not need too much time.

"I believe I shall retire now," she said, rising from the sofa. She glanced down once more at him. "Goodnight, Banning."

"I think a kiss goodnight is in order."

He stood and then bent his head to kiss her gently. She leaned into him, touching her tongue to his lips. He knew if he responded to her blatant invitation there would be no waiting for her to get comfortable with their arrangement. He drew away but his hand caressed her cheek. "Goodnight, Avis."

Something wasn't right. Avis blinked her eyes open and glanced at the small nightstand with the vase of fresh-cut flowers, remembering she was in Banning's cottage by the sea. The white cotton curtains waved like a surrender flag. Nothing seemed out of place.

Still, something felt wrong.

She held her breath and listened to the sound of the waves crashing onto the shore and a breeze rustling the leaves.

The light snore from behind her gave her a start.

She dare not turn around. When had he entered her room? And why was he sleeping here instead of the other bedroom? She couldn't help herself from gently rolling over and staring at him.

The moonlight gleamed off the sea and into the room, spilling its soft light on Banning's face. She stopped her hand from reaching out to touch the bristly black shadow that covered his cheeks. He had a face a sculptor would love, high cheekbones, a strong jaw, and stubborn chin. If she were an artist, she could draw his face all day and never be bored.

It felt strangely intimate to sleep in bed with a man she only knew from a few kisses and many arguments.

He shifted positions, thrashing his arms around until they reached her waist. With a sigh of satisfaction, he drew her close. Her head rested in the crook of his arm. While she knew she should pull away, instead, she closed her eyes and inhaled the clean scent of him.

His hand moved again, this time coming to rest on her breast. Avis waited to see if he would change positions, but he did not. She tried to ignore the tingling sensations that filled her as his thumb rubbed over the tip of her right nipple. Her breathing accelerated as her nipple tightened into a hard bud. She resisted the urge to arch her back so that his entire hand would cup her breast.

Banning's hand slipped off her. She forced herself to move to the opposite side of the bed while she had the chance. Glancing back at him, she noticed a ghost of a smile lit his face.

She should be furious with him for his trickery. Perhaps she would be later, in the morning. Or maybe she would get even with him somehow. But for now, she was content with the knowledge that his hand on her breast was a surprisingly pleasant feeling.

Chapter Nine

"Well, aren't we a slugabed this morning," Banning announced as he walked into the room with a large tray.

Avis yawned and stretched, unable to move from her comfortable place on the bed. He must be one of those odd people who actually enjoyed being up in the early morning. His cheeks were no longer covered in rough, dark whiskers, and he wore a fresh shirt and trousers. He looked good enough to eat.

Before he reached her, the scents of warm chocolate and raspberries filled the room. "Berries?"

"Yes. Mrs. Hathaway makes the best raspberry scones you will ever taste," he said.

He placed the tray on the bed table while Avis sat up. She reached for a scone before he could hand it to her.

"Greedy bugger," he said with a laugh.

"I am always starving in the morning. I could care less for food any other time of day, but don't stand in the way of my breakfast." She sat back against the pillows and took a bite of scone that melted in her mouth. "Mmm, I am in heaven!"

"And I haven't even touched you yet."

She pursed her lips. "I believe that was your hand caressing my breast earlier this morning."

Banning waggled his brows at her. "And I thought you were asleep."

"You are truly a beast."

"Good. We have our beast calling out of the way for the day. I've decided to limit you to once a day. Now move over."

He stretched his legs out next to hers and bit into a scone. "I only come up here for these," he said with a mouthful.

She sipped her chocolate and again thought about heaven. "You should bring Mrs. Hathaway to London."

"I imagine you would visit Jennette much more often if I did."

Since he was the reason she didn't call as often as she should, Avis decided it was best not to reply to his comment. It had always felt odd to visit his home in town before they had made their nefarious arrangement. She wondered how it would feel after they parted.

"What shall we do today?" he asked, turning his lean body toward her.

"I need a walk after this delicious breakfast. Shall we stroll on the sand?"

Banning flicked a crumb off the corner of her mouth then rubbed his thumb across her lower lip. "I can think of a better form of exercise."

Avis stared into his pale blue eyes. She had always thought of herself as a courageous woman. But actually going through with this idea and with this particular man scared her half to death. Her intuition told her she might get far more than she bargained for with Banning.

"Kiss me, Avis. We'll only go as far as you wish," he whispered.

She had no control of her head as it slowly lowered toward him. Using only the lightest of touches, she caressed his lips with hers. But it wasn't enough. She wanted the fire. She wanted to be seared by his passion if only to prove to herself that plain, old, spinster Avis could indeed flame Banning's desires.

As she parted his lips with her tongue, he groaned. He tasted like scones and chocolate . . . or was that her? Either way, it was delightful.

Banning deepened their kiss as he rolled her over onto her back. She stiffened and then forced herself to relax. No easy task when he trailed hot kisses down her neck. A moan escaped her. Never in her twenty-six years had she imagined a sensation as exciting as Banning's lips on her body.

As he undid the pearl buttons of her nightrail, cool air swept over her right breast. His kisses stopped. Avis peeked at him through her lashes. He stared down at her breast with a sensual smile on his face.

He skimmed a finger down her chest until it reached the tip of her breast. Tremors coursed through her body at his light touch. She wanted him to do more than just tease her like this. But what? What more did she want?

Everything.

She wanted him to do everything she'd only read about and never completely understood.

"You are a beautiful woman, Avis."

Beautiful? He couldn't be serious. But as his hand kneaded and pulled at her nipple, she truly didn't care if he was serious or only filling her head with nonsense. As long as he didn't stop what he was doing.

"Oh God," she whispered, as his mouth replaced his hand. Heat shot through her and pooled between her legs. She twisted and writhed under him. As she moved, she felt the hard weight of his shaft between them. She rubbed her hip against his long length and stilled in panic.

"What is wrong?"

"I think we need to stop." This would never work. She had felt the length of him and there was no possible way that would fit inside her.

Banning lay back against the pillow and blew out a long breath. Even from her position on the bed, she could still see the hard outline of his manhood. She couldn't take her eyes off the bulge. Would it be as large as she'd thought? Could it possibly be even larger?

"Have you ever seen a naked man?"

The question startled her out of her gawking. "Pardon?"

Banning smiled and relaxed. "I noticed your gaze wasn't exactly focused on my face. Would it help if I let you examine me?"

"Examine you?"

"Yes. I'll remove my clothes and you can do whatever you would like to my body."

Before she could say another word, he pulled his linen shirt over his head, exposing his muscled chest. Dark hairs sprinkled over his chest and she had the urge to run her fingers through them.

"Oh my," she mumbled.

"Should I continue?"

"Yes," she answered before her courage fled.

"I do love a curious woman," Banning said before he turned and stripped off his trousers.

From her current position, she could see the hard muscles flexing in his back. Her breath hitched as he rose and turned around. His broad shoulders melded into a hard chest. Her gaze lowered across his stomach, and then further down where his shaft proudly rose from a patch of dark springy hair.

She tried to keep her perusal casual, but she couldn't. Now seeing all of him in person, she knew it would never fit. Yet, feeling the moist heat between her legs increase, she would love to see just how much of him she could take.

"Do you want to touch me?"

Avis tore her eyes away from his shaft and looked up at his face. He wore an arrogant expression, which she took to mean he was quite proud of his body or at least his appendage. His eyes burned into hers, scorching her with his desire.

"May I?" she asked, scooting closer to his side of the bed.

He lay back down on the bed and stared at her as she touched the muscles of his chest. When she skimmed her hand through the hairs and over his flat nipple, he moaned. The sound gave her courage to continue. Her fingers rippled over the top of his shaft.

Banning grasped her hand, showing her how to rub her hand over its velvety top and down to the base. How would it feel to have him deep inside her? Would his shaft pulsate inside her as it did when she stroked the hard length? She felt wicked touching a man like this and yet, she liked it.

Who would ever have thought that she would be here, in this room, touching a naked man . . . not just any naked man, Banning? Certainly not her. But she was touching him, stroking him, and watching as his face tightened as if holding back his pleasure.

"How does it explode?" she finally asked.

He opened his eyes and laughed. "Explode? Let me guess . . . Sophie?"

"I needed to learn about prevention and her mother had taught her all she needed to know."

He laughed even harder. "A virgin telling another virgin about prevention and sex. You are too charming, Avis."

"But you haven't answered my question."

"If you keep up what you are doing you shall get a first-hand look at me exploding." Banning grasped her hands in his. "Not today, we agreed to take this slowly."

"Are you certain?" She couldn't explain the way her breathing felt so quick and shallow as if she couldn't take in enough air. But she was certain of one thing—it was all due to Banning. He made her nerves tingle and her heart pound. She wanted to know so much more about him . . . and his body.

"We should stop for today," he said softly.

"As you wish."

"I believe you mentioned a walk?" he said, pulling his trousers back on. "Personally, I could use a dip in the cold sea."

"A walk would do us both good." She sat back

and watched him pull his shirt over his head, covering that magnificent chest. She was right when she'd thought a sculptor would love to use him as a model. He was a perfect specimen.

"Finished staring?"

Heat scorched her cheeks. "For now."

"Get dressed and come downstairs."

He headed for the door, but she needed one more question answered.

"Banning, why did you sleep in here with me instead of in the other bedroom?"

He turned and smiled warmly at her. "Come here and I'll show you."

She quickly pulled on her wrapper and followed him into the hallway. Banning opened the door to the other room. A large desk faced the sea and stacks of paper and books lined the walls.

"I thought you might wish to use this as your study while you are here. I asked Mr. Hathaway to set it up for you."

Her heart melted with the generous gift he'd given her. She threw herself at him and kissed him soundly. "Thank you."

"Just remember your first priority is to learn about passion, and you can't do that locked up in here. Now get dressed for that walk."

"Yes, my lord." Avis held out her wrapper and nightrail and gave him an elegant curtsy.

"You're too cheeky by far," he said with a smile and then walked down the stairs.

Avis glanced back into the study he'd prepared for her. "You are too nice by far," she whispered.

* * *

They walked along the shoreline hand in hand for close to an hour. A comfortable companionship evolved as they strolled even though they barely spoke to each other. They trudged back to the cottage slowly as if they resented having to return.

Reaching the terrace, Avis shook the sand out of her boots, noting that he did the same. His strong leg muscles stretched as he pulled off his second boot. Suppressing the urge to rub her hand down his leg, she wondered if she would always feel this potent attraction to the man. Perhaps once they made love she would be able to look at him and not feel these strange sensations.

"Would you like some time to write?"

It might be best to get some time and perspective away from him. "That would be nice."

Banning turned away but not before she noticed his small frown. All she had done was accept his offer. Had she imagined the crestfallen look?

"Shall we meet for luncheon at one?" she asked. That was only two short hours from now. She hoped that would appease him.

"Yes, let's have a luncheon on the terrace." He gave her a quick bow and left her alone.

She walked into the study and the kindness of his generosity struck her again. Never had she known a man to think about a woman's needs as he had done. In her father's home, he was the ruler, the king, and the man with the power. Everything was for his pleasure and God help the person who displeased him. Especially his wife.

Avis pushed aside the dreadful memories of her past and concentrated on her story. Determined to uncover the mystery of her dull writing and fix her errors, she read the first page and saw nothing. Frustration surged in her. Perhaps it just wasn't the first paragraph, she read further. The prose was lyrical, the descriptions lush, what more could a reader want?

A knock on the door interrupted her. "Lady Selby, may I have a word?"

Lady Selby? How could she have forgotten she was supposed to be his wife? "Yes, Mrs. Hathaway. Please come in."

Mrs. Hathaway heaved a breath. "Thank you, my lady. I need to know if you wish to plan the meals while you are here."

That was a chore she certainly did not need. "Thank you, but you are doing a fine job. I will leave our appetites in your trusty hands."

The older woman blushed at the comment. "My lady . . ." her voice trailed off.

"Yes?"

"I'm sorry," she waved a portly hand at Avis. "I'm just a busy old bee who should mind her own business. It's not my place—"

"Mrs. Hathaway, if you have something to say, please feel free," Avis said gently.

Mrs. Hathaway nodded. "We're a little more informal in the country than those town servants." She cleared her throat before continuing, "It's just that Lord Selby is downstairs playing some mournful tune on the pianoforte, and you're up here staring at your papers. For a newly wedded couple, you don't seem very happy. I was wondering if everything was all right?"

"We are very well."

"If there's any problems, you just come ask me.

Harry and me have been married forty years now. There isn't much I don't know."

Avis blinked. Married forty years to the same man and Mrs. Hathaway didn't act as if that was anything out of the ordinary. Avis shouldn't unburden herself to a complete stranger. But having a few answers might help her feel more comfortable with this arrangement.

"Mrs. Hathaway, you are very astute." She glanced down at her ink-stained hands. "Lord Selby and I did not know each other very long before we wed. He wants me to be more comfortable around him before we . . ." She looked at the knowing nod the older woman gave her. "I've read a couple of books but . . . well . . . I don't exactly know . . ." Her cheeks blazed with heat.

Mrs. Hathaway walked to the desk. "I understand, my lady."

"My mother died before she could tell me what I should know on my wedding night and . . . well," she couldn't believe she was asking this but the question burst from her, "will it hurt?"

"Only a little bit the first time. But Lord Selby is a good man. He'll know how to make sure you get your pleasure out of the act too. Now let me tell you everything you should know."

The lovely old lady proceeded to tell her all she needed to know and more. Forty years of wisdom and experience illuminated the entire process, including things Avis had never dreamed of that happened between a man and a woman. By the time Mrs. Hathaway left the room, Avis felt much more confident.

Tonight she would learn about passion firsthand.

* * *

Banning stared out at the wild sea. The waves broke farther out than usual and higher than normal—a storm was brewing. He looked down at his pocket watch and frowned. Avis must have lost track of the time.

He decided to give her a personal reminder about luncheon. He strolled up the stairs and quietly opened the door to what had been a guest bedroom, not that he ever had guests here. The sight before him made him smile. Her head lay on the desk with her arm on either side. Those beautiful amber eyes closed.

After tiptoeing across the room, he glanced down at the paper where her head rested. In big letters was one word: PASSION. Under the word was a list of smeared words and phrases she must have decided meant passion. He let out a low chuckle as he read the list. The darling woman needed him desperately.

Her head jerked up. "What are you doing?"

Banning bent over and kissed her forehead. "What your cheek says."

"What my cheek says? Have you gone mad?"

"No, it's right here," he said, pointing to her cheek. "K–I–S–S–E–S. My pardon. The word is plural so you must need more."

Before he could bend down to kiss her again, she shoved the chair back and stood. "What the devil are you talking about?"

She walked to the old bureau and the small mirror there. She let out a shriek when she looked at her reflection and the smudged, faint word on her face.

"I must have fallen asleep before the ink dried!"

She rushed from the room into the bedroom and to the basin in the corner. Banning followed her to the doorway in amusement.

"This is not funny!" she said, soaping a cloth.

"I find it quite entertaining."

"Well, you are a—"

"You've already used up your beast quota for the day," he said with a laugh.

She scrunched up her face and scrubbed even harder.

"Give me that," he said, walking toward her with his hand held out for the cloth. Surprisingly, she handed it to him. The letters faded with each stroke, but her heady scent increased until he felt surrounded by it and her.

She would make a wonderful wife. He had no doubts that once she overcame her initial fears of making love she would be an energetic partner. The thought of her lying naked in his bed sent his cock thickening. He had to find a way to get past her fears before he did indeed go mad with desire for her.

"What are you thinking of? Your eyes are almost as stormy as the sea," she said, pulling him out of his erotic musing.

"You don't want to know."

"Oh?" She gave him a sly smile. "Perhaps later I shall tell you what Mrs. Hathaway and I discussed today."

"How much later?"

She only smiled mysteriously. Avis looked as if she was hiding a great surprise, and his cock throbbed in anticipation. No other woman excited him as she did. He had to get his desires under control. A lovely luncheon awaited them on the terrace. Women loved romance and he had plans to make this the most special meal Avis had ever eaten.

"Shall we dine?" he asked.

She glanced down at her wrinkled dress and sighed. "I really should change."

"Come along, Avis. This isn't London. Personally, I think you look adorable with your hair slightly mussed and your gown wrinkled." Unfortunately, the sight of her reminded him of how she would look after a quick afternoon tumble. So much for getting his desire under control.

She smiled. "All right then. Let us dine."

He escorted her to the terrace, but she stopped when she noticed the table. Pink rose petals covered the table and blew around the terrace. Two silver covers hid the delights Mrs. Hathaway had cooked for them.

"How lovely," she said, picking up a rose petal and releasing it into the breeze.

"Have a seat and I shall serve you, my lady." Banning pulled out a chair for her.

Avis let out a soft laugh and then sat. The smell of her, combined with the roses and the sea, affected him in a wholly erotic way. If he didn't have her soon, he might just explode. He forced himself to sit in the chair across from her when all he wanted to do was use the terrace wall as a brace and sink deep inside her.

Again, he forced the lascivious thoughts away. He lifted the lids, which covered the ham, warm bread, and pudding.

"Banning, why are you being so nice to me?"

He glanced over at her and smiled. "Why would I not?"

"How often in the past eight years have you actually been pleasant to me?"

She had a point there. Ever since that first kiss, he spent more time arguing with her than anything else. He couldn't tell her the truth. Besides, he could barely believe it himself. After putting off marriage for years, he had decided it was time to marry, and he had chosen her. Not that he had picked Avis because he loved her. No, she would just make marriage much more bearable than any other woman he'd met in the *ton*.

"Well?" she asked.

So why was he being nice to her? "Because I hardly think you'd want to bed me if I was nasty to you."

"True. But are not blackmailers supposed to be nasty and evil?" she asked, suppressing a grin.

"I was not blackmailing you. I merely wanted to protect you—" He stopped before he gave away everything.

"Protect me from what?"

Perhaps a little truth was in order. "From being made a fool of by Emory Billingsworth. The man has no sense of decorum and will freely discuss any woman he has ever bedded. I doubt you would have wanted your good name so abused." Or any other part of her lovely body.

Avis chewed a bit of ham and frowned. "How do you know this?"

"What would you like to know about Lady Susan Hythe and her sexual habits?"

"Lady Susan has been bedded by him?" She twisted her lips in thought. "How do I know you are telling me the truth?"

"According to Billingsworth, she prefers two men in her bed, and he has no qualms in satisfying that quirk."

Her fork clattered to her plate. Banning almost laughed at the gaped expression on her face.

"Two men. At the same time? How can that possibly work?"

"I shall explain that to you another day," he said with a laugh. She was a very entertaining woman. And he couldn't wait to show her exactly how much passion she had inside her . . . with just one man.

Him.

Chapter Ten

After an afternoon in each other's company, reading and discussing politics and art, Avis still felt confused by the two Bannings. The one she'd known and argued with for eight years, and this new man with whom she laughed and whose company she enjoyed. She wondered if he knew that each hour with him heightened her attraction and affection for him. She noticed facets of the man she never even imagined existed.

He played the pianoforte for her as she sat on the settee, staring out at the wild sea. She had heard many people at the pianoforte, but Banning had a touch that made her wish she could play.

"Is that Mozart?"

He smiled and shook his head as his fingers glided over the keys.

Avis frowned. "Hayden?"

"No."

She wondered how her music education was so lacking.

"I doubt you'll guess this one," he said. As he finished, he turned on the bench to face her.

"I give up," she said with a shrug.

"A new English composer whose music shall never leave this room."

"You?" she breathed.

"Just a little hobby to pass the time while I'm alone here."

"But you play beautifully. You should sell your compositions."

He rose from the bench and looked out the window. "I am an earl, Avis. That is my priority. This is just a hobby."

She crossed the room to sit beside him. "And one that you love."

"Perhaps I do," he said, leaning down to kiss her lightly. "But my priorities come first. And right now, you are my only priority."

He drew her into his arms and kissed her deeply, then pulled away. "Why don't you change before we dine?"

She nodded. Tonight, she would let him do whatever he wanted to her. She would not push him away but welcome his advances. She had packed her one and only gown suitable for a seduction.

The emerald dress showed off her assets quite magnificently, or so the dressmaker had told her. Mrs. Hathaway had assisted her with her gown but then departed to finish dinner. Without a lady's maid to assist her with her hair, Avis had two choices. She could either put it up into a tight chignon or let it flow down her back. She chose the latter option, knowing he would like her hair down. The warm sea air curled her brown hair into spirals, so she fluffed her tresses once more with her fingers and left it free.

The low-cut dress made her feel sensual, and tonight she wasn't about to bury the emotion. She wanted to feel bold and sensual, and she wanted Banning to find her desirable. She walked down the stairs to the small dining room in the front of the house. With a table that only sat four and a small sideboard, the room was a perfect place for an intimate meal.

Banning faced her as she strolled in the doorway. His shocked expression almost made her laugh. Instead, she only smiled at him—a long, seductive smile. She noticed the instant reaction as the fullness returned to his trousers. Her cheeks heated as she remembered touching the hard length only this morning.

"You look . . . beautiful," he said.

"Thank you. I remembered you had said you were quite fond of me in this dress."

"I would be fond of you without the dress too."

She had no reply because her mouth stopped working. He looked at her in such a manner she felt as if she were already standing naked in front of him. A slow burning heat slid into her belly and lower.

"I believe we had better eat," he commented.

As they ate, they discussed all manner of important and not so important topics. While they disagreed on the importance of repealing the Corn Law, they maintained a polite attitude with each other. And it drove Avis mad. He acted as though this was just a normal meal at a dinner party in town. She wanted this meal over with now. She wanted to throw herself in his arms and kiss him.

"Would you mind if I read your novel?" he asked, dragging her out of her ponderings.

"Pardon?"

"I would love to read your story."

Avis bit her lip. She wasn't certain why she hesitated. After all Emory had read it and even Jennette had read her story.

"I promise to be gentle with my criticism."

She laughed softly.

"Is that a yes?"

"I daresay it is," she replied. The man asked for something and she seemed unable to say no.

"Good." Banning scraped back his chair and stood. "Brandy in the salon?"

At least they wouldn't be a table apart. Maybe if she put her hand on his leg while they sat on the settee he would understand her implied message.

"Yes, brandy would be lovely."

He gave her an odd look but clutched her elbow and led her into the back room. She deliberately sat on the settee and moved into the corner so he would notice there was plenty of room for two. Banning handed her a snifter and then took a seat in a chair by the window.

"Is something wrong, Avis?" he asked with a wry smile.

She took a gulp of brandy, coughed, and nodded. "Yes," she rasped. She sipped her brandy down and stared at him. "I want you to kiss me."

"I thought we agreed to take this slower?"

"We did."

"And?"

She knew what he wanted to hear. "I don't want to take this slowly any longer," she whispered.

"Thank God. Come here."

"There isn't room in that chair for the two of us."

"You'll be on my lap, not on the chair."

Now that had possibilities. She placed her glass on the table and walked toward him. The warmth from the brandy suffused her entire body. Courage took over from fear. Tonight she would discover all the secrets between a man and a woman.

When she stood before him, he did not move for a full minute. He only stared at her. Twilight muted the room with long shadows, casting his face in darkness.

"Will you take off your clothes for me?" he whispered hoarsely.

"If you want me to," she mumbled as her confidence waned.

"Not yet."

He drew her down on his lap and continued to stare at her. He twined a piece of her hair around his finger. "You have the most unusual hair. When I first met you, I thought it was plain brown. But when light hits your hair it is brightened to shades of gold."

He moved his thumb to her lower lip. "What are you waiting for, Avis? Kiss me."

What *was* she waiting for? She inclined her head toward him and touched her lips to his. This was nice but it would never do. Using her tongue, she parted his lips and explored the warm, tangy recesses of his mouth, savoring the hint of brandy from his drink. As he responded to her, heat blazed between them. His hands flowed through her hair and down her back, heating her skin through the layers of clothes, drawing her closer to him.

It quickly became apparent to Avis that she was no longer the one in control. The moment he returned her kiss, she was lost to the fiery sensations of his lips on hers. He took the lead, and she let him. For once, it felt wonderful to allow another person to exhibit a little influence over her.

Every nerve in her body tingled with anticipation. Her courage grew with every kiss. Cool air swept over her shoulders as he pushed the small cap sleeves of her dress down her arms. She hadn't even felt him unfastening the hooks on the back of her dress. She wiggled to set her hands free and then realized how close her dress was to falling off her.

"Don't," he whispered as she reached to yank her bodice more firmly over her breasts.

Banning's warm hands skimmed down her neck in a gentle caress until they reached the top of the fabric. She watched helplessly as he slid the dress down and then unlaced her stays, throwing the garment to the floor. Her unbound nipples tightened and rasped the fabric of her shift until he pushed it down and exposed her breasts to his intense gaze.

"God, you are lovely," he murmured. He shifted her on his lap so she straddled him then kissed her neck and downward until he drew one pebbled nipple into his mouth.

She writhed with the contact, feeling his trouser-clad hardness against her most private area. Liquid fire raced through her veins. She pulled his head closer to her breast as if she could not get enough of him. And she couldn't.

She wondered what could possibly be better than

this, when his hand glided up her silk enclosed thigh and found the opening in her drawers. His thumb discovered the small nub and rubbed gently, teasingly against her.

"Banning," she whimpered.

The man she'd thought she hated was touching her most private of parts. And she loved it. She never wanted this to end. Her traitorous body and now even her mind wanted him here, wanted him kissing her, caressing her, driving her mad with desire.

"Don't think, Avis," Banning muttered against her breast. One finger slipped inside her wetness, then two.

How could she possibly think when she was burning with desire? She wanted to be closer to him. She wanted him inside her, claiming her as his lover. Glancing at him from under her lashes, his eyes were as dark as midnight. Unfulfilled need flowed inside of her. She wanted more than this, she wanted to be joined with him in the most intimate manner.

Every stroke of his thick fingers sent her higher toward something unknown. Her muscles tightened around him, drawing him in deeper.

"Just let it happen," he whispered.

She closed her eyes and her head fell forward as a violent explosion of pleasure sent her shuddering against him. "Banning," she cried out.

"That's it, my love. Shh."

Resting her head against his shoulder, her breathing slowly recovered. She'd never thought making love would feel that . . . that . . . incredible.

Banning shifted slightly under her and his

trouser-covered shaft made contact with her moist folds. If he could make her feel so wonderful, she wanted to do the same to him.

She placed a kiss on his jaw and set to work at his cravat. He didn't say a word, letting her unravel his neck cloth to find more warm skin. His pulse leaped as she kissed his neck.

"Whatever are you doing?" he asked with a low laugh.

"Whatever you'd like me to do."

A groan was his only reply as she unfastened the buttons on his linen shirt. Even through his trousers, she could feel his hardness pulsating. She wanted to give him pleasure. But more than anything, she needed to know if she had the same effect on him that he had on her.

She slid his jacket off and pulled his shirt over his head, baring his chest. "May I . . . ?"

"Anything you want to do to me, darling. Anything," he groaned.

She smiled against his chest as she kissed him. Finding a flat nipple, she flicked her tongue across it and he shuddered. Well, that was encouraging. She repeated his movements, brought the small nipple into her mouth, and suckled it.

"Avis," he moaned.

She slid off his lap to kneel between his strong legs. His muscles twitched as she kissed down his flat stomach until she reached the band of his trousers. She found the buttons and each one popped through its hole. She slid the garments down over his hips, freeing his shaft from its confining prison.

"You don't know what you're doing," Banning mumbled. "You should stop before—"

"I believe I am more than ready to see you explode," she said with a small laugh.

Mrs. Hathaway had given her more information than she requested. The housekeeper had told her men loved this, and Avis was determined to discover if that was the truth. She gripped his shaft firmly in her hand and let her tongue circle around the tip of him. He clutched the arms of the chair. A bead of moisture pooled at the very top of his penis. She brought him fully into her mouth, and he moaned in pleasure.

Banning let his head fall back to the top of the chair. This was not what he'd expected when he pleasured her a few moments ago. All he had wanted was to see her find release, and stretch her a little before he took her the first time. But this was too much. Desire coursed through his veins and down to his swollen cock. He couldn't make love to her now for he'd never last long enough to give her the pleasure she deserved the first time.

Instead, he gave into the allure of her mouth on him. The sweet sensations grew stronger as her pull on him continued. He had never wanted a woman, never needed a woman as he did Avis. He was getting in too deep with her. Marriage was one thing, but these other feelings were not supposed to be part of his plan.

"Avis, lift your head before it's too late," he bit out.

Thankfully, she did as he requested. He placed her hands back on him and closed his eyes to the most incredible pinnacle he had ever experienced.

Breathless from the experience he kept his eyes

closed in wonder. How was that possible? He hadn't even made love to her and yet, it was astonishing. He opened his eyes to see her watching him curiously. She was the most inquisitive woman he had ever met.

"Does it hurt?" she asked in a soft, curious voice.

"What? You mean when I spill my seed?"

She nodded as her cheeks brightened.

"God, no." He bent down and kissed the top of her head. "You are the most incredible woman I have ever known."

"Hardly. I'm just a simple woman whose curiosity gets the best of her sometimes," she answered with a coy smile. "That is how I ended up here with you."

Banning took his shirt, wiped his stomach and fingers dry then pulled her close. "Personally, I love that about you."

Did he just say that? He did not love her. He liked her immensely but that was all. Wasn't it?

Avis woke the next morning to the sound of rain battering the stucco and a heavy arm resting across her stomach. Not wanting to get up to a dreary morning, she snuggled in closer to Banning. After their first true passionate encounter last night, they had decided to sleep. In truth, she believed Banning wanted to give her time to rest and recover. She almost told him that she really didn't need that, but he certainly tried to be a gentleman with her, and she did appreciate his gesture.

She had thought she would have regrets about her decision to go away with the man who had brought her nothing but grief. Yet, the only thing she could think of was tonight when they might make love completely.

But for now, it was morning and as usual, the only thing on her mind was food. Memories of a warm scone melting in her mouth set her stomach rumbling.

"You're hungry," Banning's gruff voice murmured in her ear.

"It's morning. I'm always hungry." She smiled and arched her back as his hand cupped her breast.

"I'm hungry too, but not for food."

"I need nourishment."

He growled. "You're not very romantic in the morning, are you?"

She rolled over and rubbed his whiskered cheek. "No. Where is breakfast?"

"But it's a nice rainy morning, perfect for early lovemaking and late breakfasting."

The idea of making love this morning made her tremble. She thought couples only made love at night, when it was dark. "I warned you yesterday about my food inclinations. Besides, I won't be petulant after I eat."

Banning leaned back and laughed. "Well, I cannot have my lady petulant in the morning." He tossed off the covers, displaying his body to her. After he stood, he glanced over his shoulder at her. "Still want food?"

She stared at his shaft in profile to her. A small smile lifted her lips upward. "Yes."

"You are a beast, my lady, making me cover this," he said, pointing to his manhood.

"Perhaps I am," she teased.

Banning tossed on his trousers and a shirt then

proceeded to the kitchen. While he was gone, Avis had time to think about her choice of lovers. Emory might have been a good choice, but Banning was definitely the better selection. She doubted Emory would have given her time to get comfortable with the idea of making love as Banning had.

She used to wonder if her innocence and sheltered life had affected her writing. Well, she certainly didn't feel sheltered or ignorant now. The idea of Banning being completely inside her sent a rush of moist heat to her private parts.

"Mrs. Hathaway hopes you enjoy her cinnamon scones as much as her raspberry ones," Banning said as he entered with a tray.

Dear God, the man was too handsome for words. His dark whiskers and loose shirt made him look like a pirate about to ravish his stowaway.

"What are you smiling about?" he asked.

"You look like a pirate."

He gave her a sardonic quirk of his lips. "A pirate. Hmmm, I might be able to satisfy that fantasy. Am I the conquering pirate and you my willing captive?"

"I believe you should forget the fantasy and hand me a scone."

He laughed as he handed her the food then stretched out beside her. She had never felt so relaxed in her life. Perhaps it was the scones, or even more impossible, the man beside her.

It was a strange idea that a man could make her feel at ease. With Banning, she had a very good reason not to trust him—he'd blackmailed her, he had kissed her on a wager, and they argued every time they were together . . . until now. Yet, here she sat eating scones in bed with him.

"You're terribly quiet," he said then stuffed the last bite into his mouth.

"I'm eating."

"And I am finished and feel like ravishing my captive." He pulled his shirt over his head, yanked off his trousers, and rolled over on top of her.

He inched the bottom of her nightrail up over her body. The more skin he exposed, the warmer she became under his scorching gaze.

"Is this proper?"

"What?" he asked with a kiss to her bare thigh.

"Making love in the morning?"

"Highly improper," he said, kissing her belly. "But so is going away with a man who is not your husband. So I believe this must be normal for two scandalous people."

Other than living alone, she had never done anything "highly improper" in her life. Yet, ever since he'd kissed her in the study of her cousin's house, she'd done nothing but improper things.

He pulled the nightrail over her breasts and groaned. "You have the most beautiful breasts." He quickly flung the offending garment over her head and tossed it across the room.

She wanted her pirate to ravish her. Banning excited a primal part of her that wanted to be dominated by him. The bristly hair on his chest rubbed against her already tight nipples. She dropped the rest of her scone on the nightstand and welcomed his kisses. Aching need swept across her as warmth seared between her thighs.

Every one of her senses heightened with his

nearness until she became overwhelmed by him—
the rasp of his breathing, the spicy scent of him, the
sweet taste of his cinnamon kisses, and the burning
touch of his lips against her skin. She arched against
him desperate to be closer to his body, closer to him.

He trailed his lips down her neck, flicking her
rapid pulse there, before continuing to her breasts.
He laved her nipple from all sides then finally suckled her completely. Avis twisted and moved beneath
his skilled touch. Even fire would have felt cool
compared to his mouth on her breast. His touch
seared her soul, branding her as his possession.

As his mouth whispered down her stomach, she
felt adored. Safe in his arms and protected from
her memories. Even loved. His lips skimmed lower
across her stomach until he reached the apex of
her thighs and continued through the curly hair
until he found the hard little bud. She couldn't
think about anything but the sensations of his
tongue lapping at her.

The pressure built and this time she knew what
to expect. His finger eased into her wetness, spread-
ing her open for him. Then he inserted another
finger to stretch her and stroke her. Her limbs felt
like molten lead unable to move. Hot pleasure ra-
diated from her core as he brought her closer to
release.

"Banning, now. Please," she mumbled. "I want you."

"Not yet," he whispered.

She gripped the sheets as his fingers worked in
her and out, causing her to tighten against him. He
moved over her, watching her reaction to his touch.
She closed her eyes and let the shuddering release
wash over her.

His shaft slid inside just as her climax hit. She couldn't stop herself from pushing him in her farther, breaking the barrier that had kept her a virgin.

"Ow, ow, ow," she sputtered.

"Shh, Avis. The worst is over," he whispered, kissing her ear.

He could still feel her pulsating against him with the aftershocks of her release. He concentrated every ounce of self-control he had on not following her over the edge into bliss. He had to make this wonderful for her.

"How long do we wait?" she asked, then kissed his whiskered cheek.

"Until you tell me it doesn't hurt anymore."

"I believe I'm well enough. Besides there is only one way to find out."

He smiled down at her. He'd heard horror stories of men taking their wives' virginity and the wives' dramatic reactions. Slowly, he slid out and back in, waiting for a sign of discomfort from her. She closed her eyes and moaned.

Definitely not discomfort. He brought her legs up around his waist, filling her completely. She opened her eyes in surprise and gave him such a seductive smile he almost lost his control right then.

Avis was seducing him without words, purely with her smile, her kisses, a look. Her eyes closed as she arched against him. His control slipped a little more. He had to hurry her up or he wouldn't be able to keep his word to her about withdrawing. Bringing his thumb down, he rubbed the pebbled nub with her wetness. She responded instantly.

"Oh Banning," she whispered, her muscles tightening, pulsating around him.

He was losing ground fast. Her tremors continued to stroke him until he had no choice but to withdraw and spend himself on her stomach. But he had kept his promise to her. She might not get pregnant this time, but at some point they would do this properly and maybe by next year he would be a father. The idea of children with Avis warmed his heart.

He collapsed on top of her, his heart pounding in his chest. She was his now. She would become his wife.

Chapter Eleven

Avis studied the man who slept next to her. His dark whiskers seemed to have thickened in the past few hours. The storm still raged outside, but inside, under the covers with Banning, the world was safe and warm. She felt emotionally shaken from her first lovemaking experience. No one had ever told her what to expect. Men did this all the time. Even Banning didn't appear different after they had finished.

Yet, she felt different. Not physically—well, she was a little sore, but she knew that would fade. Her whole world, as she knew it, seemed off-center now. Men were big, strong beings who got their way through abusing and demeaning women. Staring at the handsome man next to her, she doubted he'd ever done anything to harm a woman.

And that was what had her so confused.

Banning was known for getting what he wanted in life and business. He charmed the women he knew. All except for her. Sparkling blue eyes blinked open and a warm smile lit his face.

"What has you frowning at me that way?"

She attempted to ease her frown but doubted it worked. "Nothing. Just lost in thought."

"About . . . ?"

Avis bit her lip. She wanted the intimacy that had formed in the past two days. Asking him about his objectionable feelings toward her might bring them back to the surface and for now, she preferred them buried.

"Avis? Are you regretting what we did?"

She couldn't let him think that, especially when it was the farthest thing from the truth. "I'm wondering why we used to be so rude to each," she blurted out.

"Oh," he muttered, a frown creasing his brow. "Why?"

"We've been getting along so well the past few days. Why is it that we haven't been able to get along until now?"

Twin dimples framed his lips. "Perhaps we always sensed what was between us."

"What was between us?"

"In the past eight years, have you never wondered what it would be like if we kissed again?"

Heat scorched her cheeks.

Banning laughed. "Can I assume your silence means you might have had that thought once or twice?"

"Perhaps," she answered, staring at his chest and not into his prying gaze. "Did you ever think about it?"

He leaned in closer to her ear and whispered, "More than I would admit to anyone save you."

"Is that the reason you blackmailed me into an affair with you?"

He went still. "Of course," he answered a bit too quickly, then turned, flipped off the coverlet and reached for his trousers.

Before he turned, Avis could have sworn she saw a tinge of pink sweep across his cheeks. "Banning?"

"What?"

"Why *did* you offer yourself to me?"

"Just as you said, because of my attraction to you." He stood, buttoned his trousers and grabbed his shirt. It was as if he couldn't get away from her fast enough.

"Banning, what aren't you telling me?" There was definitely something he was trying to avoid with her.

"Absolutely nothing." He strode to the door. "I'll haul the water up for your bath."

He left before she could question him any further. What was going on? And why couldn't he tell her? Avis pressed her lips together, flicked the coverlet off her, and reached for her wrapper. She walked to the window. The sea was venting its wrath on the beach, tearing at the sand, taking the seashore back out with it. Darkness seeped into Avis. Could he have lied to her? Perhaps he wasn't truly attracted to her at all but did this for some illicit reason.

Another wager? She shook her head in denial. A wager made no sense, as he was no young rascal out to break a girl's heart now.

Unless he wanted to break a woman's heart for some wrong she might have done to him years ago.

Banning watched the water heating and sighed. Perhaps he should tell her the truth about Billingsworth. However, he still believed she liked Billingsworth too much and wouldn't believe him. In a few short weeks, she would be his wife. Then he could order her not to see the bastard and she would have to obey him. He almost laughed aloud at the idea of Avis obeying him. She was no wallflower to let him impose his rule on her. It was one of the things he lov—truly liked about her. She wasn't afraid to let him know her true feelings on any subject.

Remembering his purpose in being downstairs, Banning searched for the copper tub and hefted it up to the bedroom. He was surprised to find Avis staring out the window. She didn't move when he entered the room.

"Are you all right?"

She nodded.

He could not stand for another conversation about why he made his offer to her so he refused to question her further. Another day perhaps, but not today. As long as she still considered Billingsworth her friend, she would never understand that he'd been trying to protect her. So instead of facing her condemnation, he retreated to the safety and loneliness of the first floor.

He was right about his decision not to tell her about Billingsworth. Exposing Avis to the gruesome details of both those nights would do her no good. It was his job as her future husband to protect her from such things. Telling her would only hurt her, harden her as it had him. The last thing he wanted was Avis becoming cynical about men.

He poured water from the kettle into a large bucket. After getting two buckets ready, he carted them upstairs. She still hadn't moved from the window.

Don't look, he told himself.

Damn. He looked.

This time he caught her wiping a tear away as if she could do it before he noticed. He hated women's tears.

He strode from the room determined to get the water for the bath as he'd promised. He brought up several more buckets and tossed the water into the tub. She had yet to say a word to him, but at least it looked as if her tears were finished.

"Your bath is ready."

"Thank you," she said with a little sob.

Damn. He wasn't totally heartless. He looked at her and couldn't keep himself from bringing her into his arms. "Why are you crying?"

"I am not crying. I don't cry."

"Avis?"

"I know you're not telling me something, and I hate it."

He wanted to deny her accusation, but couldn't. "I told you everything you need to know."

She pushed away from him. "Everything I need to know? Which means you're not telling me something on the pretense that I don't need to know. Why did you make your offer to me? Were you seeking revenge because I spurned your kiss eight years ago?"

"No. I wanted to keep you away from Billingsworth because he is truly not worthy of you." That sounded better than *he might beat you close to death.*

She looked at him with watery eyes. *"He* has always been kind to me."

Unlike Banning. Those unspoken words ate at him, twisting his stomach into a tight knot. "I only wanted to stop you from meeting him like this."

She blinked and shook her head, golden brown hair flying around her face. "But it was all right for us to meet like this?" She paused and studied him for a moment. "You never meant for us to go away together, did you?"

"Of course not, Avis. You are an unmarried woman whose reputation is important to her station. I didn't want to ruin you." Damn. How would he get out of this one?

"But you still offered yourself to me and even blackmailed me into this affair. Why, Banning? Why did you do that when you knew if anyone discovered the truth of where I was I'd be ruined?"

Because I took the one chance I had to make you my wife. He certainly couldn't tell her that. "You won't believe me if I told you."

"Well I won't know if you don't speak of it."

Banning sat on the bed and blew out a breath. There was no way out of this mess. He had to tell her something. But she didn't need to know all the grim details, only the mildest possible version.

"Billingsworth beat a prostitute when he was at Eton. I didn't want anything to happen to you."

Avis went pale and swayed until she reached for the bedpost. "Why?"

"He said she was stealing money from him."

"Well—"

Banning stood in one fluid motion. "Don't defend that man to me. I saw what he did to that woman. She was only taking what he'd promised her."

She bit her lip and blinked back tears. "I can't—"

"Don't," he warned her again. "I couldn't let you go away with him where you might be in harm's way." He reached out and slowly drew her to him.

"And I couldn't let you go to another man with this between us."

He sought her sweet lips and the forgiveness he hoped he would find there. With only a brief hesitation, she responded to him. He wanted to give her everything she wanted, needed, or secretly desired, but first, he wanted her to have a warm bath to ease her soreness.

"Take a bath while I shave," he said, pulling away from her.

"Are you staying here while . . ." her voice trailed off.

"I believe after this morning, there isn't anything on you I haven't seen."

Her cheeks blossomed with embarrassment. Slowly, she removed her wrapper, and Banning rethought his decision about shaving first. Before he could say a word, she slipped into the steamy tub of water.

"Ahh, this feels wonderful."

His cock instantly reacted to the view of Avis lounging in the bath. She soaped her face and neck before moving lower. She slipped her hands over her nipples, taking care to wash them until they puckered for her. He was about to lose his mind as the soap disappeared between her legs. Her nipples jutted out from the top of the soapy water, the thick patch of curly hair at the juncture of her legs darkened with the wetness. And now he was supposed to pick up a blade and scrape his face with his shaking hands.

"Do you want to join me?" she asked with a seductive smile.

"Hell yes."

He stripped off his shirt and trousers and then slid into the end of the small tub. She brought her slick body on top of his and proceeded to wash his neck. His head fell back as her hands skimmed over his chest and rubbed against his nipples. He never expected Avis to be so bold, and he loved her for it.

"What is this?" Avis asked, circling a scar he had tried to forget.

A day he wanted to forget for eternity but never could. "I was hit in France."

"Someone shot you?"

"That is generally what happens during war, Avis."

She splashed water at his face. "I realize that. But it was kept so quiet. Jennette never told me you were in the army."

"I wasn't. I worked for the Home Office."

"You?"

"Yes. Trey and I helped out on a few missions. During one, I was shot. Trey arranged for my transport home and stayed with me while I recovered. We worked as a team."

She rested her chin on his chest and stared up at him with a questioning look. "I thought I knew everything about you."

"Indeed?"

"Yes, indeed. Your sister loves to talk about you."

"Yes, and I love talking about her, but right now, I have a beautiful woman on top of me and no desire to discuss my sister."

He drew her face up to his and kissed her until all thoughts, all questions, were banished.

* * *

After spending two days blissfully naked in bed, they dressed and strolled on the storm-torn beach, picking up shells tossed from the sea. When they returned to the cottage he began to read her story.

Avis sat nervously picking at her short fingernails, awaiting his pronouncement. Only twenty pages or so into the story he exclaimed, "You know absolutely nothing about men."

"Whatever are you talking about?"

"This," he said, pointing to a page. "On page twenty-five you have Lord Shipley declaring his undying love for the heroine. No man would do that."

"Admit he loved her, or just admit it so quickly into the story?"

He glanced toward the window, staring at the sea with a pensive countenance. "Not on page twenty-five."

He continued reading, but her ire climbed with every "Humph" and "Not bloody likely." She strummed her fingers on the arm of the settee. She knew men. She knew exactly how conniving they could be when they wanted something.

"Avis, I realize you never had a brother, but really, no man would do this."

"Do what?"

"Fall in love at practically first sight."

"Why not?"

"Men don't do that." Seeing her look of disbelief, he added, "It's true."

"I presume you mean to tell me that you don't believe in love?" she asked in a haughty manner. Most of the stories she read contained some romance and she secretly enjoyed reading them. She had tried to use some of her friends' husbands as examples for her story but had become quickly disillusioned. The only positive model she noticed had been the Kesgraves, but they had only been married a short time. Avis imagined even her parents' marriage had a few good months.

"Actually, I believe some people do fall madly in love. However, most good marriages are based on social and economic reasons. Land, money, and social standings are the basis of a good marriage. Companionship is what makes the marriage strong. Love comes from companionship."

She had never thought Banning would be so commonsensical regarding marriage. She thought he'd be a romantic at heart especially after seeing how he'd made the extra bedroom into a study for her. "So you don't believe in love, do you?"

"I don't think it happens within two days of meeting someone."

She cocked her head and stared at his windblown hair. "So I should never have Shipley admit his love to Sarah?"

"Well, perhaps you should. It would make for some nice discord if Shipley declares his love, and she falls for another man."

"Another man? Who?"

"The answer is here on page thirty. The way you describe Haywood looking at Sarah is perfect."

"Haywood is Shipley's best friend."

"And it is so obvious to the reader that Haywood is the man for a high-spirited woman like Sarah."

Avis bit down on her lip in thought. "But Emory said it would give women the wrong impression."

Banning gave her a wry smile. "Did he now?"

Her first thought had been to make Haywood the hero, but Emory talked her out of it. He was the published author. He knew best. "Yes, and he was right. A woman of her station should be interested in a man who is at least her equal in rank."

"Very dull, my dear."

"But Haywood? He is only a squire and a gambler, while she is the daughter of an earl. A match between them—"

"Would make for a very romantic tale."

She caught his excitement. "You might be right. Whenever Sarah talks to Haywood there seems to be this . . . well, attraction."

"Just listen to how you describe his bowing over her hand. 'He took my hand in his strong grip. Shivers raced up my arm until I thought my entire body would be consumed in them. His lips kissed my gloves and searing heat scorched a mark where he caressed me.'"

Banning looked over at her and smiled. "Haywood is the hero for Sarah."

"But isn't he rather arrogant for a hero?"

His brows rose. "There is nothing wrong with a little arrogance." He placed the papers on the table next to his chair and walked toward her. "Does my criticism bother you?"

"No," she answered. "I believe you might be right about it." But could she do it? Could she write the story the way she had originally intended it to be? In her mind, all she could hear was Emory's voice telling how important it was for her peers to accept her work, and no woman of the *ton* would let her daughter fall for a man like Haywood.

"I know I'm right," he said, lifting her off the

settee and into his arms. Right where she wanted to be, for a very long time.

Her mind flashed with images of summers spent just like this, winters by the fireplace in town. Perhaps they could continue their liaison after their two weeks . . . until he decided to marry someone. Then she would have to give him up.

"So what has given you that far off look?"

"Memories of you," she whispered, and then kissed him softly.

"Memories? We've barely started making memories yet. There is so much I want to share with you."

"Oh?"

"Hmm," he said, kissing her neck. "Like making love outside. I love that."

"What else do you love?"

"Let me show you." He grasped her hand and led her out to the terrace. "That," he said, pointing to the sea. "I should have been a ship captain. I love the wildness of the sea."

He stood behind her as she looked out at the water with him. His hand reached around her waist, pulling her up against his hard length. Her nipples tightened from his close contact. Dear Lord, she was becoming insatiable.

Surely he'd noticed her breasts because his hands reached to cup each one. She arched her back as he kneaded her breasts. His lips burned on her neck. When he pulled her bodice over her breasts, baring them for the world to see, she stiffened.

"Banning, we're out of doors," she whimpered.

His mouth traced the shell of her ear, sending tingles down her back. "I own the outdoors here. No one is around for miles."

"I—I . . . What about the Hathaways?"

"They're probably doing the same thing we are," he said with a husky laugh.

She should stop him before she succumbed to this madness. But the heat from his kisses on her neck seared her mind until she couldn't think. Her wits never won when Banning was near.

He pushed her skirts up and out of the way then slipped his breeches down his hips and entered her wetness from behind her. Avis gasped at the sensation of fullness as he grasped her hips with his strong hands. Excitement rushed through her as he rocked her hips against his.

Dear Lord, she *needed* him.

She had lost control of her life. The only thing that mattered was the man behind her who could bring her such happiness and pleasure. And she wanted to please him. She wanted more than she had ever imagined. She wanted his lo—

She closed her eyes as her release washed over her.

Burrowing deep in her, he stiffened his muscles then succumbed to his own pleasure. The smell of the sea air mixed with the musky scent of their love. Thankfully, she hadn't removed the sponge from this morning. She could only hope that it would still work.

Love.

She had almost thought that she loved him. Love meant losing yourself. Losing your self-preservation. Love led to violence—no. She had to stop thinking in such a manner.

"You are the most incredible woman," he murmured.

What had she been thinking? She had so completely lost control of her sense that she let him make love to her out on the terrace. Banning made her do the most absurd things. Things she'd never even thought of until she came to know him so well. Making love outside? In the middle of the afternoon where anyone could have spied them. She had gone away with a man to learn about passion, but she was now no better than the strumpets down at the docks.

What was wrong with her?

Could she truly believe that she was falling in love with him? The idea was too impossible to contemplate. She didn't love Banning. Loving him would make her life unbearable since she could never marry him.

What did she want from Banning?

Not love and marriage. Her mother had loved her father desperately, no matter how many times he'd abused her. No man would ever be able to convince Avis that marriage was something she needed.

Banning slowly moved off her and then turned her into his arms. "What is wrong?"

How had he sensed something was wrong? "Nothing at all," she said in a completely unconvincing voice.

"Are you embarrassed by what we just did?"

She shrugged.

"No one saw us, Avis." Banning took a deep breath. "What we did is perfectly normal. We are two lovers carried away by passion."

He chuckled softly. "I should take you to the Abbey in Surrey. We have a lovely maze and could make love once we found the middle. I've heard rumors that it is quite an adventure."

"No more sexual congress outside. Besides, we only have these two weeks and driving to Surrey would take days."

He smiled down at her, then he kissed her sweetly. "I agree. We shall stay here. You can visit Surrey another time."

Another time? Perhaps he did want to continue this affair for a while longer, but she couldn't afford the risk that someone might discover their relationship. Their time would end soon and then they would part. No matter how much her heart might want otherwise.

Chapter Twelve

Avis sat back against Banning's hard, bare chest and relaxed. The last three days had been bliss. She had thought this would be a difficult fortnight, being alone with Banning. She couldn't have been more wrong. She felt relaxed, comfortable around him even when they disagreed about things. Not once did he lose his temper with her or lash out.

After pulling the white coverlet up over her breasts again, she reached for another piece of paper, read the page, and handed it behind her to him. "I believe this one is all right. What do you think?"

Banning took the paper and scanned it as she read the next page. Shaking her head, she blew out a breath.

"This just doesn't work now," she said with a sigh.

He nipped her naked shoulder with a kiss. Reading in bed had never been so much fun.

"Why?" he asked.

"Because Lord Shipley proposes. He cannot do that if Haywood is our hero."

His lips skimmed up her neck, sending shivers of desire down her back.

"Unless," she started then stopped.

"Go on," he whispered against her shoulder.

"Think of the problems that would cause Sarah. Her mother will demand she marry Shipley, but Sarah will resist because of her attraction to Haywood."

"I like that . . . and this." His lips moved to the left side of her neck.

"Stop that," she said breathlessly. "I cannot think properly when you're kissing me."

"Hmm, that is a good thing to know."

"Behave."

She had to admit editing with Banning was far more fun than doing it on her own. Just having someone to talk to about the story helped her immensely. Besides, when she tired of writing or editing, all she had to do was kiss him and they would find something much more interesting to occupy them.

"You're not working," he whispered in her ear.

"That thing prodding my back keeps distracting me," she said with a laugh.

"We could take a break."

"And do what?"

He stroked her bare arms. "I'm quite certain we could think of something."

"You're very bad for my concentration." She whimpered as he brought her earlobe into his warm mouth.

He pulled back with groan. "All right, taskmistress. But we shall continue this later."

"Most definitely."

His hand slid up her arm and stopped at the scar

on her forearm. Instinctively, she attempted to pull away from his light touch, but she paused as his thumb traced the jagged line.

Don't ask about it, she prayed.

"This must have hurt," he commented.

Avis swallowed hard and said, "I scarcely remember. I was only seven." She'd tried to reply lightly but her voice caught, betraying her.

"You must have been a brave girl." He lifted her arm and gently kissed the spot.

If only he could kiss away all the pain so easily, she thought.

After releasing her arm, he picked up a piece of paper and read. "Lovely."

"What?"

"You have the most beautiful descriptions."

She turned her head and attempted to look at him. "You really think so?"

"I really do. You are a wonderful writer, Avis." He tweaked her hair. "I wish I had your talent for writing."

"But you have your musical talent. I can't hold a tune or even read music."

"Thank you. Now back to work."

Avis smiled. "Now who is being the taskmaster?"

She penciled in a few notes to remember what she wanted to write when she had undisturbed time. Then she handed it back to him.

"Wonderful ideas," he murmured.

"I have you to thank."

"No, these were your ideas. It was evident in your writing how you meant the story to proceed."

She still found it fascinating that after working on this story for almost a year with Emory, she had

never realized why the story didn't work. Then
again, neither had Emory. She frowned. He'd been
writing for almost fifteen years and had only four
books published. Perhaps he was too much of a
perfectionist.

But Banning helped her uncover the weakness in
the story after only reading to page thirty. Without
him, she might have continued to work the story in
the wrong direction. A brief thought flitted through
her mind. It was inconceivable. She shook her head
in denial. Spending so much time in Banning's
company had started to make her disbelieve everything she knew to be true about Emory. He was her
friend. He wanted her to publish as much as he
wanted to be published again.

Emory could not have deliberately misled her.

After several lovely days spent mostly in bed, Banning was certain they would suit perfectly as a married couple. The only question was how to broach
the subject. He'd known for years that she enjoyed
being a spinster with the relative freedom the status
gave her. But she couldn't want that forever. She
must want children. After ten days with her, he
knew Avis Copley was firmly stuck in his blood and
quite possibly, his heart. He had no idea when it
had happened.

Love was not an emotion he believed he would
ever feel for his future wife . . . until now. He'd
always thought he would find a woman who would
meet his requirements for a wife. If he were lucky,
he would find a woman who was a good companion

and wouldn't drive him mad. But never had he anticipated falling in love with her.

Yet, his best friend, Trey, had fallen madly in love with Charlotte. Banning envied Trey's relationship with his wife. They had the warmth of good friendship and the passion of lovers. The looks Trey gave his wife at times bordered on obscene and yet, Charlotte always returned those glances.

Avis groaned beside him. He turned to watch her in her sleep. Her eyebrows furrowed and suddenly her arms lashed out toward him.

"No, no . . . Papa, stop . . ."

He continued to stare as the dream subsided, and she relaxed again. He wondered what her father had been doing in the dream.

Her amber eyes blinked open, and Avis smiled up at him. "Good morning," she whispered in a hoarse voice.

"Good morning. Bad dream?"

Her eyes widened in disbelief. "How did you know?"

"You talk in your sleep."

"I do? What did I say?"

"Hmm, 'no, no, Papa, stop.'"

Avis stiffened. "Did I say anything else?"

"No."

She relaxed again. "I cannot remember what the dream was about. Isn't that strange?"

He nodded. Strange indeed. He had the singular feeling that she was lying to him. But why?

"What shall we do today?" she asked in an overly seductive voice. She reached her hand out and brushed his bristly cheek.

"Shave. You are going to leave here with red marks on your body if I don't."

She stuck out her tongue at him.

"Besides you have another scene to rewrite. The scene in the park with Haywood was perfect." He felt her gaze on him as he stood to dress. She stared at his cock, already hard with desire for her.

"I had a good teacher," she said.

She lowered the coverlet, until one puckered nipple came into view and then the other. The blanket continued to expose her creamy skin inch by agonizing inch. Her brown curly bush came into view, and he was lost.

"Damn. I'm never going to get that shave."

He released the trousers he'd been attempting to get over his hard shaft and jumped back into bed.

"Wait, I need to put something in," she said, reaching for her drawer.

"I'll withdraw," he said hungrily. "I want you right this minute." He drew her hips back across the sheet and covered her with his hard, lean body.

"We only have a few more days," she mumbled before kissing him.

No, we have a lifetime, he thought but refused to say aloud. It was too soon to speak of marriage with her. She would need more time to accept the fact that they would make a perfect match. But they *would* marry.

Avis awoke to a strong rumble from her stomach and a feeling of lassitude in her muscles. She rolled over to watch Banning sleep. Never in her twenty-six years had she ever thought she could be so content.

Her stomach groaned again, reminding her that while the sun was high overhead, she had eaten nothing. A small smile stretched across her face. No one had ever been able to make her forget her breakfast before now.

Silently, she rose, dressed, and tiptoed from the room. She found a basket of scones and a pot of chocolate on the dining room table. Touching the pot, she realized that the chocolate had long since gone cold.

How hard could it be to heat something? She shrugged. Having never done one bit of cooking, she had no idea. She walked to the kitchen with the tray in her hand. At least the fire was burning so she didn't have to fight that. After a quick search of the room, she found a pot to heat the chocolate. She placed the pot on the hook near the fire, and then sat at the little wood table waiting for the liquid to warm.

She had only three more days with Banning then she would return to her dull life. Dreary days filled with writing and lonely nights in town. She had never minded this existence before, enjoying the freedom and independence her spinster status afforded her.

But now it all seemed dreadfully dull. Banning brought her to life and more than in the bedroom, though that was rather nice too. He sparked something inside her that was new, fresh, and exciting.

And in three days, she would lose these new feelings forever.

A low rumble from the pot by the fire forced her to stand and investigate. The chocolate boiled to the top of the pot. Without a thought, she reached for the handle and screeched as the pain shot through her hand.

"A towel usually helps keep the cook from getting burned," Banning said from the doorway. His smile dissipated when she turned toward him with tears streaming down her cheeks.

"This really hurts," she retorted, holding her hand.

He rushed across the room, lifted her onto the table, and took her hand in his. The warmth of his hand eased her discomfort.

"It hasn't blistered."

"It still hurts."

Slowly, he lifted her hand to his lips and kissed it. While his action didn't truly remove the pain, the gesture wasn't lost on Avis. He wanted to comfort her, and she wanted his comfort. He cupped her face in his hand, kissing away the few remaining tears.

Dear Lord, how was she supposed to leave him in three days?

"Dare I venture a guess you haven't cooked much?" he whispered in her ear.

Avis smiled. "I have never had a need. I am completely hopeless in a kitchen."

"Then you need to marry a wealthy man to keep you in servants and cooks," he murmured.

She stiffened and glanced up at him. An uncomfortable silence filled the kitchen.

"I have enough money for cooks and servants without needing to marry," she reminded him.

"True, but they can't keep you warm at night." He turned away from her, reached for a towel, then grabbed the forgotten chocolate.

Banning couldn't want to shackle himself to her,

and she definitely did not want to marry. Jennette's comment about him searching for a wife this season tumbled back in Avis's mind. But he knew she had no interest in marriage. Surely, this affair was just a diversion from his pursuit of the perfect wife . . . something she could never be.

He poured the chocolate into two cups. "Shall we dine in here this," he looked out the window, "afternoon?"

"That would be lovely." She grabbed the scones and placed them on a plate while he brought the cups of chocolate to the table.

Silence filled the kitchen again. After his brief hint of marriage, Avis found herself unable to think of any other topic. She had no desire to bring the subject up again. She wasn't about to ruin her few remaining days with him by having a disagreement.

Only the ticking of the mantel clock from the drawing room broke the stillness that filled the kitchen. Banning ate with quick, abrupt movements and a sour look on his face as if he were eating a lemon and not the delicious food Mrs. Hathaway had left them. Not that she tasted the meal either. Every bite tasted like the dry sand outside.

"I'm going for a walk," Banning said, as he rose from his seat.

"Oh?" She waited for an invitation to join him.

"I shall be back in an hour or so. That will give you some time to write."

He was leaving without her? Without even asking if she wanted to go too? He did not even look back as he left the room. Dejected, she walked up the stairs to the study he had made for her. Papers lined the desk, beckoning her to sit and write, but she could not think of a thing to write. She glanced out the window and saw the silhouette of a man, sitting on the sand, tossing shells back into the sea.

Banning picked up a small shell and hurled it toward the water. He'd known she wouldn't be amenable to marriage when they started their affair. But after ten days he had thought she would change her mind. For some mad reason he had actually believed she might be falling in love with him.

He was a pathetic fool.

She didn't love him. She only loved her writing. To her, he was nothing but a tutor in the passions of the flesh.

So why did he still want her? Why did he still believe she would make him a perfect wife? A wonderful mother to their children?

Because she would.

Avis was the ideal woman for him. His head knew that. His heart knew it too. He'd been foolish to think everything would fall into place just because he had decided it would be.

How could he have fallen for her so quickly? Although in retrospect, he'd known her for over eight years, lusted over her for years, and heard all about her from Jennette.

He had only three more days to prove to her that marriage wasn't a prison. He would give her freedom to write. He would give her children to love. He would give her any damn thing she wanted.

And if she asked for it, he might even give her his heart.

"Banning, are you all right?" she shouted over the roar of the sea.

He leaned back and looked up at her, his future wife. Her tawny hair whipped around her face as she attempted to keep it out of her eyes. Her indigo dress danced around her ankles, flirting with her calves. But her brown eyes shone with concern for his well-being.

She knelt beside him and pressed her lips together. "Do we need to talk?"

"No."

"You seem a tad, well, upset."

"I'm not upset. I needed a little fresh air and assumed you needed some writing time." He grabbed her waist and brought her down on top of him. "Since you decided to forgo your writing, there is only one thing to do."

"Banning!" she screeched.

He kissed her quickly then released her. She scrambled off him but only to sit next to him. Glancing out at the horizon, she said, "I had a strange feeling you were trying to tell me something when we were in the kitchen."

He shrugged. "I don't know to what you are referring."

"Your comments regarding my needing a husband to keep me in servants."

"Just a little jest," he said, waving his hand in dismissal.

"Indeed?"

"Yes, indeed." Banning reclined against the soft sand. Their time together was almost over. If he didn't do something quick he might lose her and he couldn't let her go without a fight. "Of course, you realize you might be ruined."

"Perhaps. But we did make every attempt to conceal our trip."

"Somerton saw us together."

"You said he would keep quiet."

"But if you are?"

"Ruined?" she asked without a look to him.

"Yes."

She glanced down at the sand and traced shapes with her finger. He sat up and turned slightly to face her, but she refused to look at him.

"Well?"

"Then I shall be ruined," she stated as if discussing the weather and not the total destruction of her social standing.

"Or you could just marry me and we'll face the scandal together," he murmured.

Avis went perfectly still. The only sign of movement was the slight rise of her chest as she took in a shallow breath. "Have you lost your mind?" she asked softly.

"Quite possibly."

"When we made our plans you knew I wanted nothing to do with marriage."

He shrugged. "That was weeks ago. I thought you might have realized just how scandalized everyone will be if they discover the truth."

"I don't care."

He didn't quite believe her. Something told him that she did care, more than she would ever admit. So why wasn't she agreeing to his rather clumsy proposal? "I think you should consider my offer."

"Why would you want to marry?"

"All the usual reasons," he said dismissively. "I need an heir."

"So you need a brood mare."

Frustration seeped into him. Why couldn't she see this was the right thing to do? "No, I need a wife."

"Then any woman will do."

"No. Any woman will not do. *You* will do."

"Why me?" she barely voiced the words.

"Because I love you."

Chapter Thirteen

He didn't just say those words to her. He couldn't have. Avis jumped up to get some distance from him. He did not love her. Her heart pounded so hard in her chest it actually hurt. This could not be happening. She should never have agreed to go away with him. Jennette had told her before she even left with him that he'd been searching for a wife this Season. Well it wouldn't, it couldn't, be her.

"No," she said. "You don't love me. You don't even believe in love."

"I never said that."

"Yes, you did. Perhaps not in those exact words but you did say marriages were based on companionship and landholdings and good social standing."

"And you have all that," he said, looking up at her, "except perhaps the landholdings."

"Well then, we should hasten to Gretna Green," she retorted sarcastically. "I am such a fine specimen of womanhood. I come from a good family." She held her finger to her mouth. "Oh, and of course, I have a fortune."

"I certainly don't need your money."

She had to convince him of the madness of his thoughts. "Love is a convenient emotion for you, Banning. You decide we should marry because I fit into your little box," she made a square in the air, "of what makes a perfect wife. So you must love me."

"This has nothing to do with your qualifications."

"Oh, I believe it does."

"I took your virginity. You may be ruined."

She released a coarse laugh. "Dear Lord, do you propose to every woman you sleep with?"

"Only when I take their virtue," he retorted.

"Did you plan this? Your sister told me you were searching for a wife. Was I just a convenient woman who might fit into your plans of marriage?" She stared down at him.

"No. And I never planned this." His anger emanated from him like the strong breeze at the shore. He eased himself off the sand to stand next to her. His hands clenched into fists. "Well? I made you an offer."

"No."

"Pardon?"

"I cannot marry you, Banning."

He drew in a deep breath. "Why not?"

"Because . . ." How could she tell him? He would only try to convince her that she was wrong. But she wasn't. He couldn't truly love her. He didn't know what love was. Marriage was a death sentence to a woman especially if she loved her husband. All her freedoms, all her loves, taken away from her until she died a pathetic old woman, or worse, a pathetic young woman like her mother.

"Well?"

"I'm sorry. I just can't." Avis lifted her skirts and ran from the shore. By the time she reached the house, she was panting.

Knowing he must be following behind her, she fled to the sanctuary of her writing room. She searched the room until she found the key on top of the old bureau. Only after locking the door did she allow herself to sit and catch her breath.

"Avis," Banning shouted from the hallway.

She watched the doorknob turn and the door rattle, but the lock held him at bay.

"Unlock this door so we can talk."

"No. There is nothing to discuss. I cannot marry you."

If only she felt as confident as her voice sounded. She couldn't marry him. But every time she thought those words, another voice in her head told her she could. Listening to that voice would only bring her ruin.

"Open this damned door or I will knock it down."

She almost smiled. As if he could knock down a locked door. But the sound of splintering wood turned her head toward the open threshold.

He stood at the entrance, his hands on his hips and an angry grimace on his face. "Don't ever lock me out again."

"Get out, Banning. I need some time alone."

"No," he answered, stepping into the room. "I want some answers."

Avis stood up and faced him. "I do not wish to marry you or any other man. You've always known that. My God, you're the one who named us the Spinster Club."

He eased toward her. "Even a spinster can change her mind."

"Not me."

"Give me one good reason."

She had plenty of excuses—reasons. But as her mind processed them, none of the explanations sounded plausible. She didn't want to hurt him, but he'd left her no choice. "I don't love you."

He stared down at her for what seemed like minutes. She trembled under his scrutiny.

"I don't believe you," he said finally.

She jerked her head upward and looked into his eyes. Those beautiful, sparkling blue eyes that normally shined with happiness, contentment, even love, now hardened like the icy waters of the North Sea.

She glanced away from his prying stare. "It's the truth."

"Prove it."

Before she could determine his meaning, he picked her up and tossed her over his shoulder as if she weighed no more than a stone. He strode to the bedroom.

"Put me down. This is not the Middle Ages where you can just take any woman you choose."

His hand caressed her bottom, kneading the flesh he found under her skirts. Even angry with him, all the sensations that flooded her senses when he was near started again. She didn't fear his show of strength, but she was madly aroused by it.

"Put me down!"

He eased her down his chest, slowly, deliberately. Her breasts rubbed against him, her nipples hardened with his nearness. She didn't want him this way, full of anger and frustration. But before she could have another thought, he kissed her with a hot passion that she couldn't refuse.

She knew she should push him away. Tell him he was a fool for trying to seduce her after she'd told him she did not love him. But she didn't. She was lost to the wondrous sensations of being seduced in a fury.

Her dress slipped from her shoulders, baring her body to his perusal. She should be stronger.

"Push me away, Avis," he mumbled against her neck. "Tell me you don't love me."

She really should do just that. She had only a few more days with him. The memories of their time together would have to last her a lifetime. She tore at his clothes with a ferocity greater than his own. Her body already ached for him to fill her, to send her to ecstasy at least one more time. She arched toward him as he took her nipple into his warm mouth. Pulling him closer, she felt as if her knees would buckle. Then they did.

He caught her in his arms and carried her to the bed. Covering her with his hard body, he mumbled against her breast. "Tell me you don't love me, Avis."

"I—ahh."

He suckled her deeply. "Tell me, Avis." He skimmed his lips across her belly, downward to her core. "Tell me."

"I—." She couldn't get the words to come out when he laved the tender nub between her legs. She couldn't think a coherent thought.

"Tell me, Avis," he said again as he sank one finger deep inside her.

She closed her eyes as her muscles tightened

around his finger. The pressure increased with each steady stroke but it wasn't enough. She wanted him one last time. Closer and closer she came to release, and then his finger was gone. The tip of his hard shaft entered her and stopped. She tried to move, but his weight made it impossible.

He grasped her hands and held them above her head. "Tell me, Avis," he whispered in her ear. "Tell me you love me."

She couldn't take another minute of this unfulfilled passion. Slowly, he eased out and again let just the tip of his cock fill her. She needed him. She wanted him. She loved him.

"I love you," she rasped.

He filled her completely, stroking her with a wildness that she'd never felt before. He glided his hands down her arms until he clutched her hands tightly to his. "Let me love you, Avis."

She went still and stared at him. The man from her dreams. All those weeks she had been dreaming of Banning and hadn't even realized it. She lifted her legs and wrapped them around his hips, letting every stroke send her higher with him. Certain she could go no further she arched her back and shuddered with abandon. He followed quickly behind her, spilling his seed inside her.

It wasn't until her heart calmed that she realized just what he'd done.

She had no protection. And she was certain he'd known it.

Banning rested his head on Avis's shoulder basking in the glow of their lovemaking. She loved him and the feeling was indescribable. Contentment filled him with every breath he took. They would marry, have a handful of children, and make love every night.

He would have the best of both worlds. A good, strong marriage bound by love not duty, and a passionate wife who wanted him to satisfy her. She satisfied him both emotionally and physically. Everything was perfect.

"How could you have done that?" she shrieked, pushing him off her. She scrambled off the bed. After grabbing her wrapper, she tossed it on and stared down at him.

"What exactly did I do?"

"You stayed inside me when I had no protection!"

He shook his head in confusion. "Why does that matter now? Even if you do get pregnant, I'll have the special license in a few days so the baby will be born just about nine months after the wedding. No one shall talk about that."

She clenched her fists in front of her. "Have you heard nothing I told you today?"

He sat up slowly and grinned at her. "I heard you say you love me."

"Under duress."

"Duress?" he asked, raising a brow at her.

"Yes."

"Call it whatever you like," he said, anger slowly welling inside him. He gathered his clothes and put on his trousers. "You might be pregnant—we'll marry."

"I am not marrying you."

"Yes, you will." He was done with this conversation.

He tossed his shirt over his head and quickly fastened the buttons.

"How exactly will you force me to marry you?"

His fingers faltered on the last button. Damned good question. Her father was dead. She had no true guardian and was well past the age of majority. Would she fall for the blackmail ruse again? He highly doubted it but what choice did he have?

"Shall I tell the world how the *Ice Maiden* is really a passionate woman who loves to swive a man until she can't think, until she confesses she loves him?"

"I daresay you won't go through with it."

He stalked her until he stood only a few inches away. Her angry breath heated his face.

"What do I have to lose?" he whispered harshly. "People love to believe you are so proper and would never take a man to bed. I know you are hot. You burn with desire and passion. The *ton* would love to hear about the woman I know."

"You bastard!"

He flinched as her hand made contact with his cheek. No more than he deserved. Still, the woman had quite an arm on her, his face hurt like the devil. Without looking at her, he turned and left the room.

He made his way down the stairs as a knock sounded at the door. "Just a moment," he shouted.

The footman wore the Selby livery, but Banning didn't recognize him. "My lord, I have an important message from your sister."

"Are you to wait for a reply?"

"Yes, my lord."

Banning scanned the note and cursed. "Tell her I shall arrive home as quickly as possible. Go around to the groundskeeper's house and tell Mr. Hathaway to ready my coach. Make haste, lad."

The boy took off running for the Hathaways' home. Banning slammed the door shut. He took the steps two at a time. So much for giving her time to calm down and think rationally. He rushed into the room and stopped dead.

Avis sat on the floor with her hands covering her face weeping. He crouched down beside her and slowly removed her hands. She attempted to twist away from him.

"Go away," she cried.

"I cannot do that." He attempted to draw her into his arms, but she turned the other direction. "Unfortunately, we must leave for London immediately. The Duke of Kendal has died."

The Duke of Kendal had been a dear friend of his family, and more importantly to Avis, her best friend's father.

"What? Oh God, Elizabeth!"

"We must pack and get back to town." He stood and started packing his bag.

Avis nodded but still remained on the floor, staring at the floral design on the carpet. "I'm sorry."

"We shall discuss this another time. We may miss the service if we don't hurry."

He held out his hands and assisted her to her feet. All he wanted to do was draw her into his arms and comfort her.

"Please remove yourself while I dress," she said in a firm voice.

"I've seen you naked before."

"Our time is over. We must go back to proper morals and values and—" She stifled a sob.

"As you wish."

He left her to sort through her emotions and change into a more suitable outfit. He packed up her papers in the other room. Unable to stop himself, he read a few pages she had written and smiled. She never needed to learn about passion, she had that in droves. All she ever needed was to let go and become the writer that was always inside her.

Now if she'd only free herself from the emotional ties that held her bound. Something or someone was keeping her from marrying him. And he was determined to discover what secret she'd kept from him.

Avis stared at the room once more before she left it forever. The white coverlet was back in its appropriate position and not twisted from two writhing bodies locked in a passionate tryst. The cotton curtains blew out like ghosts haunting the room. Or more fittingly, like the memories that would haunt her forever.

She glanced around once more. Not that she'd forgotten anything. No, she wanted to remember this room for the rest of her life. All she would have was her memories of these past few days. This was for the best, she attempted to convince herself. She had to get back to her normal routine, and no time with Banning was ever normal.

In the short time they shared, she had never laughed as much as she had with him. She felt safe, happy, and for once in her life, loved by a man. All she had to do was say yes to him. A simple three-letter word.

But life was never simple.

Marriage was a prison. She would rather live by herself than subject someone to what she feared was inside her. Being like her mother had never been an overwhelming concern to her because she'd always known she would never let a man abuse her. All her life she'd tried to control her anger. Her mother had forced Avis to learn how to restrain herself so she wouldn't hurt another person. Today, she failed. She'd hit the man she professed to love.

Fearing Banning. Fearing that he might change, might grow violent was just a cloak she hid behind. A cloak to disguise what she feared most—the truth.

She was no better than her father.

Chapter Fourteen

Neither Banning nor Avis spoke as the tension in the coach grew thicker with every mile that passed. She pulled at her silk gloves in her lap, stretching each empty finger. Even before their affair started, she had thought their parting might be difficult, but she'd expected after such an intimate time together they could still be civil. Given his stubborn silence, she realized civility wasn't an option.

They were bound to run into each other at most of the *ton's* social occasions. As it was summer, she shouldn't have to worry overmuch about Society and balls and parties in town.

The Kesgrave country party was only a few weeks away, and it was the only summer obligation she'd agreed to attend. She had also promised Jennette that she would brave her motion sickness and attend the party. Banning would be there. They might have to talk to each other, at least while others were present. She doubted they would ever speak privately again. She would never have an intimate conversation with him, or listen to him play the pianoforte, or edit naked with him, which was deliciously wicked. She'd never have anything but this blasted tension with him.

Acid burned the back of her throat. She had to get out of the coach.

"Stop the carriage, Banning."

He stared at her for a moment then banged his fist on the roof of the carriage. They came to an immediate halt. Avis didn't even wait for the coachman to open the door. Scrambling past Banning, she fled the vehicle and raced for the nearest tree. After emptying her stomach, she leaned weakly against the trunk. The fresh air slowly settled her stomach down again.

"Avis," Banning said, concern lacing his voice. He handed her a handkerchief. "Do you need to rest here for a short time?"

She shook her head. "We should be able to travel again. My stomach is empty."

"Is this a problem with motion or should we travel to the nearest church and marry immediately?" He cocked a black brow at her.

She brushed past him. "I am not with child."

"Or you just haven't discovered that you are yet," he replied softly.

Her feet refused to move further. She turned around and leveled an angry glare at him. "I have this problem every time I travel."

"You didn't on the way here."

"I slept most of the way."

"Hmm," he said, disbelieving her. "My proposal still stands. If you find out there is a child from our affair, you know where I live."

In her heart, she knew Banning would be a wonderful father to any woman's child. But *she* couldn't be trusted with a baby. Slapping his face earlier today had proven that to her.

She couldn't be pregnant, she thought rubbing the scar on her arm. While the physical marks on her had faded, the memories never would. She would never forgive herself if she hurt a child in anger. The only way to prevent that from happening was to never marry and have children. And never have sexual congress again.

No matter how difficult it would be to live without Banning, she had no choice. Only difficult didn't even start to encompass how hard this would be. She felt as if her heart had broken into shards too small to repair.

She walked back to the coach and climbed inside. The ride would take another four hours before they even reached the inn. Four more hours of his company today. She prayed he would get them separate rooms for the evening.

Banning reached down under the seat and pulled out a pillow. He placed it on his lap. Patting the pillow, he said, "Put your head down and sleep off your sickness."

She did as he suggested though her mind warred with the idea that she was succumbing to his charm again. But she certainly was not because that would mean there remained a chance she would change her mind.

As she inhaled his heady, spicy scent, her mind wandered to a future without him. Her nights would never be the same. She wouldn't wake up to his soft snore in her ear or the weight of his leg over hers. Instead, she would have her cold, lonely bed. She pressed her lips together to keep from crying.

His hand gently caressed her hair as she drifted off and she wondered if life could be any more complicated.

Banning stared down at the beautiful woman asleep on his lap. How could he have told her he loved her? He was a foolish bastard to think words of love would have any effect on her. She'd never wanted marriage, and he had known that long before he offered himself up to her. Even though she'd spoken those words of love to him, he was certain it was as she said—duress.

Damn. But her words didn't change anything. He would still marry her and just put love behind him. Love only complicated matters and led to smart men doing foolish things. He would just treat this as a business arrangement. As in any business arrangement, everyone had a price. He just had to determine her price, and he doubted it pertained to money. He twirled a strand of tawny hair around his index finger. As he released the curl, it sprang back into place.

There were several options. He could compromise her publicly. The ensuing scandal would force her hand. He knew she enjoyed her life socializing with her friends and the *ton*. She would marry him to save her reputation.

Or would she?

She was as stubborn as his own sister, and he knew Jennette would never succumb to such coercion.

Perhaps ruining her wasn't the best option.

If she were pregnant, she would marry him to give their child his name and all that went with it. He smiled at the thought of Avis carrying his baby. Or even better, the thought of making love to her over and over until she did carry his child.

Of course, knowing Avis, she would be just as likely to run off to a different country to avoid marrying him. She was a very independent woman and had the means to live anywhere she pleased.

He could always court her until she gave in under his constant barrage of flowers, poetic love letters, and stolen kisses. However, he might possibly be the world's worst poet.

Dammit!

How would he convince Avis to marry him? For once in his life, he hadn't any ideas. She was the most stubborn, passionate, intriguing, and beguiling woman he had ever met. Even now, after their disagreements this afternoon, he wanted to wake her up and make love to her again and again until she realized just how much he loved her.

He continued to dwell on his situation for hours, until the carriage rolled to a stop at the inn. With the time that had passed, he should have been able to produce one decent idea, but still he had none. Perhaps one more night together would help his cause—one room, one night with her before they had to return to civilization.

"Wake up," he whispered, careful not to jar her.

She groaned, twisting her head until it rested against his hard cock. "Not yet."

"We're at the inn."

She came awake with a start. Sitting up, she

glanced around taking note of her surroundings. "Already? I only slept for—"

"Three hours, maybe four."

"Oh."

"I shall secure us a room while you straighten up."

"Two rooms, Selby." Her voice brooked no denial. So much for one more night with her.

He climbed down and strolled toward the inn, noticing that the area seemed to be teeming with people. Strange, given that it was nearly nine in the evening.

"Welcome back, milord," Mr. Owens said enthusiastically.

Banning leaned against the desk. "We would prefer two rooms tonight."

Mr. Owens shook his head. "I'm sorry, milord. Between the duke's death requiring people to return to town and the exodus of people leaving London for the summer, I have only one room left."

Well, she wouldn't be pleased with this outcome. Now they would have to sneak her in undetected by whoever happened to be staying here too.

"Very well, one room then." He gave a cursory look around and noticed two people who gave him a quick nod of acknowledgment. Somehow, he would have to slip her inside.

"Do you have a back staircase?" he asked the innkeeper.

"Yes," Mr. Owens answered. Comprehension dawned on his face. "Of course, milord. Bring the gel around back and we'll spirit her upstairs."

"No one must see her."

Mr. Owens nodded.

Banning returned to the carriage thankful that no one was attempting to engage him in conversation. He opened the door and jumped back inside. Avis had taken the time to put her bonnet on and straighten her dress.

"This is not going to be easy," he started.

"Why?" she asked with unease lacing her voice.

"The place is teeming with people. I arranged to have you enter through the kitchen and walk up the back stairs."

Her face paled. "So I'm no better than a servant now, or a serving wench. Am I here to service your needs, milord?"

"Avis," he warned, "would you rather risk your reputation and enter via the front door? It wouldn't bother me."

"Of course not." She sighed. "I'm just a bit ill-tempered this evening."

"Come along now. Pull your veil down and hunch over as if you are ill. That way no one will see your face. Anyone who sees us will think I'm assisting Jennette inside."

"Jennette! She is a good five inches taller than I am. No one would make that mistake."

"Shall we?" he asked, impatience threading through his voice.

"Of course, milord."

"Would you stop calling me that?" Damn, the woman was exasperating. "I almost like you calling me a beast better."

They wound their way to the back of the inn, passing the herb garden and dodging the chickens pecking for food. The kitchen bustled with activities as the cooks finished preparing the evening meals.

Pots clanged and dishes clunked onto the table as silverware chimed when tossed onto the waiting trays. No one seemed to take undue notice of two strangers walking through.

"Right this way, milord," Mr. Owens said by the staircase.

Mr. Owens led them up to the second floor and looked around the hallway before waving them forward. The room was only a few feet from the staircase. Banning breathed a sigh of relief as he closed the door behind him.

"Am I to presume we are sharing a room again?" Avis asked, removing her bonnet. Long spiral strands that had escaped her chignon framed her face.

A slow burning desire spread to his loins. She hadn't sounded unduly upset with the notion of sharing a room with him once more. A sensation so strong he could barely keep from pulling her into his arms.

"Yes," Banning replied. "The inn is full. We were very fortunate that Mr. Owens had a room left at all."

She nodded. "Please tell me he'll bring us some food?"

"Of course, you must be hungry. You barely ate a thing all day. While you slept, I ate the meal Mrs. Hathaway had packed for us."

"I couldn't have stomached anything then."

"Are you certain you're up to it now? I've heard tales of women who are sick their entire pregnancy," he teased, just to see her face color.

Instead of retorting, she took a seat in a worn, green chair by the fireplace and crossed her arms over her chest. He removed his waistcoat and untied his cravat. As he unfastened the top buttons of his shirt, she stared at him from the corner of her eyes.

"Are you tired?" he asked.

"No," she answered tightly. "If I sleep tonight, I'll never be able to rest in the carriage tomorrow. I believe I shall write. If you don't mind the candlelight, that is."

"No, I don't mind."

They ate a quiet supper in their room. Unlike the last time they were here, the meal tasted like dust and Avis rushed through her supper as if she couldn't stand being so close to him.

She retired to the small table and brought out paper, her quill, and ink. Banning stripped off the rest of his clothes, noting how her posture straightened as each garment landed on the floor. He almost smiled. Instead, he lay on the bed and attempted to sleep.

Avis spent the night staring blankly at the paper on the table. She wanted to write. She needed to write. But no words came forth. Her characters were exceedingly quiet tonight, refusing to tell her what to put down on paper. Or maybe she couldn't hear them over Banning's snores.

Unable to contain herself, she sneaked a glance at him. Dark whiskers extended from his right ear to his left. She wanted to reach out and caress the hairs, feel their bristly roughness again. She didn't dare. She had caused this rift and there was no mending it.

He wouldn't want a woman who might strike him

when he angered her. He definitely wouldn't marry a woman who might hurt an innocent child.

As morning dawned, the paper still lay blank. Avis had spent most of the night watching him sleep. Captivated by him. Tears fell silently, burning her cheeks with self-damning clarity. She didn't deserve him. Some other woman would be his wife and raise his children, while she would watch from afar . . . alone.

She wiped away the vestiges of her tears.

"Wake up," she called to him. "We need to eat and continue our journey."

Banning groaned. "No."

"Yes."

He rolled over onto his stomach and put the pillow over his head. "Go away."

"I need food."

He mumbled something from under the pillow that sounded like "More than you do me." Surely, he didn't believe that. She needed him more than she could ever admit to anyone.

Banning pushed the pillow off his head and tossed the covers to one side. His damned cock had heard her voice and readied for the usual morning lovemaking. Not today, or possibly ever again.

Bloody hell. His life was a mess. He stood and stretched, giving her a full body view of just what she would be missing. Based on the slight gasp he heard, she'd taken notice.

He dressed quickly, but he did note the disappointment in her eyes as his trousers covered his erection. Good. She deserved to be frustrated. He certainly was.

"I shall go down and order a breakfast tray," he said, walking toward the door.

He took the front stairs down to the dining room. He ordered a large breakfast and decided to wait for the tray. He glanced about the room. Several acquaintances nodded at him. He would have to sneak Avis out the back door again.

"Lord Selby!"

Damn. Miss Olivia Roebuck, the biggest thorn in his side this Season, rushed over to him. Her mother followed quickly behind.

"Lord Selby, what a coincidence running into you here," she said excitedly. "Whatever are you doing here?"

"I'm returning from my estate in Southwold. I just received word of the Duke of Kendal's death."

She flipped an ironed curl back from her face. "That is why we must return also. But it will be nice to have another chance to socialize with my peers."

Before she could say anything else foolish, one of the serving girls came up with a tray for him. "Milord, do you wish me to take this up to your w—"

"No," he interrupted before she could say the word *wife*. The last thing he needed was either gossipy Roebuck interfering with his life. "I shall take the tray upstairs myself."

The girl handed him the tray with a nod and returned to the kitchen.

"My, that is a lot of food for one person," Miss Roebuck said. Her mother frowned but nodded just the same.

"Is your sister with you?" Mrs. Roebuck asked.

Now that was a question. If he lied and said yes, they might find out exactly where Jennette had been—at Lord Durham's country party. If he said no, they would think he was a glutton. Gluttony won.

"No," he finally replied. "You must excuse me. I should eat while the food is warm."

"You may join us," Miss Roebuck offered, batting her golden eyelashes at him.

"I really must not. I have some papers I need to review before I leave. Good day."

The women mumbled their replies as he walked back upstairs. Avis really didn't need to know that the Roebucks were here. She might become aggravated thinking they might see her with him. It was far better to keep this quiet.

He entered the room slowly. She had changed into a blue traveling gown, fixed her hair, and sat ramrod straight in the chair by the window. She turned her head as he walked in.

"The dining room is full of people. Unfortunately, some we both know."

"Dare I guess, it's the back door for me again?" she asked bitterly.

"Unless you prefer we walk down the front stairs together."

She blasted him a glare. "I do not believe we shall do that."

He shrugged. "I thought not."

Olivia Roebuck excused herself from the dining table. "I need to speak with the proprietor to inquire on my glove. I should hate to think I had lost one of my best gloves here."

"I shall go with you then," her mother said, stuffing more eggs in her mouth.

"No, Mother. You need to finish your breakfast."
Her mother loved her food, to excess. "The desk is
just over there," she said, pointing toward the hall.
"I will be within sight the entire time."

"Very well," her father replied. He also seemed to
be in no mood to miss a meal.

Olivia rose from her seat and proceeded to the desk.
That disgusting Mr. Owens sat behind the counter,
sorting through papers. The one thing she needed was
right on top.

"Miss Roebuck, is there something I can do for ye?"

"Oh, Mr. Owens," she said in a wispy voice as she
fluttered her eyelashes at him. All men loved when
she did that. Except the one man she wanted more
than any other. "I lost my silk glove here. Could you
look around and see if any of your maids took it? By
accident, of course."

"They dam—darned well better hope they didn't
take one of yer precious gloves."

"Please," she begged prettily.

He stared at the cleavage she showed by leaning
over the tall desk and pressing her arms to the sides
her breasts. It must have worked.

"Of course. I'll be back in a moment."

He walked back toward the kitchens, giving her
just a moment to twirl the register around and
glance down. She scanned the list but could not
find Selby's name. She continued through the past
few days until her finger paused by Talbot. That was
his surname, but why would he use that instead of
his title. Her eyes widened in realization.

Mr. and Mrs. Talbot.

Lord Selby must have a woman with him. Her
mind wheeled with the possibilities. A slow cat-like

smile tilted her lips up as a plan started to form. An excellent plan. But she would need an accomplice to complete the deed, and after a moment of thought, she knew just the woman who could help. The one woman who despised Selby, the most proper of all the spinsters in her little club—Miss Avis Copley.

With Miss Copley's unknowing assistance, her plot would work perfectly. Olivia stifled a laugh. And she would be Lady Selby before the end of the summer.

Chapter Fifteen

"Good evening, my lord," Battenford said.

"Banning!" Jennette shouted from the top of the stairs. She raced down the marble stairs and threw herself into his arms. "I am so glad you're home."

"Well, this is an unusual welcome."

"I'm sorry," she said, pulling away. "It has been a very dreadful week."

"How are Lady Elizabeth and her sisters?" he asked, removing his gloves and hat. Handing them to his butler, he moved toward the salon. He poured a brandy for them both and shoved away the memories of doing the same with Avis.

"They are as well as can be expected. I think poor Elizabeth is the worst. At least her sisters have their husbands and families, while she has no one now."

Jennette reached for the brandy snifter and took a long draught. Unlike Avis, his sister had no issues drinking brandy.

"Well, that is to be expected," he said, giving her a pointed look. "It is one of the reasons I want you to marry. I don't want you to be alone."

She waved his hand at him in dismissal. "I do have my friends. Although, that is another reason why I'm quite upset."

"Why?"

"It's Avis. She told her butler she'd decided to go away with Elizabeth. But Elizabeth joined her cousin at Durham's country party. No one has seen Avis in close to a fortnight." She bit down on her bottom lip.

Well, not quite no one. "She probably ensconced herself in a small village to write for a few weeks. She will most likely show up any day." Or minute.

"I hope you are correct. I am considering hiring a Bow Street Runner to investigate. What has me worried is that she hates to travel. It makes her dreadfully ill. I had to beg her to attend the Kesgrave party with me in a fortnight."

A shot of disappointment ran through him. He'd only been teasing her about the pregnancy, knowing it was too soon to know. Still, a part of him would have been quite pleased if it were true.

"Don't hire anyone just yet. She's bound to come around."

A footman entered the room and handed a message to Jennette. She unfolded the note and smiled. Looking up at him, she laughed. "You were right. I asked one of Avis's footmen to inform me of her return. It appears she has arrived home this very evening."

"Indeed." He drained his brandy and stood to take his leave. "I believe I shall retire early. Goodnight, Jennette."

"Hmm, goodnight, Banning. I must inform Avis about the duke's death."

"She knows." His feet stopped moving. He hadn't just said those words in front of his inquisitive sister.

"How could she possibly know?"

He tried to keep the heat from creeping across his face, but it didn't seem to work. "How could she not know? Everyone in England is talking about it, even at the inn where I stayed. No doubt that is what drew her back to town."

"Perhaps you are right."

He'd best leave before he let anything else slip. Refusing to look back at his sister, he strode from the room and up to his bedroom. He'd never felt so utterly disgusted with everything in his life. He never understood how people could whine about life being so difficult; life had been easy, until he decided to marry Avis.

The idea that she didn't want to wed made no sense. He could give her everything. It should be obvious to her how well they suit, in bed and out. Her writing wasn't the issue as he'd made it perfectly clear he would never stop her. What of companionship? Did it mean nothing to her? He was certain it did. He had seen the looks on her face when they walked hand in hand on the beach, and when they worked on her story in bed. She was happy, dammit.

Something wasn't right here.

What could possibly be keeping her from marriage? He pulled off his jacket and sat down on the bed in thought. He needed to discover what was behind her issue with marriage and assuage her reasons until she relented.

* * *

Other than a chiding from Jennette for worrying
her and a quick visit to Elizabeth, Avis spent the
remainder of the next week alone in her home.
With each day that passed, she prayed for her
monthlies to come until she believed she could not
ask God for another thing in her entire life. But still
they didn't come. She couldn't be pregnant. She
would have to marry him. She didn't want that . . .
did she?

She lay in bed, trying to imagine what marriage to
Banning would mean. A man in her bed who knew
her body and how to bring her to ecstasy. Someone
to talk to during the long winters. Someone who
seemed to respect her opinions on matters and had
no problem discussing, or rather arguing, his opinion too.

Avis bit her lower lip. Blast, she missed the cur.

He'd called on her several times in the past week
and each time she had Grantham turn him away.
So far, she didn't believe anyone had noticed his at-
tempts to visit, but she couldn't take any more
chances. Spurning his calls hurt her more than she
wanted to admit but there was no point in encouraging him when she couldn't trust herself. Not as
long as her father's blood ran through her.

As she rose to change into her morning clothes,
she realized thoughts of marriage did not matter
any longer. Her courses had started during the
night. There no longer appeared to be any reason
she might *have* to marry him. Tears burned down
her cheeks.

After the past few days, she'd expected to be crying
out of relief. She fell onto her bed and put her face
in the pillows. She wasn't with child. She pressed her

hand to her belly, there was no baby growing there. She would never have his child. She would never have him again.

She'd never felt so empty in her life.

Why had she invited guests today? With her courses only started two days ago and her emotions still in upheaval, the last thing she needed was a literary salon in her home. But she'd planned it weeks ago and it would look quite bad if she canceled. As people arrived that afternoon, she did her best to plaster on a smile and be pleasant.

Soon the salon filled with people but still there was no sign of Emory. She knew he had returned with the prince for the duke's memorial because he'd sent a note around telling of his return. They really shouldn't start discussing his book without him.

"He should be here any moment," she told her friends. Trying not to look obvious, she peeked out the window. She was anxious for the salon to start. The sooner it began, the sooner it would be over. She spotted Emory coming up the walk. Thank God, he had arrived. But glancing behind Emory's carriage, she noticed another coach. This one had an earl's emblem blazed on the door. She clutched the window frame for support.

"I believe our guest of honor has arrived," she said. Plus a very unwelcome addition.

If she barred Banning from entering, everyone would be suspicious. If she let him in, who knew what might happen. She had no choice but to invite him into her salon and hope he did nothing extreme.

"Lord Selby and Mr. Billingsworth," Grantham announced.

"Welcome to my salon, my lord," she said with an exaggerated curtsy. "This is quite unexpected."

"I am fairly certain it is not," Banning remarked as he passed her. "Thank you for the invitation, Miss Copley."

As if she would have issued such an invitation. "And Mr. Billingsworth, our honored guest."

Emory took her hand in his and placed a quick kiss on her hand. "It is a pleasure to be at your home, Miss Copley. I will need just a moment and a glass of water before I start my oratory."

A footman poured a glass of water for him as the guests took their seats. As the hostess, she felt all her guests should have the best chairs, so she sat in the rear of the room. Banning took the seat next to her. She could feel his breath caress her ear as they turned to watch Emory take his position in front. She could smell the tangy scent of him that always drove her mad.

While Emory spoke, Avis did her best to concentrate on him and not the man next to her. But try as she might, she heard barely a word Emory spoke. Yet she heard every breath Banning took. She watched from the corner of her eye every movement he made, whether it was crossing his legs or shifting in his chair. She'd only ever been this intently aware of one man—Banning.

She wondered if the swift brush of his arm against hers had been accidental. He mumbled a soft apology. She closed her eyes briefly only to imagine Banning, naked in bed and waiting for her.

Her eyes snapped open, and she tried her best to

listen to Emory. But Banning moved his legs again and one strong thigh grazed her skirts. Only this time, he didn't move his leg back into a proper position. The heat of his body swept up her limbs and farther, up her back until she had to steel herself against the assault. She shifted away from him, praying for a breath of cool air to dampen her desires.

She glanced at him from the corner of her eye and noticed the smug little smile on his face. Damn him. He was playing with her.

Minutes passed and several people asked questions of Emory. She would normally be one of the first to speak up and query an author. Tonight she could barely remember her name much less something to say.

The sound of clapping hands told her Emory's speech was finished. The crowd mingled for over an hour. When Avis glanced around, she realized Banning must have slipped out without saying anything to her. How odd. She rather thought he might do something inane such as cause a scene. Relief merged with disappointment at his exit.

"Avis, I must say you seem different tonight," Emory noted from over the top of his port glass. He had remained as everyone else departed, leaving them alone in her house.

"However do you mean?"

"Distracted. It's not like you. I do not think you asked a single question tonight."

"I do apologize, Emory. I find of late my mind to be on Lady Elizabeth in her time of sorrow."

He patted her hand softly, caressingly. "Of course, that must be it."

What was it about his reply that set her nerves on

edge? Avis pulled her hand away and looked around for her servants. Where were they? "Did you have a chance to read through my story?"

"I did."

"And?"

Emory walked away from her. "Well, I believe the story is improving."

She could hear the hesitation in his voice. "But?"

"Something is still missing. The romance between the two characters is fascinating but it is rather scandalous, and I fear you might offend some readers."

"Offend some readers?"

"Yes, your heroine is rejecting an earl for a mere mister and a gambler at that. I don't believe most marriage-minded mamas would ever allow that to happen no matter the reason."

"But they are in love with each other."

Emory rolled his eyes. "Yet they still must conform to the mores of society and society would look down on such a marriage."

He wanted her to change her story again.

Emory clasped her hands and looked into her eyes. "Avis, what is most important is getting you published. I have told you hundreds of times that even if you get your book published you must make your readers happy so they are satisfied and all too pleased to buy your future novels. You have to play the games of Society and follow their rules. The story must be perfect and offend no one. That is why my first book was so successful. I don't want you making the same mistakes I made with my last few books that I can't seem to sell."

Avis nodded, stifling the need to run to her room

and cry. Emory was right. She wanted to see her novel in print, and she mustn't offend anyone or she would never realize her dream.

Emory cleared his throat noisily, as if to regain her attention. "Would you allow me to take you for a ride in the park tomorrow?"

A ride? With Emory? He had never shown one bit of attraction toward her except in a friendly manner. Perhaps he just wanted more time to talk about his book and his time with the prince. "Of course. I would love that."

Emory smiled in a way that made her think she was about to be pounced upon. After kissing the top of her hand, he said, "Very well, I shall call for you at four."

Avis nodded as he picked up his coat and hat. After Emory left, she dismissed the servants for the night before heading to her study. She wanted her novel published so she had to make her miserable writing less offensive to the general public. Or she had to decide if writing was what she truly wanted to do with her life.

How could she do either one? In her heart, she knew the story worked the best as she had rewritten it. But what was the point of writing if no one would read her stories? She pressed her lips together, fighting the tears that threatened. She didn't want to give up writing. Creating stories had been her escape from her family life and her escape from Society's strict rules. Without her writing, what would she have?

Nothing.

A house filled with servants, a few close friends, and enough money to live lavishly the rest of her life, but she wouldn't have that fulfillment of having created something no one else could have.

The only thing she had ever wanted to do was write. What would she do now? How would she occupy her days? With no husband or children to occupy her time and no writing, the emptiness inside her would only grow. She wiped away a tear that managed to overflow with her frustration.

After she entered the room, she lit several candles on her desk until she had enough light to read without straining her eyes. Standing in front of the desk, she picked up the first page of her manuscript and scanned the story again.

"This is horrid," she cried, ripping the paper down the middle. A tear trickled down her cheek and then another. She would never be a writer, never see her books in print. No one would ever read her stories and be captivated by them, lost to another world and time.

She lifted the second sheet and started to rip it, but two large, masculine hands reached out from behind her to close over hers.

"Don't," Banning whispered in her ear.

Avis gasped in surprise. He shouldn't be here, in her study. They were alone together and all her servants had retired for the night. And yet, she felt far safer alone in the study with Banning than she had just a few minutes ago with Emory.

"What are you doing in here?"

"I didn't come to your literary salon to hear Billingsworth blabber on about how wonderful he thinks his new book is."

"Then why did you attend?"

She could feel his smile against her hair. "It was the only way you would let me into your home."

"Why should I let you into my house?"

"We still have much to discuss."

Avis took in a long breath. "I did not believe there was anything left to discuss."

"You're wrong." He wrapped his arms around her. "We have unfinished business."

She twisted out of his arms. He acknowledged her movement with a brief nod then took a seat across from her.

"Then let us finish our business and be done."

His lips turned up in a sardonic smile. "At your service, ma'am."

The look he gave her was positively sensual, and it sparked her every nerve ending to life.

"Why was he here tonight?" he asked.

"He? Which *he* are we discussing?" She glanced away from him as she played with the folds of her gown.

"Billingsworth. I told you to stay away from him."

"You are not my keeper."

"I told you once before not to be in his company."

"I shall keep the company of any man I choose."

"Why would you want to be with him after what I told you?"

"He helps me with my writing," she whispered, looking away from his prying gaze.

"Indeed?" Banning rose and picked up the pieces of her first page. "Is he the reason you believe this page is horrid?"

"It is dreadful writing."

"It most certainly is not. And you didn't answer my question," he retorted.

"Yes," Avis answered with an exasperated sigh. "Emory reread my manuscript and told me it was better but still would offend the proper ladies of society."

Banning laughed as he shook his head.

"What are you laughing about?"

"Billingsworth is a jealous ass."

"What?"

"If he gets you to give up writing he is essentially crushing his competition. He knows you will continue to support him until he sells enough books to be rid of his sponsor. It's in his best interest to keep you as beholden to him for advice as he is to you for money. Why can't you see that?" Banning placed the torn paper on top of her manuscript pile.

Avis whirled away from him. "You're mad. Emory is a fine writer. He has nothing to be jealous of from me."

"This has nothing to do with how well you write. It's all about you continuing to pay his debts."

"You're wrong. My writing will never be good enough to be published," she said, trying to keep a sob out of her voice.

"Your writing is beautiful."

"He said it was too controversial and the ladies would never read it."

"All the best writers in history were controversial."

Avis paused. His words made no sense. Emory had nothing to be jealous of from her. She only gave him a little bit of aid until he published his next book.

"You're wrong about Emory," she said. "Why should I believe anything you tell me?"

"He's lying to you, Avis. The creditors are closing

in on him. If he keeps you from publishing he knows you will still want to be around writers and will continue to support him."

Her temper flared. "He is not the liar."

"When have I ever lied to you, Avis?"

"You told me Emory was to marry Lady Hythe. You told me I was beautiful just to get me on the terrace alone eight years ago."

He smiled down at her. "I never lied about your beauty, Avis."

"You kissed me on a wager? A wager!"

"I would have done anything for that kiss," he whispered.

His warm breath caressed her ear, teasing her with its softness and reminding her of the time they had shared at the cottage. She had to get him to leave before she did something completely rash such as kissing him.

"I think you should leave now," she said.

She grabbed for the desk behind her as his lips came closer to her neck. A hot shudder swept over her body. She couldn't let him kiss her again. She pushed herself away from his tempting heat and glared at him.

He took in her mutinous expression. "Perhaps I should leave after all." He grabbed his coat and hat from the chair and turned toward the door. "Stay away from Billingsworth."

"Tell me, Selby. Does everyone do your bidding without argument?"

"Yes." He reached the threshold of the study and glanced back at her.

She cocked her head. "One more thing before

you leave. You said we still have unfinished business. What did you mean by that?"

He lifted his head slowly and smiled seductively at her. Staring at her, he strode toward her until they were inches apart. Dear Lord, he was going to kiss her. She couldn't let that happen. He brought his lips closer to hers until they were only a breath apart.

"I just thought you should know that my proposal still stands," he whispered.

He left before she could give him a proper set down for his presumptuous comment. She had to get him out of her mind, not that he made it easy. Every time she saw him, she returned in her memories, back to her time alone with him. She pushed those traitorous thoughts aside. She had to be strong. She could never marry.

Chapter Sixteen

Banning left Avis's study in a foul mood. The brief contact with Avis had irritated him because all he'd wanted to do was draw her into his arms and kiss her again. As soon as she'd entered the room, her essence surrounded him, feeding on his desire for her. He shouldn't kiss her anytime soon. He had to let her come to him, although staying away from her would be near to impossible.

As he walked toward his bedroom, he heard his mother's voice. "Banning? Is that you?"

"Yes, Mother."

"Please come into my room."

His mother sat in her salon working on a floral embroidery piece. She glanced up as he entered the room. "How was your evening?"

"Dreadful," he answered.

"Oh, then it quite possibly is about to get worse." She straightened in her seat. "You have a slight problem, my son."

"Oh?"

"Yes. You were seen leaving the Halstead Inn."

"What is so unusual about that?"

"With a woman."

Dear God, she knew. "Mother, I believe I am old enough to do what I wish with my time."

"Indeed. You should be thankful that I am informing you and you're not hearing this whispered behind some gossipmonger's fan. No one knows who the woman was, but the current speculation is that she is a lady and not a lightskirt."

"So no one saw her face?"

She tossed her embroidery, hoop and all, at him. "No. But I will not have our name bantered about by the gossips. Make sure no one discovers this girl's name."

She rose from her seat and blasted an icy blue glare at him. She reminded him of Jennette when he'd teased her to the point of anger. Only he could cajole Jennette out of her ill humor. He knew his mother would not.

"Best make certain *I* do not discover who she is or you will be married before you can snap your fingers."

"Yes, Mother."

She pointed toward the door. "Be off now."

Nothing like a good chiding by your own mother to end a perfect day, he thought sarcastically. He glanced down at his watch. Even though it was only eleven, he'd had enough of this day. He slammed the door to his bedroom suite and headed for the brandy.

He wanted to forget the past month. As if that would ever happen.

"Avis, are you even listening to me?"

Avis blinked and returned her concentration on

Emory. He sat across from her in the carriage while Bridget sat next to her. While her maid wasn't the perfect chaperone, Avis hadn't any other choices. All her friends had begged off, even Sophie.

"I must apologize, Emory. My mind drifted away from me."

He smiled at her. But his smile didn't quite reach his eyes. "I was telling you all about the prince's comments."

Of course he was. And normally, she would have been listening with great interest to him. Instead, her mind kept wandering off and thinking how much more interesting this carriage ride would be if Banning sat across from her. She clenched and unclenched her fists. She had to stop thinking about him. That part of her life was over.

Concentrate on Emory, she scolded herself.

"And then he said it was a most agreeable story," Emory said.

Emory was the perfect gentleman. After their time alone in the study last evening, she feared he might have developed an attraction to her. While only a few weeks past, she would have welcomed his attention, now she wanted no part of it.

"Avis," Emory exclaimed. "I really don't believe you are hearing a word I've said today."

"I am dreadfully sorry, Emory. You have been a perfect companion and yet my mind keeps wandering off."

He reached over and clasped her gloved hands. "Whatever is the matter?"

Avis closed her eyes and squeezed his hands. "I've just been worrying about Elizabeth."

"It will take time but she will get over her father's death. At least she has her sisters."

"You're right, of course."

Emory was a wonderful man. How could she have believed Banning's ranting about Emory hurting that prostitute? Not once in all the years she'd known Emory had he behaved poorly toward her or any other woman. But perhaps she should hear his side of the story, if he would tell her of it.

"Emory," she paused for a breath of confidence. "Yes?"

No, she couldn't ask him such a personal question. "Never mind."

"Avis, what is on your mind? You can tell me or ask me anything. We're friends."

Yes, he was exactly right. And friends told friends the truth. "I heard a rumor about you and would truly like to hear your side of the story."

He released his grip on her hands and sat back. A deep frown marred his face. "What rumor?"

"Something that happened a few years ago."

"It wasn't as it appeared," he said quickly. He clenched his jaw and fists as a bead of sweat broke out on his forehead. His eyes widened but he refused to look at her. "I—I never laid a hand on that girl. I have witnesses."

Avis smiled at him. "I knew it. With the number of boys at Eton it could have been anyone."

"Eton?" Emory released his grip and sank back against the velvet squabs visibly relaxed. "It was nothing but a simple misunderstanding, Avis."

"Will you tell me about it?"

He hesitated a moment too long before he agreed to tell her. "Another young man in my room had snuck in a strumpet. He became irate after she tried to steal more money from him than she'd originally asked for and he struck her forcefully. The misunderstanding happened because James left the room after he saw what he'd done to her, and I walked in right after him. Everyone thought I had hit her. I never could live that story down. To this day there are still people who believe I was the monster who hit her."

He stared down at his hands.

"I'm so sorry, Emory."

"Thank you, Avis. I hate talking about what happened that night. It makes me feel as if I am there again, watching the scene unfold in front of me, trying to defend myself against something I had no part in."

Avis felt a sense of guilt now for bringing it up. "Thank you, Emory. I'm certain it can't be easy to relive such a dreadful time."

Emory's explanation seemed perfectly logical to her. Not once had he acted as if he wanted anything more than a pleasant drive through the park. She breathed a sigh of relief that Banning was wrong about him.

Banning thought about his options again for getting Avis to marry him as he rode through Hyde Park. He'd finally come to the conclusion that he would have to speak with Jennette in a manner that wouldn't make her suspicious. The last thing he needed was his sister furious with him for having an affair with her best friend.

"Riding alone today, I see."

He blinked and looked over at Somerton's sardonic smile. Banning had been so engrossed in his thoughts he hadn't even heard Somerton's horse approaching.

"What happened with your lady friend?"

Anger fired in his belly. "That is none of your concern."

Somerton shrugged. "Perhaps not, but I thought it odd that you were riding here alone while she rode with Billingsworth by the Serpentine."

"What?" He just barely remembered to keep his voice at a civil tone.

"The Serpentine, Billingsworth and Miss Copley, riding with just her servant as a companion." With that, he rode away.

Banning wasted no time in turning his horse around and galloping toward the water. He pulled up a short distance from the lake and scanned the area. Being a mild day there were many people on both horse and foot. Never having paid attention to Billingsworth's carriage, Banning had no idea if there were any special markings on the vehicle.

One open carriage caught his attention or maybe he had noticed the bonnet and remembered it from their drive to Southwold. Either way, his hands twisted on the reins. He wanted to shoot Emory Billingsworth so he couldn't hurt another woman again. Knowing he was unable to shoot him, the thought of strangling Avis entered his mind. Unable to do that either, he rode off toward her house. He might not be able to shake some sense into her, but he could tell her his opinion on the subject.

Grantham opened the door and opened his mouth to speak.

Banning pushed past the older man. "I know she is not at home but I will be waiting for her in the study."

"Milord," Grantham started, but Banning was already down the hall.

He walked into the study and poured a glass of brandy as Grantham reached the room.

"Milord, you must realize how . . . how . . . indelicate this is. Miss Copley is an unmarried woman and you mustn't barge into her home in such a brutish manner."

"Grantham, go get your strongest footman to forcibly remove me if you must but I will not leave until I see her or you have me thrown out."

Grantham's back stiffened, and then he smiled tightly. "I believe I understand, milord. Would you like refreshments while you wait?"

Banning held up his snifter of brandy. "This shall do nicely. Thank you, Grantham."

He slipped into the leather chair by the unlit fireplace and waited, and waited. The minutes ticked past until one hour had come and gone, the brandy glass refilled twice and she still hadn't returned. How could she ride with that bastard after what he'd told her about him? Perhaps she liked him a bit more than she had said. Billingsworth had been her first choice as a lover after all. And even though she hadn't admitted an overwhelming lust for him, she might find him attractive enough.

Dammit.

She was supposed to be his betrothed by now. He had to keep her away from Billingsworth. There was no way of doing that unless she agreed to be his wife, and the likelihood of marriage lessened every day.

"I heard I had a visitor," her voice sounded like a soft breeze from the doorway.

He looked over at her and glared until she let out a small gasp.

"Why are you here, Selby?"

"Shut the door, Avis."

She glanced nervously between the door and him. "I don't think that would be a good idea," she mumbled.

Banning gulped down the remains of his brandy and rose. "Not a good idea?" He laughed. "But I suppose riding with that bastard in the park with only a maid for a chaperone was a brilliant idea?"

"You were spying on me?" She inched backward toward the open doorway.

"Spying? Just how many people saw you driving with the man today, Avis? You know what they will assume," his voice grew louder with each sentence. He strode to the doorway, caught her wrist, swung the door closed, and pushed her against the wood. "You know people will talk."

"Why do you care?" she whispered.

He inhaled the intoxicating scent of her jasmine perfume and sighed. "I just do."

She turned her head slightly. "I spoke to Emory about what happened at Eton."

"Oh? And what lies did the bastard tell you?"

"Don't call him that," she said in a harsh tone. "He told me about the misunderstanding."

"*Misunderstanding*? Is that what he called it?" Banning backed away from her as she recounted the lies Billingsworth had told her. Staring at her amber eyes, he realized she completely believed Billingsworth.

"That was quite a work of fiction he told you. I was there, Avis. He had no roommate named James."

Avis threw up her hands in frustration and took a step backward. Why was this so important to him? "Why does this matter?"

He moved in closer, trapping her between the door and his hard chest again. "Because the man could hurt *you*."

"He would never do that, Banning. He's my friend."

"A friend doesn't take money with no means to repay you."

"A friend doesn't ask for repayment," Avis replied curtly.

He grabbed her wrists and raised them above her head, pressing his body against hers. "Stay away from him," he whispered as he bent his head toward her lips.

Quickly she turned her head the other way to avoid his kiss. His lips landed on her neck as hot need shot through her body with his closeness. He traced the contours of her neck up to her jaw until he reached her lips. Her control slipped as his tongue found hers. Her hands itched to wind their way through his silky hair, to skim her fingers up his chest, but he held her bound to the door so she had no ability to touch him.

"Avis," he muttered against her lips. "Marry me."

He was wearing her down with just his nearness. She struggled to get out of his arms and put some distance between them, and some sense back into her head. Instead, he pressed his body closer to her.

"Marry me," he whispered in her ear. "We can

make love every night, even tonight, right here and now."

"Oh God," she mumbled, closing her eyes as his tongue lapped her earlobe. The idea of making love with him had turned her body to mush. If he let her go right now, she'd drop to the floor. She couldn't make love with him again. No matter how much her body wanted him.

"No."

Banning leaned his forehead against hers, breathing hard. "Avis, this is madness. We both want each other. We love each other. We should marry."

Avis closed her eyes to keep the tears at bay. "I just can't, Banning."

"Why?" He barely whispered the word.

"I cannot marry you or anyone."

"Why not? Are you secretly married to someone else?"

"Of course not."

"Then give me one good reason why you can't marry me," he whispered against her forehead.

One good reason. Fear? The idea of marriage, even with Banning, still terrified her. She loved him. But *she* had her father's blood running through her veins. She remembered the look in her mother's eyes when her father had hit her. The memories of her mother's broken bones and bruises, of her own bruises, would never fade. And Avis was certain of one thing—she would never want a child to go through the hell she had. She couldn't stand to see Banning's love turn to loathing when he realized the truth about her.

"One good reason, Avis," he said again.

"I just can't marry you. I'm sorry."

"That was scarcely a good reason."

This had to end. He actually mentioned love again. His proposal today was far more serious than any previous one. And she was weakening. Perhaps it would be prudent to stop this insanity now.

"I don't want you to call on me again. This foolishness needs to stop." She twisted out of his arms and finally had the distance she needed to maintain control.

"This will not stop until you are my wife." He crossed his arms over his chest. "And I will not stop calling on you."

She shook a fist at him. She couldn't cry. She wouldn't cry. No matter how she tried, she couldn't keep the tears from racing down her cheeks. How could she take a chance with him when she knew what was deep inside of her?

"I am never going to be your wife."

"Yes, you will."

Chapter Seventeen

By the time she reached the Kesgrave estate in Suffolk, Avis felt as if she would never eat again. With her nerves in a knot, she'd been unable to sleep during the drive. So her coachman had to stop every hour or two for her to cast up her accounts.

She stepped down and held her coachman's arm for a moment to steady her legs. Once she was certain she could manage on her own, she walked toward the old stone house. Leaded glass windows lined the building, giving it an ancient feel. Carved in the wood above the entrance was the date 1593.

The door opened before she even reached the front step. The butler showed her inside and into the elegant drawing room. Lord Kesgrave and his wife Charlotte smiled at her as she walked toward them.

"Avis," Charlotte said. "It's so lovely to see you again. I am pleased you decided to join us for the week."

"Miss Copley." Lord Kesgrave nodded at her.

"Jennette arrived ahead of you but awaits your presence in the billiard room."

"Thank you, my lord." Avis glanced toward Charlotte and noted the softly rounded belly that announced her impending motherhood. "You look very well, Charlotte."

"I feel wonderful. I assume you wish to retire to your room to refresh yourself?"

Avis nodded. Nothing sounded better than a cup of tea and no rocking motion. "Yes, thank you."

Charlotte led her into the large hallway where a footman stood in wait. "Show Miss Copley to her room."

Turning toward her, Charlotte said, "Since you are a dear friend of Jennette, I put you in a room near the Selbys. I'll have some tea sent up to you."

Avis tried to control the nervous twitch that suddenly attacked her eye. Just how close would she be to *him?*

"I would be happy to show you around our home once you have settled in," Charlotte said.

"Thank you."

Avis followed the footman through the hall to the oversized staircase, glancing at the large portraits of Lord Kesgrave's ancestors that hung on the wall as she walked. The footman led her down a long hallway with bedrooms on each side.

Every room had a nametag, Lady Selby's room, and then Jennette's room. Thank heavens. For a moment she had been certain his room would be next to hers. The footman opened the door to her room and she stepped inside.

The bedroom teemed with yellows. The marigold bedspread on the four-poster bed matched the velvet curtains, which lined the windows. Pictures of tulips and daffodils provided a beautiful accent to the landscape painting over the bed. Avis knew with one glance at the picture that Jennette had painted it.

"Ma'am?" a voice called from the hallway.

"Yes?" Avis opened the door a crack and saw her maid, Bridget. "Please come in." She held the door open as the maid came in followed by a footman carrying her small trunk.

As her maid unpacked her clothes, Avis relaxed and sipped her tea. Finally, her stomach settled down. Bridget helped her change into an ivory silk dress with bluebells embroidered on the hemline and then redressed her hair. As Avis collected a few extra pins in case her hair became unruly, her maid unpacked the rest of her gowns.

"The blue gown for dinner, Bridget."

"Yes, ma'am. I will have it brushed out."

Avis left the room to find Charlotte for her tour of the house. Her fingers trailed down the polished cherry handrail as she descended and scanned the area for Banning. Uncertain how to proceed after he left in a bit of a temper the other day, she decided it might be necessary to avoid him as best she could.

As she reached the last step, Charlotte withdrew from the drawing room. "I believe Jennette is looking for you. I shall lead you to her."

As they walked along, her hostess rambled on about the estate and its history, but Avis's mind remained on Banning. At some point she would see him, and then what? The crack of a cue hitting a ball revealed their proximity to the billiard room.

"Here you are," Charlotte said. "I must go see to my other guests, but I shall have some refreshments brought in for you both."

Avis strolled into the room and stopped. Banning leaned over the table with a long cue in his hand ready to knock a ball. His buff breeches accented his muscular thighs and buttocks. A small sigh escaped her. He turned his head toward her and instantly stood upright.

"Miss Copley," he said in an unemotional tone.

"Lord Selby. I understood your sister was looking for me."

"I believe she is." He placed his hand on his hip and stared at her. "I did not think you would come all this way. With your dislike of traveling, that is."

"I promised your sister."

"Very well then." He turned back to the table to take a shot. "Since you have not mentioned it, I trust there were no complications I need to be aware of?"

Complications? Is that what a child would have been? With her courses only just finished, she did not want to think about her reaction to them again.

"Complications? Whatever are you talking about, Banning," Jennette said, entering the room like a floral scented breeze. She hugged Avis tightly. "I'm so glad you are here with us."

Jennette pulled away, glancing at the two of them. "Now what were you discussing? Complications?"

Banning chalked his cue. "I happened upon Miss Copley a few weeks ago in Hyde Park. She had fallen off her horse."

Jennette whipped her head toward Avis. "*You* were riding?"

Of all the excuses, he managed the one that his

sister would never believe. "I thought to overcome my fear of horses," Avis said with a glare to Banning.

"And did you?"

"She agreed to let me work with her while we are here." Banning gave Avis a smug grin. "In fact we shall start tomorrow at eight, Miss Copley."

Jennette laughed. "Well that should be something to watch. The way you two argue no doubt you'll scare the poor horse to death."

Avis continued to glare at Banning. "I don't believe that will be necessary, my lord. I prefer to keep my distance from horses."

"The only way to overcome a fear is to face it straight on." He gave her a knowing look. "Tomorrow morning, meet me at the stables at eight."

Banning turned to Jennette. "Are we playing?"

"It would be quite rude to Avis."

"I don't know how to play, so please go ahead," Avis replied.

"Why don't we teach you?" Jennette asked with a mischievous gleam in her blue eyes.

"Yes. A splendid idea." Banning crossed the room to the cue holder and picked up another cue. "You and Avis shall play while I tutor her."

No! The word seemed to catch in her throat. In fact, she appeared unable to utter a single word or sound. He must have taken that for concurrence because he handed her the cue with an arrogant grin.

"Jennette, you may go first," he said then turned to Avis. "Watch how my sister leans over the table and takes her aim. It's a very simple game."

She watched as Jennette hit the ball with her cue and it crashed into others, scattering them across the table. She would never be able to do that. Jennette took two more turns until she missed.

Avis leaned over the table as Jennette had, but before she could line up her shot, a muscular body pressed against her and strong hands guided her own hands. She trembled with his nearness. How was she supposed to take her turn with him so close? She glanced up and noticed Jennette pouring the tea that had arrived.

"Get away from me," she hissed.

"Take your shot," he answered in her ear then quickly kissed the nape of her neck.

The stick shot forward and nicked the ball, sending it only a few inches and nowhere near another one. Before he could move away, she elbowed him in the ribs. A small grunt from him was her only satisfaction.

"Don't worry, Avis. You shall get better. Banning is wonderful at billiards. He taught me everything I know."

He'd taught Avis a few things too. Banning's closeness was her undoing. Every chance he had, he held her arms or her hands. He would stand over her, or worse, lean over her, pressing his strong body against hers.

"Not quite like that," he said as she bent down to eye the ball on the table. He squatted next to her. "I want to make love to you right now," he whispered, "on the billiard table."

Avis jumped to her feet, heat scorching her cheeks. Banning rose with a grin that she yearned to smack off his face.

"Stop it," she said.

"Is my brother bothering you?"

How could he have affected her to the point of forgetting that Jennette remained in the room? The man was driving her mad! Avis turned to Jennette. "His advice is not always welcome."

"Banning, let her try it alone."

"As you wish," he said, dropping into the nearest chair.

Avis gulped and then stared at the balls again. She tapped her fingers on the edge of the table, frowning. Perhaps she needed some advice. She sneaked a glance at him. Based on his scowl, she'd better try it by herself. She whacked the ball, surprised to see it crash into another ball and then fall into the pocket.

"Well done, Miss Copley," Banning said.

She resisted the urge to stick her tongue out at him. "Thank you, my lord."

"Oh for pity sakes, call him Banning," Jennette said. "I hate all this formality. You've known each other for years."

Speaking his Christian name in front of others made their relationship appear far too intimate. "It is highly improper of me to call your brother anything but Selby."

Jennette waved a hand in dismissal at her.

"Who else is coming this week?" Avis asked Jennette.

"You should know just about everyone."

"I did not see your mother," Avis commented. "Is she here?"

"My mother and Trey's mother are currently in the salon planning Banning's downfall."

Avis glanced over at him. His lips turned down into a deeper scowl.

"His downfall?" Avis asked.

"My mother believes it is well past time he marries. He disappointed her greatly by not choosing a bride this Season."

"I *am* in the room, Jennette," he growled.

Jennette walked past him and flicked his head. "I believe I noticed you were here. Anyway, Lady Kesgrave, the dowager Lady Kesgrave that is, is marvelous at matchmaking."

"Well, I wouldn't trust my future to either of those ladies," Banning said.

"I am certain you will find the perfect woman when the time is right," Avis replied.

"I'm sure I have," he muttered.

Jennette turned back to him. "You have?"

He smiled at Avis and then Jennette. "Slip of the tongue. I'm sure I will."

Banning watched Jennette and Avis leave the billiard room to change before supper. He needed a little time alone to get his base urges under control after the close contact with Avis. The woman drove him insane. It took all his concentration to focus on the billiards and not her lush body. He'd meant every word when he told her that he wanted to make love to her right here. But he couldn't believe he'd said that to her while Jennette was in the room. Insanity. Surely, that had to be the cause of his actions.

Ever since he'd met Avis he'd felt insane, mad with lust and now crazy in love with her.

"So here you are," Trey said, entering the room. "How was the billiards?"

Banning shrugged. "Jennette made me Miss Copley's tutor for the game."

Trey raised a chestnut brow at him. "Indeed?"

"Yes."

"So when is the wedding?"

"What?"

Trey laughed as he pulled the billiard balls out of the pockets. "I may have left London, but I still hear the gossip. Something about you being seen at an inn with a woman of quality."

"Don't remind me." Banning rose and grabbed a cue. "And what makes you think it was her? It could have been any woman."

"Just a hunch." Trey placed the balls on the table. "Of course your defensive attitude more or less confirms it."

Damn. "The woman is driving me mad. She has no intention of marrying . . . ever."

"Ever?"

"Ever."

"Odd," Trey replied. "I don't believe I've ever met a woman who really had no desire for marriage."

"Well, she doesn't."

"Why not?"

"Damned if I know." Banning leaned over and took a shot. But he did have an idea what caused her wariness. Absolute fear. But fear of what? Him? Marriage? "She's scared of something but won't confide in me."

"Perhaps you should speak with your mother. She might have an idea as to the cause of Miss Copley's reluctance."

The idea of asking his mother anything about any woman held no appeal. She would assume he cared for Avis. Which while true, he had no intention of divulging that information to his mother or anyone else. If his mother discovered his true feelings for Avis, a wedding would be planned whether or not Avis wanted it. Then again, he might save that idea as a last resort.

"If you have done what I believe you have," Trey said, taking aim, "you really should force the issue with Miss Copley."

"And how exactly do I force the issue with her?"

Trey hit the ball with his cue, scattering the others across the table. "Compromise her publicly."

Banning laughed aloud. "I doubt even that would convince her to marry me."

Trey pointed the cue stick at him. "Then perhaps you need to make her jealous."

Make her jealous . . . he tasted the idea in his mouth for a moment. But could he do that? "You make a good point, Trey."

"It does happen on occasion," he replied with a laugh.

Banning left the room to change into his formal evening attire. As he walked down the hallway, he noticed her room nearly across from his. How convenient. He wondered if she'd taken notice of his bedroom.

For once, Trey might have the right idea. If Banning gave his attentions to another, it could serve to make her jealous. He definitely would not compromise her. Perhaps by making her jealous she would acknowledge her feelings for him and confide in him the true reasons for her fear of marriage.

* * *

"And then Mrs. Dilworth said . . ."

Banning stopped listening. Miss Roebuck's conversation had run the gamut from tiresome to exceedingly dull.

"Lord Selby, did you hear me?" she asked in her high-pitched voice.

No, and he didn't want to either. "I apologize, my mind wandered." His mind hadn't wandered; it had been on Avis as she sat at the opposite end of the table entertaining the people around her. Her brown eyes positively sparkled as she discussed politics with Lord Fallston.

"I asked if you would join me in a game of piquet later."

"I must decline, Miss Roebuck. I am already promised in a game of whist." Or least he would be once he found his partners. Olivia Roebuck might be perfect for making Avis jealous, but she was driving him insane with her mindless chatter.

Her full lower lip stuck out farther than normal. "Oh. Perhaps another time then."

"My apologies to all for being so late!"

All heads turned to see Emory Billingsworth sketch an exaggerated bow to all the diners. Banning whipped his head toward Trey. His friend only shrugged as if he didn't know why Billingsworth was in his dining room.

"Mr. Billingsworth," Trey's mother rose and greeted him. "How lovely that you decided to join us in the country."

"I could not disregard your invitation, Lady Kesgrave." Billingsworth kissed the dowager Lady Kesgrave's hand. "I heard this was *the* country party to attend this summer."

"I certainly hope so," she replied.

A footman readied a place setting for him at the table. Banning's temper flared as Avis immediately turned her attention to Billingsworth. Damn her. She appeared genuinely pleased at his arrival.

He was unable to do anything but watch their every moment. Billingsworth had never done anything to make Avis suspicious of him but now with creditors skulking ever closer, he might try to do something unforeseen. A marriage to Avis would solve all of Billingsworth's money issues. Banning had no choice but to watch her and make certain Billingsworth did not force his advances on her. But would he be able to remain detached around her?

Could he pretend to pay her no heed while bestowing attentions on another?

Chapter Eighteen

Avis knew she shouldn't care. Banning could do whatever he wanted. He could marry Miss Roebuck for all she cared. Avis pressed her lips together and clenched the napkin on her lap.

Her separation from him at the dinner table hadn't bothered her until he smiled at Miss Roebuck as if she were a princess. Perhaps he would even stop pursuing her in favor of Miss Roebuck. Not that Avis didn't deserve his desertion, she did. But the idea of him with that little tart made her heart ache.

"Miss Copley," Emory said. "You look truly lovely tonight."

At least he had noticed her icy blue gown with the beautiful décolleté neckline. Banning had barely spared her a glance. Then again, with Miss Roebuck's generous bosom all but overflowing her ivory gown, it was no wonder he hadn't noticed her.

"Thank you, Mr. Billingsworth. Tell us more about your trip to Brighton."

"Unfortunately, the duke's death cut my time with the prince short as Prinny felt the need to pay his respects." He sounded more irritated than distressed by the passing of a well-respected duke. "But Prinny was a gracious host. I believe I may have a few new patrons for my books."

"Lovely," she said, glancing up the table at Banning. He met her gaze with a questioning look.

Emory leaned closer to her and whispered, "Shall we take a turn on the terrace after dinner?"

He had never asked such an improper question. And yet, if Banning had asked her to walk on the terrace she would never have been able to refuse.

"There is gaming set up after you men have your brandies."

His thin lips turned up into a smirk. "I shall take your answer to mean, not tonight, but perhaps during the ball."

She momentarily thought about enticing Emory to make Banning jealous, but she truly didn't have the heart for it. Besides, something about Emory's request didn't feel quite right. Ever since she'd returned from Southwold, she sensed something different about Emory. A difference she wasn't fond of in the least.

"If you must," she replied.

"Oh, I really must," he said with a quick glance at her breasts.

Emory must have had too much to drink tonight based on the looks he was sending her. She swore she'd felt his leg brush up against her several times during the meal. Thankfully, dinner was over and she left with the other ladies, retiring to the drawing room for tea and conversation. As she approached the room, Miss Roebuck stopped her.

"Miss Copley, I am so happy to see you here."

"Oh?"

"Well, yes. You lend an air of respectability and moral conscience to the party."

She did? What was the little tart after? "Why thank you, Miss Roebuck."

Miss Roebuck continued into the drawing room as Jennette sauntered up to Avis. "What did she want?"

"I have no idea. She seems to think I lend a moral conscience to the party."

Jennette hid her laugh behind her fan. "Of course. The spinster who wanted to give herself to a man without marriage is the moral conscience of the party."

Avis tapped Jennette with her own fan. "Do be quiet."

"Bask in your glory, Avis," Jennette said with a snicker.

They sat together on the settee as the others drank tea and talked about their husbands, or hoped-for husbands. Jennette and Avis remained quiet during that particular discussion. All the women glanced toward the door as the gentlemen filed in.

Games of whist and chess were set up around the room. Avis took a turn around the room but no game could keep her interest tonight. Instead, she walked toward the terrace door and looked out into the black night.

"Did you enjoy your dinner?"

She saw Banning's reflection in the window as he stood next to her. "Very much. I assume Miss Roebuck must be a wonderful conversationalist based on the looks you were giving her."

"Jealous, Avis?"

"Hardly," she said as her temper flared. "Just mortified that you would look at a woman in such a lecherous manner in front of a roomful of people."

"And yet, I've looked at you in much the same manner any number of times."

"Never in front of so many people."

"That you noticed anyway."

"You are truly a beast to talk to me in such a manner, Selby."

"Perhaps, but at least I have the sense to stay away from someone I've been warned about," he whispered harshly.

"Emory is my friend," she countered.

"He is a bastard who hits innocent women."

Before she could whisper a retort, Jennette approached them with a frown. "What is wrong with you two?"

"Nothing," Banning said. "Goodnight."

Avis watched as he strode from the room, praying no one else took note of the anger in his eyes.

"Is everything all right?" Jennette whispered.

"Of course," she replied in a light tone that betrayed her true feelings. "Just another quarrel with your brother."

"Of course," Jennette replied.

"I believe I shall retire, too." She walked out of the room and down the hall. As she passed the study, she heard a man's voice call out her name. She shouldn't stop. He was part of the reason she was in the mess she was.

"Please talk with me for a few moments."

She hesitated, remembering his conduct of late. If she walked into the room and someone came upon them, she would be ruined.

"Please," he said softly. "It shall only be a moment. No one will see us."

"Very well." Avis walked into the study and found

Emory sitting in a chair by the fireplace. His elbows were on his knees and his hands propping up his head. "Are you well, Emory?"

"I don't know." Slowly he looked up at her. "I fear I am losing my friendship with you."

She sat down across from him. "Why?"

"Ever since I told you what really happened at Eton, I've had an odd feeling that you didn't believe me."

"Absolutely not." She reached over and grasped his hands. "Emory, I did—do believe you."

"But someone put doubts about me in your head."

"No," she replied. "Selby doesn't know what he is talking about. I've known you for years and I do believe you."

"Selby," he muttered contemptuously.

Her anger at Banning continued to grow. The nerve of that man trying to make her doubt a good friend. If he hadn't already retired, she would give him a piece of her mind.

"Emory, please believe me."

He appeared to weigh the sincerity of her words, and then he smiled up at her and squeezed her hand. He brought her hand up to his lips quickly. "I do, Avis. I do."

"I must leave before someone finds me in here with you."

"Of course." He stood as she rose. "Goonight, Avis."

"Goodnight, Emory."

Banning stared at the closed door of his bedroom as he paced the carpet. Every time he saw her with that bastard, his blood started to boil. Not even five minutes after he left her in the gameroom, he heard them talking alone in the study. Five bloody minutes!

He stopped and listened as footsteps sounded outside his room. As he opened his door, he watched her door close behind her. Before she had a chance to lock the door or ring for her maid, he stormed into her room.

She gasped and turned around to face him. "What are you doing in here?"

"You just can't take a warning, can you?" He stalked her.

"If you mean about Emory, then you are right." She stood her ground, glaring at him with her brown eyes.

"You would rather take a chance on him abusing you in the heat of anger than—"

"That is the difference between you and him," she interrupted, pointing a finger at him. "You are the one in a temper when we talk, not him."

"And yet you trust me not to hit you in anger, don't you?"

She looked away from him. "I do," she whispered.

Banning walked over to her. "Then why don't you believe me about Billingsworth?"

"Because he has never done a thing to make me believe he would hurt me," she said tightly.

"Not yet," he added. Banning turned away from her in frustration. She would never believe him. "All I ever wanted to do was protect you."

Avis laughed coarsely. "No, Banning. All you ever wanted was for me to obey your every command like a little lap dog."

He turned back and stared at her until she glanced away. Silence filled the room as a minute passed. "Do you really believe that?"

"Yes," she whispered.

His heart sank. "Bloody hell, Avis. Nothing I say or do will ever change your mind about me or marriage or even that damned bastard, Billingsworth." He walked to the door. "I'm done. I rescind my offer of marriage."

"What?" she asked as he reached for the doorknob.

He looked back at her pale face. "You have your wish. I will stay out of your life."

"You don't want to marry me?" She blinked several times as if trying to keep the tears at bay.

"No," he lied. Silently he prayed she would stop him. But she didn't. With no other choice, he opened the door and departed the room. He strode across the hallway still hoping she would come to her senses.

Banning had never felt so out of control in his life. Once he'd taken her to his bed, she was supposed to realize her folly and understand that wedding him was the answer. Only Avis never did the expected.

He sat in the chair by the window looking up at the inky night. Stars twinkled like diamonds on black velvet. Could she have feelings for Billingsworth? She defended him tirelessly. The only conceivable answer was she did have feelings for the bastard. Feelings stronger for Billingsworth than they ever would be for him.

His entire life he'd always known the right thing to do and went after whatever he wanted with a passion. He knew the right thing to do was to marry

Avis. Not just the right thing, but marrying her was what he wanted above all. He just hadn't a thought of how to accomplish it.

He had rescinded his offer of marriage. Avis sank into a chair by the window and stared outside. In the distance, a wood owl hooted its sad song. The sound only made her feel even more desolate. She wrapped her arms around herself.

He did not want to marry her.

Her heart cried out that this was her fault. She had pushed him away. Her fears had forced her to make a decision. Now she wondered if she'd made the correct choice. All her life she'd been so afraid of being like her father that she'd hidden away her passions under a cloak of conservative behavior. But Banning unlocked the door to her desires.

She didn't want to be the prim old spinster any more.

She wanted to be the passionate woman who had loved Banning until he couldn't move in the morning. And the only man she wanted in her life was him, which meant she had to confront her fears . . . *all* of them. She could do this. After spending almost a fortnight with him she'd only hit him once.

Recognizing how weak that argument was, Avis sank her head into her hands. She *had* hit him and whether it was once or a hundred times made no difference. He would want children, and as an earl, would need an heir.

As the pink rays of dawn lifted from the horizon, she still sat in her chair wondering what to do. Her heart refused to let her give up on him. She needed

Banning. And something told her he needed her too. So she would do her best to confront her fears and even tell him what scared her about marriage. Perhaps if he knew he could help her conquer them.

She looked over at the small clock on her night-stand. She only had an hour until she was supposed to meet him in the stables for her first chance at overcoming her fears. Somehow riding a horse seemed far less frightening than confronting the demons inside her.

Avis went to her dressing room, looked at her clothes and laughed. She didn't even own a riding habit. Now what? Jennette was several inches taller and much thinner so her habit would never fit her. But she might just have an idea. Avis raced back to her room and pounded on the wall that adjoined the two rooms.

"What?"

"Come over here," Avis said to the wall.

She heard grumbling from the room next door but Jennette opened the door and entered. She wore her wrapper and her wild, raven hair had come out of its queue during the night.

"Why am I in here when the sun has barely risen?"

"The sun rose hours ago, Jennette. I need your help." Avis quickly explained her problem.

"You mean you intend to let Banning help you ride?"

"Yes."

Jennette frowned in thought. "Charlotte is nearer to your size, though a bit thinner. Anything she has might be a tad tight, but I know she would let you wear it. She certainly can't at this point in her pregnancy. I shall return in a moment."

As Avis waited, she heard the door to Banning's room open and shut, and then his heavy footsteps stopped in front of her door. She held her breath to hear if he would knock or just come in. He did neither. His footsteps receded down the hallway.

A few moments later Jennette flung the door open. She had taken the time to change into her jonquil gown and had tidied her hair. "I have a lovely riding habit for you."

She held a forest green habit over her arm. "You look so good in dark green. Charlotte said this one was always a little big on her so it should fit you better."

Avis took the habit to her dressing room and with trembling hands changed into it. The bodice clung tightly across her breasts while the rest fit her just fine.

"Well?" Jennette inquired from the bedroom.

"It will have to do," she answered, walking toward her friend.

Jennette twisted her lips. "If you were trying to entice my brother that habit might just do it. I'm surprised you managed to get the buttons to hold across your—"

"Oh do be quiet, Jennette. I want to learn how to ride again. Now help me with my hair."

"Why didn't you call Bridget?"

"I have no idea. Just help me."

Jennette pulled Avis's hair up into an artful chignon then placed a hat with a feather on top of her head. "Perfect. Now get down to those stables."

She could do this. Her stomach rumbled but she ignored the sound. It was nearly eight. She had to be on time. As she reached the stables, she slowed her pace to catch her breath. Glancing toward the open pasture, she noticed a figure galloping off. Her heart sank into her stomach.

He hadn't waited for her.

First, he recanted his proposal, and now he could not even teach her how to ride. Her shoulders slumped as she wiped away a tear. Perhaps she had truly waited too long. He had offered her marriage and even after she'd rejected his proposals, he still had called on her. He'd been a true gentleman, and she had ruined everything.

She had no idea how long she stood there, staring out into the open field, before she realized that Jennette had joined her.

"Are you all right?" she asked gently.

"I have been stood up."

"And normally if my brother had done such a thing you would be ranting and raving about what a cad he is. Yet, you're just staring out at the pasture with a far away look in your eye."

Avis blinked. "Well, I didn't think I needed to remind you about the callous behavior of your brother."

"If you say so." Jennette wrapped her arm around Avis's shoulder. "You haven't set your cap on Banning, have you?"

She pulled away with a jerk. "Jennette! Your brother is a cad. I cannot believe you think I have fallen in love with him."

"I never said that," Jennette said with a slight grin.

"Well, I haven't."

"Of course not. The fact that he was fawning all

over you when we played billiards and you barely
voiced any complaints caught my attention."

Avis stopped her gait. "I don't know why we're arguing like this. I do not have feelings for Banning."

Jennette didn't look convinced but asked, "Forgive me anyway?"

"Of course."

"Come inside and eat some breakfast. It will
make you feel better," Jennette urged with an encouraging smile.

Avis nodded. They walked back inside where delicious aromas wafted from the breakfast room.
Eating wouldn't make her feel better but it would
quiet the noise from her belly; she doubted food
would ease her heartache.

Banning walked his horse into the stables and
handed the reins to a stableboy. "Take good care of
him, John," he said, ruffling the boy's hair. He walked
back to the house with a slower than normal stride.
He'd hoped the ride would have eased his frustra-
tions, but it hadn't.

As he walked inside he decided to see if the breakfast room was empty so he might not need to
change before eating. He peered around the corner
and saw Avis in a green riding habit, and his sister in
her morning gown.

"Don't you dare try to hide around the corner,
Ban," Jennette said, pointing a knife at him.

Damn, they noticed him. "I wouldn't wish to
offend you ladies. I haven't changed yet."

"Nonsense. Neither one of us will be offended."

"I need to speak with Charlotte about the plans

for later," Avis said and quickly left the room before Banning could even sit down.

"What is going on between you two?" Jennette demanded.

"Nothing," he said. "Absolutely nothing."

"You were sniping at each other in front of a room full of people last night."

"It was just a little disagreement, Jennette. Nothing more."

Jennette twisted her lips. "I know how the ladies get around you, Ban. They fall over you as if you were a Greek god. You had better not be playing games with Avis."

"Those ladies want my title and my fortune. Would Miss Copley want either of those from *me?*"

"I suppose not," Jennette mumbled. "Still, there had better not be anything going on between you two."

"Yes, *Mother.*"

"Oh be quiet, Ban. She is my best friend and I'm worried about her. She hasn't quite been herself for the last month or so."

"Why not?"

Jennette went silent for a moment. "I am not entirely certain. Ever since her birthday, she's been acting oddly. Yet, she won't confide in me or any of her friends."

Now might just be the time to glean a little information from his baby sister. He pulled the chair out and sat down. A footman instantly filled his teacup and then carried a plate overloaded with food for him.

"So why is she so intent on remaining a spinster?"

Jennette shrugged and sipped her tea. "Why are you so interested?"

Patience. Patience. "You always wanted me to take an interest in your friends. Now that I am, you question my motives."

"Touché." She studied him for a moment, ate a bite of eggs and finally said, "Her father beat her mother."

Banning clutched his knife. "And Avis?"

"Mostly her mother," she lowered her voice to a whisper. "But he had no issue with hitting his daughter either. Haven't you ever noticed the scar on her arm?"

"Yes, I just assumed she'd fallen as a child . . . oh, damn." His stomach roiled with the thought of what she must have gone through as a young girl.

Jennette leaned in closer and whispered, "She wanted to sit on his lap and give him a hug. But he was too busy for her. He thrust her away and she fell, hitting her arm on the raised hearth."

Banning fisted his hands. "Was there more?"

"Most likely, but that's the only time he left a physical scar on her. I know her mother suffered at least a broken arm at one time."

"How did her mother die?" He hated asking the question but something prodded him to do it.

"She fell down the stairs." Jennette stared at him. "At least that is what he made certain the servants said."

At least he now understood her reluctance toward marriage. How could he blame her? How could he trust him if she couldn't even trust her own father? She had never had a good man as an example in her life.

Not that he was such a remarkable example for her. He tried to blackmail her into their affair when she wanted to back out. He manipulated her into telling him she loved him. He even tried to make her jealous. God, he *was* a cad.

Was it any wonder she trusted Billingsworth over him? Banning knew Billingsworth had never done anything untoward to her except take money she willingly gave him.

"I need to change," he said as he rose from his chair. "What activities are planned for today?"

"An outdoor luncheon and several games for the children and the adults. More people should arrive during the day and into tomorrow. There is also the hunt on Thursday morning and the ball that night."

"Very well. I shall see you later." Banning left the room and decided to change, then search out Trey.

He found his friend relaxing outside as Charlotte directed the servants preparing for the luncheon. Trey nodded his head toward his wife. "She is amazing, isn't she?"

"Yes, I believe she is. Then again, she'd have to be in order to be married to you."

Trey chuckled. "Very true indeed. Have you succeeded in making Miss Copley jealous?"

"Not quite. What do you know of her family?"

"Miss Copley's?"

"Of course." Banning shook his head. Trey might possibly be the most exasperating friend he had.

"Not much. The late Lord Watton did not inherit much from his wastrel of a father. He made a fortune from his investments."

Not the information Banning was looking for today. "What about his family life?"

Trey shrugged. "Sorry. My mother or even yours could shed more light on that subject. I only met the man once that I remember."

On to the more pressing business. "Why is Billingsworth here?"

"My mother thought he would be an interesting conversationalist."

Damn interfering ladies. "He can only talk about himself and his damned books."

"Very true. But it is enjoyable to watch your reaction to his presence, especially when he speaks with Miss Copley."

"Watch yourself, Trey," Banning warned.

"Selby, how are you today?" Charlotte asked, walking toward him.

He took her hand and kissed it lightly. "You look beautiful today, Charlotte. I think pregnancy suits you."

"Why thank you, Selby," Charlotte replied. "Perhaps someday you will be anxiously awaiting the birth of your first child." She pointed to a nearby garden bench. "Oh look, there is your mother and Lady Kesgrave. Perhaps they are plotting your future marriage. Shall we go and find out?"

"No."

"Lady Kesgrave is quite the matchmaker."

"Not for me."

"Augusta, have you shown this to Charlotte yet?" Lady Caroline Selby asked in a hushed tone.

"Just before you sat down with me," the dowager Countess of Kesgrave replied. "My daughter-in-law is quite intelligent and sees the wisdom in Sophie's note."

Caroline stared at Sophie's letter and smiled fully. Her heart brimmed with happiness at the idea of this match. Sophie's visions were becoming quite the thing in town and while Caroline had never contemplated speaking to her about her children, this note was everything she could have ever asked for and more. Sophie requested Banning and Avis be paired for every possible function—dinner, dances, anything.

"Miss Copley is perfect for your son, Caroline." Augusta leaned back and smiled.

She looked over at her dearest friend. "I couldn't ask for a better woman for Banning than Avis."

"She couldn't possibly know you wanted that match. Perhaps Sophie is a much better match-maker than either one of us," August said with a laugh.

"Perhaps she is."

Chapter Nineteen

"Avis?"

Avis turned at the sound of Emory's voice. The hallway appeared deserted except for the two of them so she used his given name in reply. "Yes, Emory?"

"May I escort you out to the luncheon?"

"That would be lovely."

He held out his left arm until she felt forced to twine her arm with his. Her skin suddenly felt as if a hundred bugs were crawling on her. For no reason, all of Banning's warnings replayed in her mind.

"With the dreadful weather this summer, Lady Kesgrave couldn't have picked a nicer day for an out of doors luncheon."

"I believe you are right."

"How is your story coming along?"

"Very well. I have made a few more changes. I am quite pleased with the way the story has developed."

He slowed their pace and turned her toward him. "I would very much enjoy another reading."

"Another reading?" He'd read this story twice already.

He smiled until his white teeth gleamed. He tugged her closer to him. "A private reading, just you and I."

"Highly improper, Emory," she said with a tap of her fan on his arm and a smile.

"You're six and twenty now, Avis. Surely you must be curious about the physical side of love."

"The physical side of love?" she squeaked.

He stepped closer until there wasn't a breath of air between them. "I can satisfy all your desires, Avis. No matter how lurid."

The sound of footsteps down the hall broke them apart. Emory winked at her before continuing out the door.

Avis remained rooted to the spot unable to believe the conversation she'd just had with him. She glanced down the hall and noticed the shadow of a man about to turn the corner. Knowing she couldn't face anyone at this moment, she walked unsteadily into the billiard room.

"Avis?"

She closed her eyes praying the owner of that deep voice would just turn around and leave. As his hands curled around her shoulders, she knew he wouldn't leave her . . . ever.

"Why are you trembling?"

"That's what you do to me," she whispered.

Banning chuckled softly against her ear. "Perhaps, but I think there is more to your nervousness than my presence. Did something happen?"

"Nothing important."

"Indeed?"

"Yes," Avis said softly as she savored the heat from his body. Just his presence made her feel safe and secure.

"Well, I suppose when you're ready to tell me the truth, you will."

She wanted to tell him but the words wouldn't form. She knew what his reaction would be to Emory's explicit suggestion. "You really should leave, Banning. Someone might see us like this and . . ."

"Of course," he replied in a sarcastic tone. "God knows we wouldn't wish to put your reputation at risk. There's no telling what you might have to do to repair it."

Cool air rushed over her arms with his departure. She sighed. He was always there for her. When she needed his support or comfort, he was near. And she had pushed him away . . . again.

She couldn't pretend any longer. She needed him.

But now, she had to get back to the party before people noticed her absence. Proceeding outside, Avis glanced around and noticed many more people than had been at dinner last night. Two large tables were set with linens and china under large white tents. Small vases of fresh flowers accented the middle of the tables. She walked past the table and noted her place card and Banning's on her right.

"Avis," Charlotte called to her. "Come and meet some of Trey's family."

Avis walked over to the group of people and Charlotte quickly introduced her to Lord Kesgrave's cousins. A woman about her age stared at her for a moment.

"Miss Copley, I believe we came out the same year." She shifted the infant to her left arm. "I was Mary Clarke then. I'm Mrs. Martin now."

Avis smiled, trying to remember the woman. "Of course. We ran with a different set though."

Mary lifted her brows. "I should say so. You and your friends were only attending the Season because your parents forced you. While my friends and I were doing everything we could to catch a husband."

"And it looks as though you did."

"Yes," Mary said with a contented sigh. The infant in her arms stretched. "This is Ethan Michael."

A small girl with blond ringlets pulled on Mary's skirts. "Mama!"

"And this would be Sarah, my oldest."

"Mama!" the little girl cried out again. "I have to tell you something."

"Well?"

"Not in front of her," Sarah said, pointing at Avis. "It's . . . it's . . ."

"Private?" Avis asked.

Sarah nodded her head vigorously. "Yes."

"Avis, would you mind holding Ethan while I talk to my daughter in private?" Mary asked with a grin.

Before Avis could deny her request, Mary held the baby out for her. "But I really don't know anything about infants."

"He's fast asleep. Just hold him."

Mary bent down so Sarah could speak in her ear. All the while, Avis stared at the little bundle in her arms. The breeze lifted the sweet smell of powder and the sour stench of milk toward her. And yet, the scents only made her smile. She had never held an infant so small and the warmth of emotions that washed over her was a complete surprise. He smiled in his sleep and her heart felt tugged by the action.

His fingers clenched into fists as he reached for his mouth. She smiled when his fingers finally found their destination. Holding an infant was far more precious than she had ever imagined.

"I can take him now," Mary said, straightening back up again. "I must go and take him inside for his nap."

Reluctantly, Avis returned Ethan to his mother. She blinked away the tears that formed as she thought about children. She would never know how it felt to have a baby stare up at her with nothing but love in his eyes.

She glanced around until she found Banning. He didn't seem to notice her as he was engaged in conversation with Miss Roebuck. Surely someone had stabbed her heart for it to hurt this much. Never in her twenty-six years had she regretted her decision to remain a spinster . . . until the past month.

All she had to do was forget her concerns and say yes to him. It seemed so simple . . . and yet, she'd never faced such a daunting demon.

Other people married and seemed happy. Charlotte, Mary . . . well, two people married and appeared happy. Perhaps they really just kept up appearances. She suddenly felt compelled to know the truth.

Avis found Charlotte resting in a chair on the terrace. She rubbed her belly as she sipped her lemonade.

"Avis, are you enjoying the luncheon?"

"Very much. You have a lovely home."

"I am happy you decided to come all this way.

Jennette told me about your illness when riding in coaches." She pointed to the chair next to her. "Please sit with me for a few minutes. Trey insisted I rest for awhile."

Avis sat down and pulled out her fan. "It must be wonderful to have a husband who cares so much for your well-being."

"He certainly cares more for me than my first husband."

"You were married before?"

"Unfortunately, I was. It was not a love match," Charlotte answered with a shudder. She closed her eyes and sighed. "But that part of my life is over and now I have the man I love."

"You seem very happy," Avis commented.

Charlotte laughed softly. "How could I not be happy? I have a loving husband and soon a baby that I never believed I would have."

"You want nothing else out of life?" All her friends wanted so much more and yet, no one seemed as happy as Charlotte.

She patted Avis's hand. "You and Jennette have such great passions for life. I am a simpler person. I have my husband, my friends, and horses to ride when I'm not with child. My husband values my opinions on the estate so I certainly don't feel useless. I have my hobbies to keep me busy when Trey is not around. What more could I want out of life?"

Avis had no idea. Once again, her life felt empty. The only time she'd felt such happiness, Banning had been with her. And now, he had rejected her . . . and it was all her fault.

"I dare say you should go rescue Lord Selby from Miss Roebuck," Charlotte said, pointing toward the table. "He looks as if he wants to stuff his handkerchief in her mouth."

"I doubt that would keep her quiet," Avis replied with a grin.

Charlotte laughed. "You might be right. Now go, my darling husband is here to escort me to the table."

Lord Kesgrave nodded at Avis as she stood to take her leave. She sauntered over toward Banning and Miss Roebuck.

"Well, Miss Roebuck, don't you look pretty this afternoon. I believe pink must be your color."

"Thank you, Miss Copley."

"Miss Copley." Banning nodded coolly toward her. "I believe we are seated next to each other today."

Miss Roebuck's bow-shaped mouth pushed out into a pouty smile. "Why, my lord, I believe you are mistaken. I just checked the tables and you are sitting on my right."

Avis knew Banning was right and wondered if Miss Roebuck could have exchanged the cards. Avis noted the devious gleam in Miss Roebuck's eyes as she spoke. It was as if she had been formulating a plan. Avis shook her head at the absurdity of that idea. Indeed.

Banning barely made it through the luncheon without strangling the woman sitting next to him. All the while, Avis sent him curious looks from the far end of the table. Luckily, he didn't have to worry about her and Billingsworth since her seat was away from the bastard. By the end of the luncheon, Avis appeared most sullen. He hated this.

Trying to make her jealous was tearing him apart, but he needed to win her. He had to find some way of getting through to her heart.

Unfortunately, his performance gave Miss Roebuck the wrong impression. As he rose from his seat, she did the same and wrapped her arm with his.

"My lord, will you escort me to the seats over by the archery competition? I would so love your company while we watch the players."

"Alas, I am one of the players so I cannot keep you company."

Thank God for Trey's idea of a competition. He had paired off couples to compete together and the winners would start off the dancing tomorrow. Banning had no idea who his partner would be, but at least he knew it would not be Miss Roebuck.

"Good luck then, my lord. I fear my archery skills are so poor I didn't dare risk anyone's life."

"I must find my partner," he politely bowed over her hand and then left to find the list posted on a tree. As he approached the willow, he saw Avis scanning the list of names.

"Oh, dear," she muttered.

"Is there a problem?"

She turned to face him, a grimace planted firmly on her face. "I daresay there is. I'm partnered with you."

He wondered if this was Charlotte's idea since Trey believed Banning should be making Avis jealous. He wasn't about to complain though because it kept him away from Miss Roebuck's clutches, and Avis away from Billingsworth.

"Well, then." He held out his arm for her. "Shall we find our bows?" A familiar sensation of warmth raced up his arm as she linked hers with him. He would have to thank Charlotte for partnering them together. They walked toward the field already set up for the match.

"Did you enjoy your luncheon with Miss Roebuck?" she asked tartly.

Perhaps jealousy might work with her. "I did indeed."

"I do hope you have some aim?" she said, reaching for a bow.

"A bit," he replied. "Though as I get older, my eyesight does decrease. Did you know Miss Roebuck is only nineteen?"

"A pity about your sight. Though you are now, what? Thirty?"

"Hmm, one and thirty."

"And you haven't started to use a quizzing glass yet?"

He smiled at her ribbing. "Not yet. And you? Please tell me that my partner will not hit another player."

She chuckled softly. "At least I can still see the target and my target isn't a child barely out of the nursery," she mumbled.

Banning almost laughed at her snide comment regarding Miss Roebuck. He wondered if he'd be able to concentrate on anything with Avis so near. Already the heady scent of her jasmine perfume surrounded him. It was taking every bit of focus he had to make certain no one else noticed his blatant attraction to her.

"I owe you an apology for missing our riding lesson this morning. Meet me at the stables in the morning so we can overcome one of your fears."

She looked up at him, confused. "*One* of my fears?"

"The least significant fear. We'll work on the others later."

"Oh?"

Banning smiled at her as he placed the arrow in the bow. Each couple had the opportunity to shoot six arrows toward a target. The two top scoring teams would then get their chance against each other. When Avis's turn approached, she sighted her target and released the arrow, narrowly missing the bulls-eye.

"Blast," she mumbled.

"Quite nice, actually." Banning sighted his target and let his arrow fly. He smiled as the arrow flew straight into the center.

"I'm much better with a rifle or a pistol," she said, readying her next shot.

Better than me, no doubt, he thought.

He pushed away the dreadful reminder of his own fear. He'd lived the past few years dreading that someone would reveal the truth about him.

Banning understood, since his conversation with his sister, that Avis's own fear was a palpable thing. He empathized with her desire for spinsterhood, even though he knew that in this, she was wrong. He'd never hurt her.

Her next arrow hit the target perfectly. "Remind me to never get you angry with me again," he said with a grin.

"I should have warned you years ago about my archery skills." She let out a giggle as her last arrow took flight. Again, she missed though this time by a larger distance. "Don't make me laugh or we shall never win."

"But then you will have to open the dancing

with me," he said close to her ear. "I hear it may be a waltz."

"A dance is a dance," she said with a smile.

"Oh no. A waltz is like a seduction. That is why it was so frowned upon." Banning didn't wait for her reply. He took aim and released his arrow straight for the target, pleased with not only the shot but with how the woman at his side now reminded him of the Avis back at the cottage. Funny, light-hearted and warm. Perhaps she was finally coming to terms with their relationship.

"I daresay with that shot I may have to dance with you."

He smiled at her. "You shall at that. Twice if I have my way. And I always get my way."

Chapter Twenty

Avis slipped into the Kesgrave study, sank into a chair by the fireplace, and sighed. Finally, she had some solitude. She hadn't wanted to go to her bedroom because her chatty maid would be waiting for her and the other rooms in the house were still active with gaming and other amusements. But she just couldn't take another moment being around people. At this point, facing her motion sickness in order to escape everyone held a certain appeal.

She glanced up at the clock—nearly midnight. The gaming would end soon and then everyone should be off to bed. Once the house quieted, she would make her way upstairs. Perhaps by then Bridget would be too tired to make conversation as she helped her undress.

She picked up a book on the table and just made out that it was a poetry volume. The light from the two candles burning on the desk didn't illuminate the room enough for her to read. She placed the book back on the table and relaxed deeper into her seat.

With nothing else to do, her mind reverted to her

conversation with Emory. It seemed odd that after three years of close friendship, he suddenly appeared to want more from her. Emory was a good friend but she felt no attraction to him in a physical manner. Perhaps before Banning she might have been able to feel some attraction for Emory. But now, she knew what desire was and she felt none toward him.

How was it that she had reached the age of twenty-six without attracting a man only to suddenly have two men after her? Very odd, indeed.

The door flew open and she covered her mouth to suppress her sound of alarm. Hopefully the darkness of the room would keep her place secret.

"What exactly am I supposed to do?" Banning asked, following behind Lord Kesgrave into the study.

"You have no choice."

"She won't agree."

Avis wondered whom this *she* was and what she wouldn't agree to.

"Compromise her," Kesgrave said. "In front of a large number of people."

"She'll hate me forever if I do that."

Kesgrave poured two brandies. "Damnation it's dark in here."

Blast! If he lit more candles, he would unknowingly reveal her hiding place. While she wasn't normally one to eavesdrop, this conversation held her interest.

"Ban, if you mean to protect her from him I don't think you have much choice."

"She may never agree to marry me anyway. I'm starting to believe she may have feelings for him."

"You went away with her for a fortnight. Surely she must have some feelings for you?"

They were talking about her! She must be more tired than she realized if she only now determined the subject of their conversation. A burst of anger flared her to action.

"I cannot believe you told him about us," Avis exclaimed, jumping out of her seat.

"Good evening, Miss Copley." Kesgrave moved back to the brandy. "Care to join us?"

She ignored her host, instead, glaring at Banning. "You've ruined me!"

"Avis, I trust Trey with my life. He would never tell a soul about us."

"That is not the point. You told him—"

"Actually, Miss Copley, I deduced what had happened between you two."

She turned back toward Kesgrave. "Why would you have deduced such a thing unless he," she pointed at Banning, "told you something?"

Kesgrave smiled warmly at her. "I helped Banning prevent you from speaking with Billingsworth the night of your cousin's ball."

"And from that you assumed we were lovers?" she asked sarcastically. "It all makes sense now."

"No," Kesgrave answered with a low chuckle. "Banning was seen leaving the Halstead Inn with a lady of quality. It seemed a simple enough deduction that you were the woman, especially after your lengthy disappearance with him at your cousin's ball."

"We were seen?" she whispered.

"Not entirely," Banning said, stepping closer to her. "No one saw your face, only mine."

"Why didn't you tell me?"

"I didn't want you to worry needlessly."

"Oh my God," she mumbled, holding her trembling hands together. "This is my punishment for rash behavior."

"No, it is not," Banning replied, caressing her cheek with his gloved hand.

"I bid you both a goodnight," Kesgrave murmured. He drained his brandy and then headed for the door. He closed the door behind him, leaving Avis and Banning alone in the study.

If Lord Kesgrave had figured out their secret, chances were good someone else might too. Then her life would be ruined. The urge to lay her cheek against Banning's chest became almost too much for her. She wanted his comfort. She desperately needed him to tell her everything would be all right. But he couldn't do that because her life was such a dreadful mess.

She couldn't stop her head from dropping to his shoulder. He encased her in his strength and comfort. Lately, Banning appeared before her every time she needed reassurance. She was coming to depend on him far too much.

"Trey won't speak of this."

"I know," she whispered.

She should leave before someone discovered them. She pushed against his chest to ward him off.

"Goodnight, Banning."

"Don't go."

She turned back to face him. His blue eyes sparkled at her in the dim candlelight. "I have to. We both know what happens when we're alone in a room such as this."

He smiled, walking closer to her. "A study?"

"Yes," she answered, taking a step away from him.

"Is there something wrong with that?" He stepped nearer to her again.

This time she could smell the rich aroma of the brandy he'd been drinking. She slowly backed up until her bottom hit the closed door. He stalked her, never taking his ardent gaze off her.

"We just cannot leave this room without a kiss," he whispered. "It's what we do."

But could he leave it at just one kiss? Could she? Memories of making love with him overwhelmed her senses, the taste of him, the spicy scent of the soap he used, the feel of his chest hairs tickling her breasts, the sound of his moans when she kissed him, and the dark look in his eyes as he watched her reach her climax. She wanted him again. Who was she fooling? She had never stopped wanting him.

And she never stopped loving him, either.

He lowered his head slowly as if waiting for her to reject him. But she felt powerless to do anything but watch his full lips come closer to hers. His lips grazed hers, a mere whisper of a touch. A tease of a kiss.

She grasped his lapels and pulled him closer, if only for a moment. Seeing the smug smile on his face just before he passionately kissed her should have cooled her desire—it didn't. She couldn't take this further than a kiss, but that didn't mean she had to be the one to break the exhilarating contact.

His lips trailed a path to her ear. After circling the outer shell, he whispered, "Come to bed with me, Avis."

Oh dear Lord, how she wanted to do that.

"I want you," he muttered. "Right now. I want to feel you naked in my arms again."

He tempted her with his words of passion. It would be so easy to give in to his allure. But it would not be smart.

"No, Banning."

He smiled against her cheek. "You want me, Avis. I feel your heart pounding against my chest. I hear your ragged breathing. Tell me you don't want me."

"I can't do that."

"Then we should go to my room."

"I can't do that either."

"Why?"

Such a simple question, but one with far too many answers. "I cannot marry you so this isn't the right thing to do. Besides, you rescinded your offer of marriage."

"I might be willing to make another offer."

"I might not be willing to accept it," she said with regret.

"I'm not like your father," he whispered in her ear.

She froze in disbelief. He did not just say those words. He couldn't have because no one knew except her best friends and they would never tell him. Except one.

"Did your sister tell you about him?"

"Yes."

She pushed him away as white-hot anger flowed through her veins. "She had no right to talk to you about my private life."

"You are getting upset over nothing." Banning attempted to pull her back into his arms, but she shrugged her shoulder out of his grasp. "Besides you should have trusted me enough to tell me about this."

"My family life is of no concern to you."

"It is when it prevents you from being happy and marrying me." He softened his voice. "You are not like your mother. And I am nothing like your father."

"You're right, I am not like my mother," she said, thrusting the door open. She glanced back at him. "But I am just like my father."

As the door slammed behind her, Banning grabbed the brandy and sank into the nearest chair. How could she believe she was anything like her father? Her father was a monster. Any man who needed to beat his wife and child to prove his manhood disgusted him.

He had no idea how to prove to her that she was wrong. She had none of her father's traits. She was a loving, passionate woman. He sipped his brandy. Somehow, she had to see how much love she had for people. Including him, he hoped.

How had he gotten himself so involved with her? He never thought he would fall in love as deeply as he had. And now that he had, he wouldn't let her walk out of his life without a fight. He wanted her as his wife, as the mother of his children, as his lover for the rest of his life.

Talking to her seemed the most sensible solution. Yet, every time he tried to speak to her lately, she pushed him away. Unable to think of anything he could do, he drank. And drank until the pink fingers of dawn slowly spread upwards from the horizon.

The alcohol infused him, turning his ineffectual musing into anger. Anger at her, fury at himself.

This should have been easy. His father had warned him of all the women who might throw themselves at him in order to become the next Countess of Selby. But not Avis. No, she had to make this harder than anything he had ever attempted. He compromised her, and she still would not concede to marriage. He had told her that he loved her and she wouldn't agree to marry him.

What else could he do?

He needed to find something to ease the anger and frustration warring in him. Looking outside, he realized exactly what he should do.

He strode to the stables, woke the stableboys, and kicked them out. Then he moved every horse into the fenced field and set to work in one of the stalls. There was nothing like a little hard labor to work off his ire. He tore off his jacket and cravat, loosened his shirt, and set forth to clean the stables. After he finished one stall, he removed his damp, linen shirt and started on the next stall.

"I do have some lads that are paid to do this."

He looked behind him to see Trey leaning against the wall with a smirk on his face. Banning frowned. "Leave me alone."

Trey's smug grin turned into a full smile. "Something tells me that my leaving you and Miss Copley in the study last night did not end the way you had hoped."

"Get out."

"And miss your misery?" he asked with a laugh.

Banning took a deep breath and attempted to ignore his most annoying friend. Unfortunately, Trey's chortles made it impossible. He turned and faced him. "What is so damn funny?"

"If I remember correctly, you took great amusement at my contorted courtship. It is a pleasure to watch you have the same issues."

"Bloody hell," he mumbled. "Some courtship. The woman wants nothing to do with marriage."

"There's always Miss Roebuck," Trey said then fled the stables before Banning could throw something at him.

He didn't want Olivia Roebuck or any other young, silly girl. He wanted the passionate woman who warmed his bed only a few weeks ago. He only wanted Avis.

Avis took a deep breath then headed for the stables. A footman had told her Banning had been down there for an hour. After spending hours contemplating the situation, she finally knew she had to tell him everything. He deserved to know why she couldn't marry him.

As she walked along the pathway, she hoped he'd decided to wait for her this time. She walked along the stone path, noticing the horses out in the fields. They really were beautiful creatures, just large— very large—and very high off the ground.

Lord Kesgrave approached her, returning from the stables. "I would think twice about going down there if I were you."

"Is something wrong?"

"Selby is in a mood."

She had never really seen Banning in a foul mood. Other than the day she refused his offer of marriage. "I see," she replied. "How bad?"

"He is mucking out the stalls," he answered as if that said it all.

"Oh."

Kesgrave held out his arm. "May I escort you back?"

Avis bit her lower lip. She had to face her fears and one of them concerned horses, and another involved the man in a black mood. "No, thank you. He promised to help me overcome my fear of horses today. And he shall keep that promise."

"As you wish, Miss Copley." Lord Kesgrave continued up the path without her.

With a breath for courage, she walked to the outbuilding. The door creaked open. She wrinkled her nose as the acrid smell of horse manure wafted past.

"I told you to get out of here, Trey."

"I am not Trey," Avis said softly.

He whipped around, his blue eyes icy with rage. Perhaps Lord Kesgrave had underestimated Banning's mood.

"What are you doing here?"

"I believe we were scheduled for a ride." She licked her lips. "If you can actually get me on a horse," she joked.

"This is not the best time." He turned his back on her, continuing to rake the hay out of a stall. The muscles of his back strained with the movements.

"Banning?"

"I want to be alone." Using a pitchfork, he tossed fresh hay down in the clean stall.

"Are you angry with me?"

Her question halted his movements. "I'm angry with you, with me, everyone."

"I'm sorry," she whispered. She approached him slowly, carefully as if she expected him to bolt. Her hands slid around his waist as he stiffened. "I never wanted to hurt you."

He remained silent. She let her head drop to

his back. Every muscle in his back tensed with the contact.

"I'm sorry."

"Enough, Avis." He twisted out of her arms and faced her.

Seeing his bare chest set her heart pounding. She wanted him. But not just for the pleasure she knew too well would happen. She wanted to comfort him. She had to let him know just how much she loved him.

"I think you should leave."

"I really don't think I should," she replied, stepping toward him.

He backed up until he reached the wall of the clean stall. His eyes darkened like the sky before an approaching storm. "Avis," he warned.

She drew her gloved fingers up his chest until she reached his neck. Twining her hands behind him, she stood on her tiptoes to kiss him. His lips, normally soft and pliant when he kissed her, remained hard, immobile. She deserved his anger.

Pulling back from him, she looked into his eyes. "Take away my fears, Banning. Please," she whispered.

Something flickered in his eyes and then his muscles slowly relaxed. "Very well. Shall we work on your fear of horses first . . . or me?"

Avis bit her lip. The more time she spent around him, the more her fear lessened.

"I've never been afraid of you," she whispered. "Only *my* anger. How much did Jennette tell you about my family?"

"Enough." His gaze fell to her scarred arm.

"Then can you understand my fear that I might be like my father? How can I marry someone when my anger might get the better of me? What if I hit a child? Our child?"

He blew out a sigh. "I understand your fear, Avis. But you have more control than you give yourself credit for."

"What if I don't have the control you think I have?"

"I would be there to help you," he whispered.

Avis let her head rest on his shoulder. "Every time I think I can do this, I remember my parents' marriage."

"And the fear returns?"

"Yes."

He kissed the top of her head gently. "Shall we try a horse, then?"

"I believe it might be easier to get me on a horse than to bring me to the altar just yet."

"I thought as much." Banning turned away and grabbed his shirt and jacket. "Come along, Avis. Your lesson is starting."

She followed him out to the yard and watched as a boy saddled a mare for her. The horse seemed larger the closer she got to it. "Banning," she whispered.

He turned and flashed her a smile. "You can do this, Avis."

She swallowed and took a step toward the mare. "What is her name?"

"Buttercup, and she is a very gentle horse." Banning grasped her hand and brought it to Buttercup's head. "She can sense your nervousness. Try to calm yourself."

"I can't."

"Yes, you can. I will be here with you the entire time." He held out his hand to her. "Are you ready?"

Avis blew out a breath to relax, as if that could possibly happen when standing between her two biggest fears—a horse and Banning. "Yes," she finally said.

He helped her up and then winked at her. "Did you fall when you were young?"

She nodded.

"How old were you?"

"S—Six," she muttered. Her hands grew damp as she clutched the bridle.

"You can do this, Avis." Banning moved toward the front of the horse.

"Where are you going?"

"I'm going to lead the horse so she doesn't startle." He grabbed the lead and slowly walked around in a circle.

The entire time Avis forced herself to keep her eyes open and breathe. The slow canter wasn't dreadful. In fact, the more Banning led her around, the more she started to enjoy the sensation of the horse under her and the view from the saddle.

"How are you doing?" Banning said, looking back at her.

"I am doing fine . . . better than that, I'm actually enjoying it."

He smiled at her. "I thought you might. Should I let go so you can lead her?"

"No!"

A chuckle was his only reply. After a few more rounds in a circle, he stopped Buttercup and turned back toward her. "Had enough for one day?"

"Yes." She smiled down at him. "But I wouldn't be averse to trying this again some time."

Avis glanced down the field and noticed the group of men with their rifles riding across the grass. She had forgotten about the hunt. After Banning helped her down, she said, "Why didn't you join the hunt today?"

He stiffened slightly and looked away from her. "I must have forgotten."

"But weren't you out here when the men left?"

"I wanted to teach you how to ride," he said quickly.

"But you love to hunt. I remember years ago at a country party at Talbot Abbey how you talked about the entire hunt from start to finish. My goodness you must have gone on about it—"

"Avis, I didn't want to hunt today. I have to go now." He stormed off, leaving her standing near Buttercup unsure what to do next.

A stableboy took the reins and led the horse away while Avis remain motionless, watching Banning stride toward the house. What was it about the hunt that angered him so? Even Jennette had remarked on how much pride Banning took in his hunting abilities, so why the change? Avis halted her steps.

We both know you'd never use a pistol.

Somerton had said those words outside the carriage at the inn. Could Banning have an aversion to pistols now? If so, what could have caused that to happen?

Slowly she walked to the house and then toward her room to spend the rest of the day mulling over her situation. Banning had helped her overcome one of her fears. But could he assist her with her biggest fear of all? She wanted that above all else. She missed him when he wasn't near. She missed his smile, his humor, and his conversations. More than anything, she missed the look of love in his eyes for her.

As she neared her room, the sound of children crying made her stop in front of the open door. Mary Martin stood in the middle of the room, a screaming infant in one arm, and a raging two-year-old pulling at her other hand. Tears fell down her cheeks.

"Do you need some assistance?" Avis asked.

"Oh please," Mary answered. "Our nursemaid fell ill. Sarah has soiled herself. Ethan is screaming for no apparent reason."

"It's all right. I will help Sarah change—"

"No!" Sarah shouted. "Don't want you. I want my mama."

"Would you mind terribly if I help Sarah?" She held out the red-faced infant to Avis.

Avis's eyes widened. "I honestly do not know much about little babies."

"Just walk him around and maybe he will calm down for you."

Avis stared at the boy and then reached for him. She could do this. How long could it take to change a small girl? Five minutes, maybe ten.

"Hold him up to your shoulder, maybe he needs to pass some gas," Mary said, showing her how to lift the baby up. "Pat him on the back."

Avis slowly patted Ethan's back and walked the room. Mary and Sarah left for the nursery. As Avis paced and patted the infant, she noticed the lovely smell of powder and soap. She couldn't help but rub her cheek against his bald head.

"Shh, Ethan," she murmured. "Mama will be back in just a moment."

He replied with a loud belch that made Avis giggle. After a few more gaseous sounds, he calmed himself. His blue eyes grew heavy with sleep.

She eased herself down into a blue chair by the window. The moment she sat, Ethan stirred. "Shh, please stay asleep," she whispered.

He stretched his chubby arms over his head and opened his eyes. He stared at her for a second before deciding she definitely wasn't his mother. As his mouth opened, Avis realized, she had no idea what to do. She stood and lifted him up to her shoulder, patting his back again as she walked the room. The motion did nothing to calm him.

"Please go back to sleep, Ethan," she mumbled in his ear. She placed her hand on his bottom to shift him and finally understood his problem. "Dear Lord, I have no idea how to change a nappie."

She glanced around and noticed a pile of clean, folded nappies on the bureau. How hard could this be? Nursemaids did this many times a day.

Too bad the nurse was sick. It should be she, not I, changing this nappie.

Gathering hold of herself, Avis grabbed a clean cloth and set Ethan on the floor. As she removed the wet nappie, she paid strict attention to how it was folded and pinned.

She lifted his legs to place the clean cloth under him and attempted to pin the nappie correctly. It took her three tries, but she finally did it.

"I did it, Ethan. I know that means nothing to you, but it does to me."

After picking him up, she held him close and inhaled that sweet, clean baby scent. He let out a few more cries before dropping his head to her shoulder and drifting off again. Avis refused to sit down, afraid he might awaken. Instead, she slowly walked and swayed across the room.

"I want this," she whispered to herself with a bit of surprise.

Chapter Twenty-One

"Miss Copley, what a beautiful gown," Olivia Roebuck gushed. "I cannot wait to be married so I may wear something other than these dreadful pastels. At least as a spinster no one notices what you wear."

Avis counted to ten in her head. "Thank you, Miss Roebuck," she bit out.

"I do so wish I could start the dancing with Lord Selby as you will." Miss Roebuck sighed.

After spending most of the afternoon with Mary and her children, Avis wanted that dance with Banning. And she wasn't about to give it up. Smiling, she said, "Well, hopefully he will ask you for a dance later."

Miss Roebuck's eyes glittered. "I am most certain he will at that."

Something about the cold tone of her voice made Avis suspicious. As the girl walked away, Avis decided to keep her eye on Miss Roebuck. Before she could follow her, Banning stepped in front of her with a glass of lemonade.

His eyes twinkled as he scanned her from head to

toe. "My goodness, Miss Copley. I might even like this gown better than the emerald one."

Her lips twitched as she took the lemonade from his outstretched hand. "I rather thought you might like this one."

He leaned in closer to her. "I would like it off of you too. More so, I believe."

"I think I have heard that before." This time her lips stretched into a full smile. She sipped her drink to cool her ardor. After speaking with Mary today about marriage and children, Avis finally had made a decision regarding marriage. And just coming to a decision made her feel so much more relaxed tonight. When the ball ended tonight, she would sneak into his room and tell him.

"I believe our dance is about ready to start." He held out his arm. "Shall we?"

They walked to the edge of the dance floor. Lord Kesgrave stood near the orchestra with his wife and announced them.

"May I present to everyone the winners of the archery competition, Lord Selby and Miss Copley."

Applause filtered throughout the room as Avis and Banning walked to the middle of the dance floor.

"Since my wife is in a delicate condition, Lord Selby and Miss Copley will start the dancing."

Banning held his hand to hers as the orchestra started a waltz.

"I am very much out of practice," she whispered to him.

"I believe you shall manage quite perfectly." They glided across the floor and people slowly joined them.

"You are truly a wonderful dancer."

"Thank you." He smiled down at her, revealing his lovely dimples. "I daresay you are doing quite well considering you haven't danced in ages."

She couldn't remember the last time she'd danced. The candles flickered, reflecting the shimmering fabrics of the dancers. Avis noted everything—the swish of the silk from the gowns as the dancers turned in rhythm, the warmth emanating from Banning, and the strong hold on her back. Somehow, she knew she would remember this dance for the rest of her life. The dance ended far too soon for Avis. He left her with Jennette, who had a very amused look upon her face.

"How was the dance," she asked with a chuckle, "with my brother?"

"Quite nice," Avis replied, not willing to give out any further information. She glanced around the room and noticed Lord Durham walking straight toward them.

"I believe this is our dance, Lady Jennette," he said with a smile.

"Yes," Jennette answered tightly. She took his arm and walked to the dance floor. Unfortunately, that left Avis alone and Miss Roebuck seemed determined to speak with her again.

"Miss Copley?"

That tinny voice sent a shudder down her back. "Yes, Miss Roebuck."

Miss Roebuck linked her arm with Avis and propelled them toward the terrace door. "Might I have a word with you?"

"Outside?"

"Yes." As they reached the doors, she continued,

"I have a small problem with which I need a woman of your stature to assist me."

"My stature?"

"Yes. Everyone knows that you are most mindful of your reputation."

"Oh?"

"Yes." Miss Roebuck patted Avis's hand. "You're a woman above reproach."

"Am I?"

"Of course. You are the perfect spinster."

"But I live alone," Avis added.

Miss Roebuck stopped and looked at her. "Exactly. Yet you still manage to keep your reputation and mores higher than most of the married women here."

"What is this about, Miss Roebuck?"

"I need to confront someone in regards to a rather delicate situation. I'd hoped you would stand up with me so I do not lose my courage."

"Of course." Oh dear, someone must have insulted the poor girl's intelligence. Though Avis wondered how the woman even noticed.

"There he is," she said, pointing toward Banning where he stood leaning against the balustrade.

"Lord Selby?"

"Yes."

This could not be good. Miss Roebuck pulled her toward him.

"Good evening, ladies," he said as they approached him. He frowned at Miss Roebuck and then gave Avis a questioning look.

"Lord Selby," Miss Roebuck answered stiffly with a nod.

Avis remained silent as apprehension filled her.

Could Miss Roebuck have seen them? Or heard them talking?

"Lord Selby, I asked Miss Copley to accompany me because I believe it is time you were brought to task for what you have done."

Avis felt the blood drain from her face. How could Miss Roebuck have seen them?

Banning stiffened. "What exactly have I done, Miss Roebuck?"

"Oh! As if you didn't know." She turned toward Avis. "Can you believe he is acting this way after he used me so?"

"Used you?" Avis asked. She doubted Banning had done anything untoward to this young lady.

"He took me to his estate in Southwold, telling me all manner of sweet tales, including how he would marry me." Miss Roebuck wiped a very forced look-ing tear from her eye.

"I what?" Banning roared.

Avis stepped between them. "Now, now, Lord Selby. I am quite certain we can determine exactly what happened." Because she would never let this little witch compromise herself with him. "Now, Miss Roebuck. Are you trying to tell me that you were the woman Lord Selby was seen with at the inn in Stowmarket?"

"Yes, I was there. Even the innkeeper saw me there."

"You were there with your parents," Banning rasped.

"No, my lord. I was there with you." Miss Roebuck took Avis's hand. "Do you see why I needed your help? He ruined me and now wants nothing to do with me. He even signed us in as Mr. and Mrs.

Talbot. I just assumed he meant to marry me. I never thought he would ruin me so."

Dear Lord, she had to do something. If Miss Roebuck spread her venom to anyone else, Mr. Roebuck would demand Banning marry the chit.

"Miss Roebuck, did you really go to Southwold with him?" A small smile tugged at Avis's lips.

"Of course."

"Oh, do tell me about the place. I have heard it is very lovely."

Banning cleared his throat. "Miss Copley, I really do not think—"

"It was a beautiful estate," Miss Roebuck interrupted.

"Large?"

"Huge! Twenty bedrooms, a lovely conservatory, gardens, and pathways. And servants, too many to even count!"

Avis smile coyly. "Twenty bedrooms? My, that is rather large."

Banning glanced over her head. "Avis, be careful," he whispered.

"And yet," Avis continued, tapping a finger on her lip, "I seem to recall there only being two bedrooms in Southwold."

"Avis, don't say—"

"And only Mr. and Mrs. Hathaway, the caretakers."

"Avis!"

"Oh my God! You went away with *my brother*!" Jennette's voice sounded from behind her.

Avis slowly turned around to see at least fifteen people standing agape behind her. Including Jennette and her mother. Heat scorched Avis's cheeks as she stared at the crowd.

"Well, that is what I was trying to explain to Miss Copley," Miss Roebuck said to Jennette. "I went away with your brother, and he needs to marry me now."

Lady Selby approached them with a satisfied look upon her face. Jennette trailed behind her. Looking at Miss Roebuck, Lady Selby said, "My dear girl, you most certainly *did not* go to Southwold with my son. Banning, Miss Copley, I believe we need to have a discussion in Lord Kesgrave's study."

"But what about me?" Miss Roebuck whined. "He ruined me!"

"He did no such thing," Lady Selby said with a wave of her hand. "If you had been to Southwold, you would know, as Miss Copley did, that it is a mere cottage. There are not twenty bedrooms and a legion of servants there."

Lady Selby cast a sideways glance at Avis. "So the real question is, exactly how did Miss Copley know?"

Miss Roebuck's eyes grew large.

Avis attempted to gain control over her erratic breathing, but nothing could stop the short shallow breaths. "Jennette told me all about it?"

Jennette glared at her. "My brother," she sputtered again. "You went away with my brother. I can't believe you would do such a thing. You two hate each other."

"To the study, all of you," Lady Selby commanded.

Banning gripped her arm and led her past the whispering crowd. "I tried to warn you," he murmured in her ear.

He had tried to warn her? Of course he did. But she hadn't taken heed and now had completely ruined herself. What should she do? She smiled knowing exactly what she needed to do in this situation.

They continued down the hallway. The crowd had thinned to only Lady Selby, Jennette, Lord Kesgrave, Banning, and Avis.

"Before we talk all together, I would like a word in private with Miss Copley," Banning announced.

Lady Selby turned and flashed a glare at him. "Five minutes."

"Very well."

His hand burned through the back of her dress as he propelled her into the room alone. Shutting the door behind them, he turned and said, "What do you want to do?"

Banning paced the room, waiting for an answer, hoping it would be what he desired. Avis sank into a chair and covered her pale face with her hands. Her shoulders shook. Damn. He never wanted to force her into marriage. Some persuasive coercion perhaps, but never force.

"Avis," he murmured, dropping to his knees before her. "Whatever you want to do is all right with me. If you want to ride out the scandal, we shall. If you want to marry, we shall do that. Just please stop crying," he said, tugging her hands away from her face.

Only she wasn't crying, not even a tear. Her shoulders shook as she attempted to keep her laughter inside. The woman must be having a hysterical fit. He had driven her over the edge of sanity.

"Avis?"

"I am such a wicked woman, Banning." She gave him the barest hint of a smile. "I just compromised myself in front of close to twenty people. And I enjoyed it."

"I do so love a wicked woman," he said, squeezing her hands with his.

"The look on Miss Roebuck's face was worth any scandal I shall have to endure."

He almost smiled at her . . . almost. Until the true meaning of her words hit him. After all that they had been through, could she possibly mean to choose a scandal over marrying him? His heart stopped for what seemed like minutes. He'd been certain she would accept marriage now.

"Oh Banning, this is not how I wanted to tell you."

"I understand," he said with sigh. This insane courtship was utterly over.

"I wanted to tell you tonight, after the ball," Avis continued.

"Well, it doesn't matter now. You've made your decision."

The door swung open and his mother and sister entered. "Your five minutes are now finished," his mother announced. "Get up off the floor, Banning. Your proposal is not needed."

He dusted his knees off before rising to his full height. He turned toward the unyielding face of his mother. Her blue eyes glinted with some undistinguishable emotion.

"What do you mean my proposal is not needed?"

"You and Miss Copley will be married as soon as we return to London. Unless you both prefer to go directly to Surrey and be married at the estate."

"Mother, Avis has decided—"

"Avis has no family except for young Watton," she said with disdain. His mother looked down at Avis and frowned. "Your mother was a dear friend of mine. Very dear. If she were alive today she would be mortified by your actions."

"With my brother," Jennette mumbled from her spot near the window.

"Shh," Mother reprimanded Jennette. Turning back to Avis she continued, "Since your mother is not with us, it is my duty to make certain you behave according to the mores of Society. You ran off with my son. Now you shall pay the price for your impulsiveness."

"Mother, that is enough," Banning stated. "You have no right to interfere in her life, or mine."

"I am only doing what is best for you both." She dropped to the settee with a sigh. "You are officially ruined, Avis." She looked up at Banning. "And I expected better of you."

Avis cleared her throat. "Your son has been a perfect gentleman. For the past few weeks, he has done nothing but ask me to marry him. *I* have dismissed his proposals."

His mother arched a surprised brow at him and nodded. She pinched the bridge of her nose as if attempting to prevent a headache. She speared Avis with a sharp look and sized her up thoroughly, "I understand completely. Banning, please accept my apologies." She waved her hand around the room. "Everyone leave the room but Avis."

"Mother—"

"Out, Banning," she said, pointing toward the door. "You may go tell everyone that your future wife will join you after a conversation with her soon to be mother-in-law."

He glanced over at Avis. She nodded in agreement but said nothing to him. He hated the idea of leaving her alone with his mother. She had a way of getting exactly what she wanted, and she wanted him married and a grandchild on the way.

Avis watched as everyone left the room, including a very piqued looking Jennette. A talk with Jennette would have to wait until after this conversation. The room filled with silence as Banning closed the door behind him. A clock ticked away the minutes.

She glanced over at Lady Selby who stared at her silver gown as if she could find the answer to some problem in the folds of her dress. Her manner reminded Avis of both Jennette and Banning. While her hair had turned mostly to silver, a few black strands threaded through the silver. Finally, Lady Selby looked up at her with her striking blue eyes.

"I believe I understand your reluctance toward marriage, Avis. After all, I was a *very* close friend of your mother."

Point taken. "Lady Selby, I *was* reluctant to marry your son."

"Was?"

Avis smiled. "Yes, was." She glanced down at her skirts, straightened them and continued, "I've had the chance to do some much needed thinking on the subject. I . . . I had my doubts, and I rejected Banning's offers at every turn. But he was so persistent and . . . I believe marriage to Banning shall suit me."

"Yes, I think it will." Lady Selby smiled fully. "Banning must love you deeply."

"Really?"

"Why else would my son have gone away with a woman of your station? He knew the risks, and my son is many things, but he is no fool."

Avis bit down on her lip. It was an interesting thought that he had planned to marry her even before they had left. He had disavowed planning to marry her when he made his first offer. At least that was what he told her on the beach the morning of his clumsy proposal.

Besides, they had barely known each other before they had gone away . . . or had they? There wasn't much she hadn't known about Banning. And very likely, he knew as much about her.

Lady Selby read the play of emotions on Avis's face and said, "Decisions that last a lifetime are never easy, Avis. But I am happy to see you have made the right choice. My son would never lay a hand on a woman in anger."

"I know that," Avis replied. And she did. "But what if I am like my father, Lady Selby?"

"You are the perfect combination of both your parents. You have your mother's big heart, but your father's determination. If a man hit you in anger, no matter how much you loved him, *you* would find a way to leave him."

"And if I hit a man, or worse, my own child?" After spending most of the afternoon with Mary and her children, Avis doubted she ever would. Still, Lady Selby had a right to know the woman she might get as a daughter-in-law.

"Even the most unflappable mother will get frustrated with her own children. They instinctively know how to get you angry. And sometimes, you have to walk away. Let the nursemaid handle the situation."

"Thank you, Lady Selby." Looking at the silver-haired woman, Avis knew Lady Selby understood her fears. And as long as she had the chance, she would ask the provocative question. "Why do you think my mother stayed with my father?"

Lady Selby gave her an understanding smile. "You may not remember, but I tried to help your mother many times when you were young."

"You did?"

"I wanted to help you and your mother escape from your father. I offered her money. She could have left him and gone to America or stayed in a small town in England. But she loved your father, too much. She thought she could change him."

Avis wiped away a stray tear that had fallen as Lady Selby spoke. At least she did not want to change Banning. She loved him for all his faults and strengths.

"Thank you for telling me that, Lady Selby."

The woman smiled kindly at her. "You are very welcome, my dear. You have no idea how happy I am that Banning chose you. He needs a strong woman."

Only Avis didn't feel very strong. All her life she'd hidden her fears behind her independent facade, not needing anyone. But she did need someone. She needed Banning. She needed his warm and loving family.

"Come along," Lady Selby said as she rose from her seat. "It is time to announce your engagement."

Avis's heart felt light for the first time in weeks. She couldn't wait to tell Banning how much she loved him and wanted to marry him. No duress this time, only honest emotions.

They walked out of the room together. Instead of Banning waiting for her, Jennette stood in the hallway, her arms crossed over her chest and an angry look in her blue eyes.

"I want to talk to you, Avis." Grabbing Avis's arm, she pulled her back into the study.

"Be quick, Jennette," her mother said. "We need to make this announcement soon."

"This really shan't take long." Jennette closed the door behind her.

Avis walked back toward her glass of sherry still on the table. Something told her that she would need a little fortification for this talk.

"How could you?" Venom fairly dripped from Jennette's voice. "How could you make your scandalous proposal to my brother? My brother! The man you supposedly hated for his one innocent little kiss eight years ago."

"He kissed me on a wager back then, hardly innocent." Avis sank back into the same chair she'd been sitting in for the past half hour. "Jennette, I never made a proposal, proposition, or tendered your brother any offer."

"Oh, so you two just happened to meet each other at the coaching inn and decided to run off to Southwold."

"Not quite." Avis sipped her drink. "He blackmailed me into an affair."

Jennette cocked a black brow and gave her a questioning look that reminded her of Banning. "He blackmailed you," she said with a coarse laugh. "That is lovely, Avis."

"It happens to be the truth!"

Jennette rolled her eyes. "You two can't stand being in the same room for more than five minutes without arguing and yet you expect me to believe that my brother blackmailed you into an affair."

"He did." Avis stood and faced her best friend. "He overheard you and Sophie talking and decided, in his usual arrogance, that he would be a better partner for me than Mr. Billingsworth."

"And you just agreed?"

Looking away, Avis bit her lip, remembering that night in her cousin's study. "Not until he kissed me," she whispered.

"He kissed you?" Jennette paced the room, frowning. "I really do not believe I want to hear about that."

"Oh? You can't believe your brother did something so underhanded?"

She stopped and laughed. "I take no issue with that. I just don't want to hear about my brother kissing you or anyone else," she replied with a delicate affected shudder.

Avis finally smiled.

Jennette stared at her for a moment. "Do you love him?"

Avis closed her eyes to keep her tears at bay. "Yes," she answered softly. "More than I ever thought possible."

Before she could open her eyes, Jennette enfolded Avis in her arms. "You're going to be my sister," Jennette said warmly.

They both sat down on the settee. "Tell me everything," Jennette said. "Just keep the kissing talk to a minimum."

Avis laughed then grew serious. "Banning knew a few things about Mr. Billingsworth of which I had no knowledge and decided it would be best to stop me. Then he offered himself in Billingsworth's place."

Avis stopped to sip her sherry, remembering that night as if it happened yesterday. "Now that I think about it, I honestly don't believe he originally meant to replace Billingsworth. He looked almost as shocked as I was when he made his offer."

"And you just accepted?"

"I refused him, of course."

"Then he kissed you and convinced you to change your mind?"

"Not quite." Avis explained about the fake engagement between Emory and Lady Hythe, and how Banning blackmailed her. She thanked God every day for Banning's meddling. If not for him, she might never have discovered love, passion, and a man she wanted to spend her life with.

The door swung open and Lady Selby entered with a frown plastered on her face. "Girls, enough. We must find Banning and get this engagement announced."

"We are done, Mother."

They split up in order to find Banning more quickly. She searched for him but could not locate him. She did, unfortunately, find Emory Billingsworth. Or rather, he found her.

"Avis," he said with a wicked smile. "That was quite a surprise on the terrace."

"It was for me too."

He clasped her arm above her elbow and led her outside. "I must admit my disappointment, though."

"Oh?"

"Well, yes." He turned her around to face him. "I had hoped to court you once we returned to town."

"Why?"

Emory gave her a patronizing smile. "I find myself attracted to you."

"Are you indeed?" Where was everyone? It was a warm night, people should be milling about, but no one appeared on the terrace with them.

"Yes, shall I prove it?"

Fear raced down her spine. "I hardly believe that is necessary."

Emory slithered closer to her. She stepped back until she reached the balustrade and her choice became limited to jumping over the edge and into the unknown, or standing up for herself. He leaned in closer to her.

"Don't, Emory."

"Don't what?" He smile revealed a row of small white teeth that gleamed in the moonlight.

Avis felt as if a rabid dog had cornered her, baring his teeth in madness. She sidestepped him but tripped over a small container of flowers. Thrown off balance, she reached out and grabbed the closest thing, his jacket. His hands clutched her bottom.

"I want you—"

Before she could finish her sentence and tell him to get his hands off her, he pulled her up against him and lowered his lips to hers. He smelled of gin, and she tried to turn away, but his lips held her immobile.

Shocked by the force of his kiss, she stood still unable to move an inch.

Chapter Twenty-Two

Banning gulped down another glass of brandy in Trey's study. He couldn't believe it was over between them. Based on her comments regarding a scandal, he knew that they were at the end of the road. He could do nothing more to convince her to give them a chance. As he reached for the brandy bottle, he spied two figures walking across the dark terrace. A brief shot of moonlight highlighted the couple strolling together like lovers seeking a retreat.

Avis and Billingsworth.

She certainly didn't waste any time in finding a replacement lover. Then again, Billingsworth had been her first choice. Some inexplicable force drew Banning toward the terrace, as he had to discover what was happening out there. He slipped into the shadows just close enough to watch their interaction.

"I want you . . ." she said to Billingsworth.

She clutched Billingsworth's lapel as they kissed. She didn't try to push him away. A more graphic demonstration of the truth wasn't possible.

She doesn't love me.

Damn her.

She had always defended Billingsworth to him. No matter how many times Banning had tried to warn her against him. Banning's shoulders sagged as he turned away from them and started to walk back inside. He had reached his limit. He had pursued her endlessly, thinking she just needed a little prodding to realize how much love she had in her.

But he was wrong.

He took a long swig out of the brandy bottle, hoping the alcohol would numb his mind. It really was over. But his mind or possibly his heart wouldn't let him walk away yet. Something just wasn't right about that kiss, but he couldn't figure out what.

Damned brandy had addled his mind already.

He stopped before the study door and turned toward them again. He watched the exchange between Avis and Billingsworth, but he was too far away now to hear them. As Billingsworth dragged Avis from the terrace, Banning knew his instinct was correct.

Avis finally came to her senses and her balance, and thrust Emory away from her. She wiped her mouth with her gloved hand. "Don't you ever touch me again!"

Emory only gave her a sardonic smile. "It couldn't have been that dreadful if it took you that long to push me away."

"You shocked me."

"Good. You needed a jolt to get Selby out of your system. Now that you have, you can reject this forced engagement."

Avis stared at him. When had he changed so drastically? "What if I don't want to reject the engagement?"

Emory's brown eyes grew dark with rage. He grasped her wrist and led her down the terrace stairs into the garden. Avis attempted to twist out of his grip but his hold was tight enough that she would surely have a bruise there tomorrow.

"Emory, release me this instant!"

"No." After finding a private area, he released her wrist and grabbed her by the shoulders. "He will force you to stop writing. He will end our friendship."

Avis had no doubt that Banning would attempt to end their friendship, but she knew Banning would never want her to stop writing. There was only one way to convince Emory that she would indeed marry Banning.

"I love him, Emory," she whispered.

"Love him!" he shouted.

"Shh," she said quietly. "Someone might hear you."

"Good. Then he will discover us and reject you."

Nothing seemed to be getting through to him. "Emory, Banning and I love each other."

"What the bloody hell do you know about love? You're a spinster, Avis. He's the first man you've laid with so you think you must be in love. But you're not. You're a woman of independent means who would suffocate under a controlling man's thumb. You won't marry Selby."

"I shall invite you to the wedding so you can watch me marry him," she said, knowing she was baiting him.

Emory's face contorted as his hand clenched and then raised. Before she knew what was happening, his fist connected with her jaw. The force of the blow knocked her off her feet. Looking up at him, she saw that his rage billowed out from him like dark clouds before a storm.

"You will not marry Selby." He reached for her again.

Unsure of his intentions, she rolled away from him. "Avis!"

She looked up to see Emory's face blanch. His eyes widened and his mouth dropped before he raced away from her. Avis blinked as strong arms lifted her from the ground.

"Are you all right?" Banning asked softly.

She could only nod against his chest. "How did you find me?"

"I saw you from Trey's study," he said gently caressing her hair. "I was about to return to town when I heard a commotion and saw him dragging you off the terrace."

"Avis!" Jennette ran toward them.

Slowly, Banning released her. He turned toward his sister and said, "Take care of her."

"Where are you going?" they asked in unison.

"To take care of a problem." Before either woman could say a word, he left them.

Avis gingerly touched her jaw. She flinched from the pain radiating up her face.

"Oh my God! What did that monster do to you?"

"He . . . he hit me," Avis said as hot tears burned her cheeks. "Jennette, he hit me. He's just as Banning warned."

Jennette crouched down and looked at Avis's cheek. "What do you mean, as Banning warned?"

They brushed her off and sat on a nearby bench.

Avis told her friend the story Banning had told her about Emory and the prostitute. "I didn't believe him," she whispered. "I never would have imagined Emory hitting anyone, especially a woman."

Jennette only nodded as if she had no idea what to say.

"Why did you come out here?" Avis asked.

"I was looking for you both." Jennette clasped her hands together on her lap. "Mother is frantic about getting the engagement announced."

"Do you think Banning went after Emory?"

Jennette nodded. "Emory most likely headed for town."

"Oh God, Emory will kill him."

"I would think you'd have more faith in your betrothed."

"I do, but I have reason to believe he is terrified of guns," Avis replied.

"Why would you think that? He loves the hunt."

"When was the last time you saw him hunt?" Avis asked.

Jennette's brow furrowed. "I don't know. Maybe four or five years now that you mention it."

"I overheard someone talking to him and this man said Banning would never shoot him."

Jennette leveled Avis an intense look that reminded her of Banning. "Then we must stop this."

"How?"

"I'd suggest by leaving for London now."

The carriage rolled into London late the next day without ever having caught up to Banning. Not a surprise since within an hour of being in the coach, her sickness came upon her. Stopping every hour or two did nothing to hasten their arrival.

"I cannot face him just yet, Jennette," Avis said, plucking at her skirts.

"Why ever not?" Jennette scrutinized her. "Never mind. I can see exactly why you wouldn't want to call on him. You're still green."

Green and miserable. And not just from the carriage ride. Before she confronted Banning she needed to think through everything. She couldn't get the words he said when he found her out of her mind.

"I was returning to town . . ."

Why was he returning to town before the announcement of their engagement? No one would have believed it without him there. Had he planned to leave her?

She shook her head. She was in no condition to reason out a thing now, save her bed and sleep.

Jennette signaled the coachman and told him to take Avis home directly. Her home. Where she would be alone. Blast it all. She didn't want to be alone any longer. She wanted all that Banning had shown her the past month, love, affection, companionship—him.

"Shall I stay with you?" Jennette murmured.

"No," Avis replied with a forced smile. "I will be quite all right. Tomorrow I shall confront your brother."

"And demand that he stop this foolish idea of revenge."

Avis laughed at the idea of demanding anything of Banning. He did not seem the type of man who would change his mind because of a woman spouting orders at him. Chances were that attitude might only make him dig his heels in deeper.

* * *

The next afternoon she'd prepared herself to face him again. "Ready my carriage, Grantham," she shouted down the hallway from her study.

"Yes, ma'am. I shall inform Bridget you wish to go out."

"No. I will go alone."

Grantham pursed his wrinkled lips and nodded.

Avis ignored the look of censure in his eyes. Knowing she had a few minutes before the carriage was ready, she pulled out her quill, dipped it into the ink, and quickly wrote out all the reasons he shouldn't duel to defend her honor. She couldn't risk meeting him without her thoughts in order. After sanding the paper, she folded it and placed the note in her reticule.

Now she was ready to face Banning.

As she departed the coach, the black lacquered front door opened to Banning's house. Battenford stood stiffly in wait for her. She walked up the six steps, breathing in deeply.

"Good afternoon, Miss Copley," Battenford said with a genuine smile. "I'm afraid Lady Jennette is not at home." He glanced backward then leaned in closer. "She is visiting Lady Elizabeth," he said softly to avoid being overheard.

"Thank you, Battenford." *Say it. Tell him why you are really here.* "Actually, I am here to speak with Lord Selby."

"I'm sorry, he is not at home."

"Oh," she said deflated. "Will he return soon?"

Battenford shrugged. "I'm sorry, miss. He didn't say when he would return."

"Thank you."

She walked down the steps slowly and entered her carriage.

"Ma'am?" her driver called out.

"Yes?"

"Home?"

"Lady Elizabeth's house."

At least at Elizabeth's house she could drown her sorrows with her two best friends. Perhaps one of them could give her some meaningful advice. Although, she knew Jennette's opinion would be that Avis should have stormed the study and stayed until Banning returned home.

The short drive allowed her enough time to calm her emotions. She briefly wondered if Elizabeth's aunt would permit her to enter the house. Until their engagement became official, she was a scandalous woman. All the proper ladies of the *ton* would scorn her.

"Avis!" Elizabeth peeked out from the salon as Avis stepped into the hallway. "I'm so glad you came to visit."

Avis gave her a tremulous smile. "Oh, blast," she cried and hugged Elizabeth. "I thought I had cried out all my tears."

"Come along. I have tea and cakes and everyone is here." Elizabeth led her into the room.

"Oh, Avis," Sophie and Victoria murmured at the same time.

"We will get this all straightened out," Jennette said in her usual authoritative manner. "He went out looking for Billingsworth. Had he returned home by the time you went to see him?"

Avis shook her head still attempting to control her tears.

"Can I assume by your tears that you have heard the gossip?" Sophie asked quietly.

"What gossip?" How much worse could it be than compromising yourself?

A hush fell over the room. Avis sat on the sofa and glanced around at the pale faces of her friends. "What gossip?"

Jennette spoke first, "The betting book at White's is being flooded with wagers."

"And?"

"About you and Banning," Jennette finished in a whispered tone.

"And about a duel between Billingsworth and Banning over you," Elizabeth said.

"So I'm officially ruined."

Banning's carriage rolled to a stop on St. James Street in front of White's. Somerton had agreed to keep a watch in the club for Billingsworth. After only a day back in town, the bastard had already been seen here.

He entered White's and found a quiet table in the corner. Several men nodded to him, or saluted him with their drinks, but he ignored them. After ordering a bottle of claret, he sat back and examined the room.

"Selby," Somerton greeted him.

"Somerton."

"May I?" he asked, pointing to the empty chair.

"Of course." Banning waited until Somerton took his seat before interrogating him. "Where is he?"

"Patience, man."

"I don't seem to have any of that left."

"I hear congratulations may be in order," Somerton said then poured himself a glass of claret.

"Not bloody likely."

"Oh?"

"I believe most people realize that Miss Copley was a spinster because she wanted to be. Apparently, she still wishes to remain unmarried."

"I find that difficult to believe," Somerton commented then sipped his claret.

"Why?"

Somerton drained his claret and then rose with a sardonic look on his face. "Even I heard the rumor that she compromised herself to save you from the delightful trap set by Miss Olivia Roebuck. Odd behavior from a self-proclaimed spinster, wouldn't you agree?"

Somerton waited for a response but finally added, "Billingsworth is in the gaming room. And by the by, the betting book is aflame with wagers that you and Miss Copley will be married by weeks' end. Since I put down a large amount on that bet, I would appreciate a Thursday wedding."

"I'll do my best, Somerton." Banning only hoped he'd still be alive by Thursday.

Somerton nodded and walked toward the gaming room. Banning knew he had to walk into that room and confront Billingsworth but his feet wouldn't move. He had always known that one day Billingsworth's violent nature would show itself to Avis. Rage billowed over him as he thought about the consequences—pistols at dawn. His blood iced over.

He scraped back his chair and strode to the back

room. Scanning the room, he finally found the bastard with his back to the door, playing whist. Banning clamped his hand down on Billingsworth's slender shoulder.

"I believe we have a meeting to discuss," Banning whispered harshly in his ear.

Billingsworth gave him a leer. "You mean to defend that whore's honor? She's a bloody vixen in bed. She couldn't get enough of me, you know."

Billingsworth stood and turned toward Banning. "And I daresay with you out of her bed, Miss Copley will be begging me to marry her and set her reputation straight."

"Like bloody hell she will." In one swift movement, Banning let his fist fly into Billingsworth's chin.

Billingsworth fell back against the table behind him with a loud crash, breaking several dishes as he landed. Slowly he stood, and Banning was waiting for him.

"She will keep writing," Banning said. "She will marry me. And she won't give you another farthing."

Billingsworth's eyes widened. A thick vein in his neck bulged and pulsed in anger. He clenched his fist, and started toward Banning.

Before Banning could punch him again, Somerton pulled his arms behind his back and dragged him away from Billingsworth.

"Stay away from her, you bastard," Banning hissed.

"Selby," Billingsworth called, "to whom shall I send my friend?"

"Me," Somerton answered from behind Banning. "Come along, Selby." He continued to pull Banning until they were both outside.

"I suppose I should thank you for getting me out

of there before I killed the man," Banning said as Somerton released his arms.

"You have the morning for that pleasure." Somerton smiled viciously. "I would offer to do the job for you, but I do have my reputation to think of. What would the *ton* think of me?"

"As if you cared."

Somerton shrugged. "Not a whit."

"Do you care about anything?"

"No. Not really."

"I thought as much." Banning's carriage slowed to a stop in front of them.

"He only wants her money," Somerton said.

"I know."

"I'll talk to his second and set everything up," Somerton said in a serious tone. "And I'll do my best to force the issue of weapons—swords only. I'm sure he only baited you so you would hit him first. Being the insulted party, it is his choice of weapons."

"He knows."

Somerton frowned. "Then you know it will be pistols. Drink a good amount of coffee or tea, no more claret today. I'll see you in the morning."

The carriage door shut behind him as the vehicle rolled across the cobblestones toward his home. Leaning back against the velvet squabs, he closed his eyes. He rubbed his hands over his face to erase the images he saw every time he closed his eyes. He would have to pick up a gun again. Possibly kill another human being. And even though the world might be a better place without Emory Billingsworth, the idea of shooting the man made Banning's stomach roil.

Banning knew he had no choice. She *would* be

his wife for this. Opening his eyes, he attempted to focus on the seat across from him, wishing the carriage would stop spinning.

By the time he arrived back at his home, the world had slowed its whirling pace. He stepped down carefully from the carriage and made his way up the steps, holding tightly onto the iron rail.

He had only hours to prepare himself to face his worst fear.

Chapter Twenty-Three

Battenford opened the door as Banning approached. "Good evening, my lord."

"Evening, Battenford." Banning continued down the hallway without stopping.

"My lord—"

"Tomorrow. I am in no mood to discuss anything at the moment." Assuming he'd be in any condition to talk tomorrow.

"But—"

"*Goodnight,* Battenford," he said as he reached his study. There was one candle lit in the room and he saw no need to light another. Crossing the threshold, a soft object bounced off his head. "What the—" Before he could even finish, another one hit him directly in the face. He looked down at the two pillows on the floor.

He slowly glanced up just as another pillow flew across the room, which he easily deflected. He stared at Avis. Her brown eyes glared nearly black with rage, as her chest rose and fell in quick succession.

"I take it there is a problem?"

"You bastard!" she shouted. "You ruined me."

"Nothing more than you deserved after your little display on the terrace at Trey's house."

She flung another pillow at him. "I deserved being deserted? I deserved having everyone in the *ton* give me the cut direct because I was protecting you from that little tart?"

He caught the pillow and hurled it to the ground. Stalking her, he said, "Yes, you deserved that. Possibly even more."

"For what? Foolishly opening my mouth to protect you from Miss Roebuck?" Avis stepped back as he came closer.

"For kissing Billingsworth on the terrace, perhaps?"

"You saw that and you didn't assist me?"

He cocked his head at her. "You didn't look as if you needed any help. You were clutching his jacket as though you hadn't been kissed in years."

"I tripped, you stupid fool. He grabbed me and kissed me."

"And I suppose he forced you say you wanted him?" Confusion flashed across her face, widening her eyes.

"I wanted him to get his hands off my derrière."

"And you were struggling ferociously to get out of his arms," he added sarcastically.

Out of pillow ammunition, she stood her ground until he stood directly in front of her. "You said you were returning to town after you rescued me. Did you plan on standing me up?"

"At least I saved you from being beaten by the bastard."

"And now you're going to face him to defend my honor? Yet you would not even stay at the ball long enough for our engagement to be announced."

"It was my understanding you wanted to ride out the scandal."

"I never said that. When we talked about scandal, I thought we were discussing the fact that even if we announced our wedding there would still be rumors flying."

He stepped forward as she stepped back again. This time, she ran into the table, knocking herself off balance. Banning reached for her, but she was just a breath too far away and he tumbled down on top of her.

"You oaf!" She pummeled his shoulders with her fists.

Grabbing her arms, he pinned them above her head and weighed her body down with his. "Enough!"

"Hardly. I still cannot believe you think I wanted to kiss him."

"Oh? Why wouldn't I believe it? He was your first choice after all. You believed him over everything I told you about him. So why are you here, Avis?"

"To stop the duel and demand you marry me," she said in a tone that sounded nothing like an order.

"You demand it, do you?"

The urge to kiss her neck became too much for Banning to ignore. Slowly, he bent his head and touched his lips to her erratic pulse.

"Stop that this instant! We need to talk."

"Never," he whispered against the hollow of her neck.

"I don't want you touching me," she said in an unconvincing voice.

"But you just demanded I marry you. If I do, you

are mine. Mine to kiss, touch, caress, fondle, make love to, any time I desire."

"Not against my will."

"Even against your will." He placed feathery kisses down the deep line of cleavage exposed to him. "Not that I would ever need to force you. You are a very passionate woman," he murmured against her breast.

"Are you going to marry me or not?"

He smiled against the soft skin of her breast. She had finally come to him. A brief feeling of relief skittered through him. He'd never felt so lucky because he would now have everything he'd ever wanted. Assuming he lived through the meeting at dawn.

Avis held her breath, waiting for an answer. Even when he brought her fully covered nipple into his mouth, she refused to breathe. Or maybe she'd just lost the ability to take air into her lungs.

"Are you?" she asked again.

He lifted his head up and stared at her. A small smile lifted his sensual lips upward. "No."

"What?" She twisted and attempted to draw herself upward but his weight kept her trapped.

"No."

She turned her head as he bent to kiss her mouth. She refused to kiss him. All logical thought and reason flew out the window once he kissed her.

"Why not?" she asked. "This is all your fault."

"Is it now?" He arched a black brow at her.

"Well, most of it."

"If I remember correctly, I asked you to marry me weeks ago in Southwold."

"You did not. You said you needed a wife. A brood mare to have your children."

"Which I do," he whispered, placing a kiss on her chin. "Beautiful boys and girls with their mother's curly hair."

"Then you will ask me to marry you?"

He shook his head with a grin. That arrogant man was playing games with her!

"I'm afraid my reputation is in tatters over being compromised on the terrace at Trey's house."

She slapped his back and laughed. "Your reputation is intact. That is just one of the many joys of being a man. Your reputation is enhanced while mine is ruined."

Lifting his head, he kissed the end of her nose. "No, I'm afraid my reputation is not undamaged. It appears since you kissed Billingsworth on the terrace, I've taken to drinking and sitting in darkened rooms. And worse, taking swings at men in White's. I might even have my subscription revoked for that."

"Whom did you strike?" she asked softly.

"A bastard of a man."

"Billingsworth?"

He nodded.

"Did he call you out, then?" Avis frowned. She'd thought Banning had called Emory out for his attack on her.

"I really don't feel like talking about him right now."

"Banning, did he call you out?" she demanded. Fear flickered through her entire body, knowing she couldn't lose him now. She was too close to having everything she now wanted in life.

"Yes."

"Damn you, Banning!" She twisted in his arms but could not move off him. "You cannot meet him."

His eyes narrowed. "Why not? Afraid I might kill him?"

"No. I am terrified that you will be killed," she whispered.

He lowered her head toward his lips and kissed her softly. "No more talk of Billingsworth. We have far more important things to discuss."

"Such as?"

He rolled her back onto the floor. "Special licenses."

"Oh?" She would let him change the topic of conversation for a short while, but she would talk him out of this duel. She couldn't let him do this, not for her.

"Hmm, would Thursday be soon enough to marry me?"

"I don't remember being asked."

"If I'm not mistaken, we both demanded that we marry each other. Do we really need a proposal?" He slipped her gown over her shoulder. "After all, we both have been compromised."

"True," she replied sweetly. "But a proposal is rather nice."

"All right then." Then he nipped her shoulder. "Propose to me," he said in a teasing tone.

"Not me, you beast." She couldn't help but laugh.

His white teeth gleamed in the dim room. Then he sobered. "Will you marry me, Avis?"

"Yes," she whispered.

His brows furrowed. "Do you want to marry?"

"Only you, Banning." She kissed him softly. "I never wanted to marry anyone until you showed me that I do have the patience."

"Love gives you the patience, sweetheart."

"Your love," she whispered. "Only your love."

"I want to compromise you again," he murmured in her ear. "Right now."

"What about your mother and your sister?"

"Damn."

He kissed her neck until she shivered with desire. Passion, she decided, was far better than she'd ever imagined. His lips skimmed across her bare shoulder.

"Banning," she moaned.

"I must find a new house for my mother and sister just as quickly as I can."

"I cannot wait that long. Did you close the door?"

Banning shot a glance behind him. "Damn."

"Go close the door," she whispered. "And lock it."

Chapter Twenty-Four

Banning turned the key and the lock clicked. He tossed his jacket on the chair by the desk. This was utter madness. With a duel only hours away, the last thing he should be doing was rutting like an animal. And yet, he couldn't stop himself from making love to her no matter how much he knew he should. As he walked back toward her, he untied his cravat and unwound it from around his neck.

"Stand up, Avis."

She looked at him with passion blazing in her brown eyes. "Why?"

"Because I want you naked in my arms. No barriers between us ever again." He reached down and pulled her to her feet. Turning her around, he unhooked her gown and slid it over her arms and down her hips. The blue muslin pooled at her feet like water from the sea.

She shivered as he completely unlaced her stays and they followed the dress to the floor. Her shift and petticoats were next until she stood before him in only her clocked stockings and shoes. He turned her back to face him.

"Do you have any idea how long I've wanted you?" he whispered.

"I believe I do."

"Take off your stockings for me."

She only smiled at his request. Taking a seat on the sofa, she unhooked her garters and threw them on the pile of clothing. She put one leg on the table allowing him a lovely view and then slid her stockings down one slim leg then the other. His cock pressed tightly against his trousers. Once she had completed the task, she stood up completely naked. He clenched his fists to keep from tossing her on the sofa and driving himself into her right then and there.

"Undress me," he muttered, even though the thought of her fingers on him made him tremble.

She smiled up at him, and he almost forgot about taking this slow.

"I would love to do that."

She skimmed her fingernails up his chest, over his nipples until she reached the buttons on his linen shirt. With quick movements, she released each one and then pulled the shirt out of his trousers and over his head. He closed his eyes as her nails trailed a path to the buttons on his trousers.

"You'll need to sit so I can remove your boots."

He moved to the sofa and groaned as she turned her perfectly rounded bottom toward him and pulled at his boots. A gentleman should have offered to do the job himself, but this was far too enticing. Each movement exposed flashes of her womanly folds and forced him to hold the fabric of the sofa to keep from touching her yet.

Finally, each boot hit the floor and she turned to remove the trousers. He smiled as her eyes widened when his cock sprang from its confinement.

"Come here," he said softly.

Avis straddled him, anxious to be closer to him, dying to have him enter her now. But another part of her wanted their time to go slowly. She wanted to savor their lovemaking as they did in the cottage those weeks ago.

The moment their lips touched, all thoughts were gone. His hands burned her back as he pressed her closer to him. Their tongues warred for possession and domination until he broke the contact and kissed her neck. Avis could scarcely breathe as his lips trailed down to her breasts.

"Banning," she murmured as he suckled her breast. "I've missed you so terribly the past few weeks."

"I wanted to take this slowly with you, Avis," he said, after breaking his wondrous contact with her nipple. "But I find I can't. I want you now."

She smiled against his forehead. "Please don't wait any longer."

He lifted her up and brought her down on his hard shaft, filling her completely, making them one once more. She never wanted this to end. She never wanted to be without him again. How could she have thought for one moment that she could live without him? She would have him forever and nothing would stand in her way now. He nuzzled her neck, nipping at the sensitive skin there as she lifted her hips and brought herself down on him.

Pleasure built as they increased their speed until

she felt forced to close her eyes and let her release wash over her. He grasped her hips and thrust into her one last time, spilling his seed into her.

"I love you," she whispered spent against his chest.

"I love you too."

She lifted her head and stared at his blue eyes, filled with love for her. "I'm sorry," she mumbled.

His eyes darkened with confusion. "Sorry? About what?"

"Not talking about my fear of marriage with you."

"What changed your mind?" he asked, caressing her hair.

"A lot of things." She kissed the tip of his nose. "You. Your mother. An old acquaintance of mine."

"How did I help you?"

Avis smiled and wondered how he couldn't have known how he helped her. "You taught me that love is patient. Love is worth taking a risk and more importantly that love is worth facing a fear."

He kissed her softly on the lips. "And my mother?"

"She told me about her marriage and a little more about my mother's marriage."

"And this friend of yours?"

"Mary and I talked for most of an afternoon with her children in the room. She also had a father who believed it was all right to strike his wife and children. But she also told me if you find the right man it will never happen."

Avis blew out a long breath. "More importantly, I think I have learned to trust myself."

"Yourself?"

"Oh, Banning, I hit you in anger." She caressed his cheek with her hand. "The man I loved. I was terrified that I would hurt you again, or worse, an innocent child. But the more time I spent with Mary the more she helped me realize I could do it. I could have the man I love. I could have children to love and cherish." She looked up at him through teary eyes. "I could have everything I was always too afraid to believe possible."

"I'm so glad you became reacquainted with her."

Avis let her head drop back to his shoulder and sighed. "So am I. I discovered I want so much more out of life than just writing. I want you. I want children with you. I want our love and companionship forever."

Banning held Avis until she fell asleep against his chest. Slowly, he lifted her into his arms and placed her on the sofa. She stirred, blinked her eyes open for a moment before smiling and closing her eyes again. After placing a soft blanket over her, he dressed, then sat down behind his desk.

He should have sent her home this evening. He shouldn't have made love to her tonight. If he were unable to go through with this duel, which was a frightening possibility after the last time he needed to use a gun, what would happen to her? His reputation would be ruined and marriage to him would reflect poorly on her. She might be pregnant. If he didn't return from this meeting, she would be left alone, pregnant, and scorned by Society all because of him.

He couldn't let that happen.

Banning reached into the bottom drawer of his desk and slowly pulled out the box. He stared at the dueling pistol box he had managed to place on his desk. This was the closest he'd been to holding a gun in his hands since that unspeakable night in Whitechapel. Even now if he closed his eyes, he could relive every detail. But he had to do this. Her honor, and his, was at stake. And more importantly, he couldn't let Billingsworth get away with this any longer.

Avis let out a small sigh from the sofa. Her hands tucked under her cheek and a few curls fell across her forehead. She was beautiful. And his. No one would malign his future wife, kiss her or strike her as long as he could breathe.

Even if he had to face his biggest fear.

Love is worth facing a fear. Her words haunted him. If she could face her fears of marriage then he had no choice but to face his.

He rubbed his hand across the smooth cherry box. Lifting the lid, he saw the two Manton pistols lying in the red silk lining. How appropriate that the lining would be the same color as spilled blood. Would the grass at the field be the same color in a few hours?

Warm fingers caressed his cheek. He turned toward her warmth wondering how she approached him without making a sound.

"You can't do this."

"Are you defending him again?" he whispered.

She turned his head toward her and pointed at the purple bruise on her jaw. "He did this."

"I know."

She blinked several times. "Did you bait him on purpose? To protect my honor?"

"Perhaps."

"Very honorable but you are not picking up a pistol for me." She kneeled down next to him and drew the blanket around her. "I know, Banning. I know you no longer like pistols or rifles or hunting."

Banning closed his eyes but that only served to bring back unwanted memories. "I have no choice, Avis."

"You do." She let her head fall to his lap. "I can't lose you now that I finally decided to set my own fears aside and marry you. I can't let you do this for me."

He caressed her tawny hair and smiled down at her. "If I don't meet him, my honor and your reputation will be in tatters."

"If you meet him, my reputation will be ruined if people believe the duel was on my account."

"Assuming I can even pick up the damned pistol," he muttered under his breath.

Avis lifted her head and then rose to her feet. She grabbed his hand, leading him to the sofa. "Tell me what happened."

Perhaps talking to her about what happened in France would help. But he couldn't tell her about the other incident.

Banning blew out a long breath and closed his eyes. In his mind's eye he saw it all again, as if it happened only yesterday and not six years ago. He'd never told anyone about what happened in France. Not his sister, not his parents. Only Trey and Somerton knew the truth.

Feeling her clasp his hand in comfort, he began, "I believe I already told you that I was shot in France."

"Yes, as were many people. Yet none of them seem to have the aversion to guns that you have now."

"Trey and I had tracked down a spy who lived outside of Paris. Our mission was quite simple, either bring the man back to England or kill him."

"Oh my," she whispered.

He rose and walked toward the window, staring out at the dark garden, but not seeing anything except his memories. "We tracked him to a house in a small village. All the information we received told us that he lived there alone. We decided the two of us could easily grab him and spirit him back home."

Banning paused to gather his thoughts. "We crashed through the door and found the man standing in his kitchen. I drew my pistol and aimed for him, not intending to shoot him."

"Oh," Avis whispered. "Then you accidentally shot him?"

"No. The man pointed his gun at me." Banning closed his eyes reliving every moment. His heart pounded in his chest as if it were happening here and now and not six years ago. *Tell her,* his conscience shouted. *Tell her what a monster you are.*

"Just as I pulled the trigger the man's young son flew toward his father to protect him and took the bullet in his heart. He was only ten years old, Avis."

"Oh, Banning." She stepped behind him and hugged him, her soft, warm arms holding him tight. "What about the man?"

"He shot me."

"And then Kesgrave shot the man?"

"Yes."

She rested her head on his back. "It wasn't your fault, Banning."

"Yes, it was," he bit out. "We should have known about the boy."

"How could you possibly have known?"

"Somerton had been scheduled to meet up with Trey that afternoon. He had the information on the boy. But we decided to get the mission completed so we could go home sooner."

"That's how Somerton knew about it," Avis commented.

"Yes."

"But how did Billingsworth discover all this?"

Banning shook his head. *Don't tell her. She'll hate you for the coward you were.* "I'm not certain."

"So all this time you've had this fear and guilt and never told me about it?"

She sounded a bit miffed by his secrets. He turned around and lifted her chin up. "If I remember correctly, you didn't seem to be in any hurry to tell me about your father, or your own fears."

Avis glanced away. "True enough. I never believed in all the tales of love that I'd heard and read about through the years. I saw what my mother went through in the name of love. She loved him, Banning. Your mother even told me that. Yet, she couldn't leave him in order to be happy."

"Maybe she had to fight her own fears."

"Perhaps she did."

"I still have to meet him," he whispered.

"No, you don't." She looked up at him with tears in her eyes. "The only thing he wants is money. If I offer him a large sum—"

"No."

"Banning, I can't let you do this when all we have to do is pay him off."

Banning moved away from her. She didn't understand any of this. Honor. Reputation. Courage. Right now, he had none of those things.

Avis started to dress. There was only one thing to do and she would do this herself. Now that she finally had Banning she wasn't about to let a stupid duel get in the way of her happiness.

"Are you going somewhere?" he asked, coming up behind her.

"I need to return home."

"No."

She turned and faced him. "I shouldn't have stayed this long, my servants will be worried."

He tilted her chin up. "You are not going to him."

"I will do whatever I have to in order to stop this duel. You will not fight over me." She twisted out of his reach and strode for the door, determined to leave before he stopped her.

As she reached the door, he whispered, "I'm not fighting this duel over just you."

She halted and blew out a breath. "I'm sure that girl at Eton would appreciate the sentiment but wouldn't require you to defend her honor at this point."

"It's not just her either," he said softly.

"There were more?" *Please say no.* She couldn't bear to hear another story about a woman beaten by him.

"Yes."

Avis turned and leaned against the door. "What happened?"

"If I had been there only a few minutes earlier . . ."

"What would that have done?" she murmured to keep him talking. He raked his fingers through his hair, giving him a wild look. Her stomach clenched at the sight of him.

"Maybe I could have saved her."

"Who?"

"I don't know her name. I never learned her name."

"Banning, what happened?"

He sank in the chair by the fireplace and dropped his head into hands. "It was two years after I came back from France. Trey and I had been down in Whitechapel, gambling and drinking, but I'd had enough and decided to head for home. I was walking up the street looking for a hackney when I heard a noise from the alley that caught my attention. It sounded like a wounded animal so I went to investigate. When I walked back there I saw him."

"Emory?"

He nodded. "I had heard the rumors that he spent a lot of time in the taverns down there but I never expected our paths would cross the one night I decided to go there. When I reached the back of the alley I was in shock . . . he was beating her, Avis. Not just one time. Over and over again."

She didn't want to ask but knew she had to. "What did you do?"

"I couldn't do it." He picked up the glass from the table next to him and hurled it at the fireplace. "I couldn't do it, Avis."

She walked over to him carefully as if he were the wounded animal. He flinched when she touched his shoulder. "What couldn't you do?"

"I had brought a pistol with me for protection. I never thought I would need to use it, but you know how Whitechapel is. I assumed if anyone tried to rob me, I could go for either my knife or just point the gun at them and they would run off. But I knew as soon as I saw Billingsworth's enraged face . . . I knew he wouldn't be stopped by just a gun pointing at him. I would have to shoot him.

"The pistol was in my greatcoat pocket. My hand curled around the handle. I pulled it out and froze. I couldn't point it at him even to protect that poor woman."

"What did Emory do?"

"He pulled a gun on me and told me to get out of there."

"And?"

"And I ran like a coward. I finally found the nightwatch but by the time we arrived back there Billingsworth was gone and the girl was dead." Banning rose and walked away from her. "Because of my cowardice that girl died."

Avis ran to him. "No. Because of Emory that girl died. Why wasn't he arrested?"

"When he was questioned he had three people, all peers, who supported his alibi. God only knows how he paid them off, but he did."

"So that's how he knows about your fear of guns," Avis muttered.

"Yes."

"I have to do this, Avis. I can't let him get away with murder any longer."

"I know," she whispered. "I know."

"I shall be fine. Somerton is my second and the surgeon will be present just in case."

He kissed her softly on the lips and she savored the sweetness, absorbing every detail of his mouth, of his body.

"I want to come with you."

"No," he ordered. "If you are there my concentration will be on you and not where it needs to be."

She pressed her lips together but nodded in agreement. "Very well. But I don't want to leave. I need to be here when you get home."

"I want you to be with my family."

"Banning, why do you think Emory has changed so over the last month?"

He stiffened with her mention of Emory. "The creditors are demanding payment. I believe he knew that if you and I were courting he would be the loser. You have given him too much money the last few years but it still wasn't enough."

"Still, it seems rather dramatic to go to such lengths as kissing me and then striking me," she mumbled.

"I believe the man may be going slightly mad. There is a rumor that no one wants his newest manuscript."

"Oh no." Avis kissed Banning's hand and rubbed her cheek against it. Fine hairs tickled her face and made her smile. "Do you really think he was jealous of my writing?"

He nodded. "I do."

The knocked sounded loudly on the front door. They both turned their heads and Avis frowned. "Who would—"

"Somerton." Banning moved away from her.

"Already? It's only a little past four."

"And it will be getting light soon." He opened the door just as the footman appeared. "Show him in."

The footman nodded and walked away only to return with Somerton in tow. Somerton sauntered into the room, noticed Avis and smiled. "Miss Copley, good morning."

"Somerton," she replied.

"Will you excuse us, Miss Copley," Somerton said. His usual casual yet caustic demeanor was gone, replaced by tight-lipped seriousness.

"She can stay," Banning replied before Avis had even opened her mouth to deny Somerton's request.

"Thank you, Banning."

Somerton shook his head. "Very well. We finalized everything. Anderson requested pistols, of course."

"Of course," Banning commented. His jaw tightened and he inhaled sharply.

"I did my best to request swords, but Billingsworth has no skill with them according to Anderson."

Banning shrugged. "I'd thought as much."

"Watch your step this morning, the grass is still wet," Somerton said, testing the grass with the toe of his boot.

"I will." Banning stared down at the box in Somerton's hand.

"Just think about Miss Copley," Somerton said. "Think about your future, the children you will have, the nights making—"

"Enough," he interrupted. He understood the point Somerton tried to make.

Banning looked up as Billingsworth's carriage rolled to a stop. Anderson jumped down and then held out his hand as Billingsworth stumbled out. Billingsworth took a step or two, as if unsteady.

Somerton chuckled. "Bloody stupid man. Perhaps drinking was the only way to foster his courage."

Somerton walked toward Anderson to work out the final details, the primary being the task of verifying Billingsworth was sober enough for the meeting.

Beads of sweat dampened the gloves on Banning's hands. His pulse thrummed through his veins. He could do this. Just think of Avis. He watched the meeting as Anderson and Somerton nodded their agreements on some matter. Then Billingsworth picked up one pistol, held it, tested it, and then did the same with the second gun. After choosing the first one, Somerton returned.

"I will load this and we can get this over with. Billingsworth says he is fine for the meeting but be careful. A drunkard can sometimes be worse than a coward. A drunkard can fire too soon."

Banning nodded, staring at the gun in Somerton's hand. This was different. No little boy was going to throw himself in front of Billingsworth. Pick up the pistol, he told himself.

Somerton held out the pistol for him. Banning reached out his hand and took the gun. The gun felt heavy and cold even through his gloves.

"Take your gloves off," Somerton reminded him.

He did and then felt the cool ivory handle and a little jump of tension skipped up his arm. He closed his eyes and inhaled deeply to calm his agitated nerves. But nothing would stop the little quiver in his hands. He just had to get this over with and live through it.

"Gentlemen, please take your places."

Banning and Billingsworth stood back to back.

"Did you know she came to see me this morning?"

Billingsworth whispered. "I think she wanted me to swive her, but I refused. I'll have plenty of time to have her after she's free of you."

Banning's fingers flexed around the handle of the gun. "She was with me."

"Will you actually be able to fire that thing?" Billingsworth mocked. "I remember another time when you just couldn't get that pistol in your hand. That girl was a good fuck but she actually thought I'd pay her for her services. Stupid girl."

"Twenty paces," Anderson called out before Banning could reply.

Damn him. Billingsworth's taunts were not about to distract him.

"Turn and fire!"

He turned and faced Billingsworth. Banning lifted his pistol into position and aimed for Billingsworth's right shoulder. *Do it. Pull the damn trigger.* Just as he did, a bullet tore past his ear, hitting nothing on him. He looked over at Billingsworth as he dropped to the ground, clutching his right shoulder.

Anderson rushed over to him and spoke in hushed tones. He stood and announced, "Honor has been satisfied."

"No," Billingsworth moaned.

"Yes," Anderson replied tightly. "The duel is over."

Somerton slapped him on the back. "I knew you would find the courage to pull that trigger. Damn shame you didn't kill him, though."

"I thought you were his friend?"

Somerton laughed coarsely. "It's always better to keep your enemies close so you can watch them. You should know, I talked to Anderson and Wilkerson, and both decided to recant their stories with a little persuasion. Billingsworth wasn't with them that night. He blackmailed them to tell the magistrate that story."

"How did you find out about that?"

Somerton gave him a half-smile. "You really don't want to know."

"Then at least tell me why you did it?"

"Because what they did was wrong and it was about time the truth came out."

"Since when do you care?"

Somerton only grinned again. "Oh, don't be fooled, Selby. I don't care."

"Thank you."

Somerton nodded.

All he wanted to do now was go home to the loving comfort of Avis's arms. The whinny of a horse brought his attention to a black carriage rolling away. He could only smile.

"Banning!" Jennette called out from the salon. "Are you all right?"

He walked into the room where his mother, sister, and future wife sat and said, "I am quite well. The man couldn't sight a pistol to save his life."

Avis gasped. "Did you kill . . . ?"

"Would you care if I did?" Banning shrugged out of his coat and handed it to the footman. "Perhaps I should rephrase my question, would you care if I didn't kill him?"

She frowned and looked down at her lap. "I suppose I should care either way. He was a dear friend of mine until a few weeks ago." Avis glanced at him, her brown eyes bright with tears. "But I would definitely care if *you* had been killed."

Jennette sighed. "What happened?"

"Yes, Banning, please sit down and tell us exactly what happened this morning," his mother requested.

"I would like to speak with Avis alone first," he said.

"Ahh," his mother said softly. "Come along, Jennette."

His mother took Jennette's hand as his sister muttered, "I just want to know what happened."

"Soon enough. Give your brother time with his betrothed."

She shut the door behind them, leaving Banning and Avis alone and in silence. As soon as the door clicked, Avis jumped out of her seat and into his arms.

"Oh God, I have been so dreadfully worried about you, Banning." She wrapped her arms around his neck as she kissed him softly.

"Really?"

"Yes."

"I thought I asked you not to come to the duel."

Redness tinged her cheeks. "You did."

He kissed her forehead. "How should I handle my disobedient betrothed?"

"Disobedient?" she asked innocently.

"I saw the carriage."

Avis looked into his sparkling blue eyes and sighed. "I had to be there, Banning. I had to know that you were all right."

"I know," he said with a smile. "I did it, Avis. Thanks to you."

"All I did was listen to you," she said.

"Anderson and Wilkerson have agreed to recant their stories about what happened."

"How did you manage that?"

"I didn't. Somehow Somerton did."

"Oh. So Emory will be arrested then?"

"Yes."

"So he'll never bother either one of us again?" Avis whispered.

"Never." Banning held his future wife tight against him, savoring her warmth. "From now on, we'll face our fears together."

"I have no fears with you by my side," Avis whispered and then kissed her future husband.

Epilogue

Avis checked the small clock on the table in the salon once more. After four months of marriage, she shouldn't still be waiting with such anticipation to see Banning. But today was different.

Where was he? He'd said he would be home by four and it was ten minutes past that now. She'd waited three weeks to be sure and now she was certain.

"Blasted weather." Banning's voice rang out from the front hall.

"Banning?" She stood and waited for him to enter the room. As he entered, a smile deepened those dimples she loved.

He crossed the room and brought her into his arms just as he did every day. Only this time it felt different to her. His lips caressed hers with such tender passion she almost thought she'd cry.

Oh, she'd better tell him quickly before he guessed from her tears. Breaking away from his kiss, she looked up at him and smiled.

"So, are you ready to tell me yet?" he said with a smug grin.

"You know?"

He brought her back into his arms and kissed her again. Lifting his lips off hers, he smiled. "Of course, I know. We are married, Avis. You can't keep a secret like that from your husband."

"But—"

"Avis, we've made love at least three times a week for the past seven weeks. Not once did you tell me we couldn't because of your monthlies." He clasped her hands and led her to the sofa.

"And you're not upset that we didn't wait longer?"

"Of course not! I would have been happy if you were already four months along or even five," he said with wink. "Although, my mother might not have been happy about such an early delivery."

Avis chuckled softly. "No, she wouldn't have been pleased with that. No one would have believed the baby was early after my admission on the Kesgraves' terrace."

"Are you happy about it?" he asked tentatively.

"More than I thought possible. I'm not like my father after all. I think I'm a perfect combination of both my parents."

Banning looked genuinely relieved as his smile deepened.

They both looked up as Battenford approached the salon holding a silver salver in his hands. "This just came for you, my lady."

Even after all these months, she still hadn't become used to hearing Battenford call her that. "Thank you, Battenford."

"And congratulations, my lady," he replied with a slight smile before he left.

Avis laughed. "Does everyone in this house know?"

"Quite possibly," Banning answered.

She picked up the letter and placed it on the table next to Banning. "It's from the publisher, and I can't stomach a rejection on such a happy day."

"Maybe it's not a rejection," he reasoned.

"Of course it is."

Banning grabbed the letter and opened it before she could protest.

"All right, tell me the bad news," she said before walking to the window.

"Well, he said the book was very well written—"

"But he didn't love the characters," she finished for him.

"No, he loved the characters." Banning looked back down at the paper.

"Then he didn't love the plot."

Banning chuckled. "No, he loved the plot."

"Then the book was too sensual for the modesty of the times."

"No, that's not it either."

Avis turned to face him as frustration flowed within her. "Then what is the reason this time?"

"He loved everything about the book and can't wait to publish it."

Avis grasped the top of the wingback chair for support. "He what?"

"He's going to publish your book." Banning rushed over to her, picked her up, and twirled her around in his arms. "You're going to be a published author."

After all these years, it felt so . . . anticlimactic. Getting her work published was something she'd wanted for so many years that she'd thought she would be jumping up and down with joy. She wasn't unhappy, but she now realized getting published was only part of what she'd really wanted.

And the rest was standing in front her with a huge grin on his face because she'd fulfilled her dream.

"Avis?" Banning questioned. "Are you all right? This is what you've wanted forever."

"I'm overjoyed," she replied with a big grin. "Not because my story will be in print but because I have you and now a child will be entering our lives and—" Her voice caught with the incredible fulfillment she felt now.

"I have everything I was afraid to even dream of," she whispered with a watery smile, "because of you."

About the Author

Christie Kelley was born and raised in upstate New York. As a child, she always had a vivid imagination and the bad drams that go along with it; or perhaps the dreams were caused by her five brothers and three sisters. After seventeen years working for financial institutions in software development, she took a leap of faith and started her first book. Seven years later, *Every Night I'm Yours* was bought by Zebra Books.

She now lives in Maryland with her husband and two future romance heroes. Come visit her on the web at www.christiekelley.com.

Put a Little Romance in Your Life With
Georgina Gentry

Cheyenne Song
0-8217-5844-6   **$5.99**US/**$7.99**CAN

Apache Tears
0-8217-6435-7   **$5.99**US/**$7.99**CAN

Warrior's Heart
0-8217-7076-4   **$5.99**US/**$7.99**CAN

To Tame a Savage
0-8217-7077-2   **$5.99**US/**$7.99**CAN

To Tame a Texan
0-8217-7402-6   **$5.99**US/**$7.99**CAN

To Tame a Rebel
0-8217-7403-4   **$5.99**US/**$7.99**CAN

To Tempt a Texan
0-8217-7705-X   **$5.99**US/**$7.99**CAN

Available Wherever Books Are Sold!

Visit our website at **www.kensingtonbooks.com.**